"This is private property,"
Jake taunted,

knowing damn well that his voice was too harsh. He couldn't help it. His hands shook. His belly was on fire. He wanted her so badly that if he weren't careful, he'd take her right there in the doorway.

She smiled, and he was lost. "I know," she answered. "I figured I'd negotiate with the owner to stay just a little while longer."

"Negotiate?"

Amanda stepped forward. "Yes," she answered, her voice slowing, thickening like warm honey. "I thought we could talk a little, and maybe share something to drink...."

Jake managed to raise an eyebrow. "Are you talking bribes here, woman?"

Her smile widened, and her eyes darkened. "If that's what you want to call it."

Dear Reader,

When two people fall in love, the world is suddenly new and exciting, and it's that same excitement we bring to you in Silhouette Intimate Moments. These are stories with scope and grandeur. The characters lead lives we all dream of, and everything they do reflects the wonder of being in love.

Longer and more sensuous than most romances, Silhouette Intimate Moments novels take you away from everyday life and let you share the magic of love. Adventure, glamour, drama, even suspense— these are the passwords that let you into a world where love has a power beyond the ordinary, where the best authors in the field today create stories of love and commitment that will stay with you always.

In coming months, look for novels by your favorite authors: Kathleen Eagle, Marilyn Pappano, Emilie Richards, Judith Duncan and Justine Davis, to name only a few. And whenever—and wherever—you buy books, look for all the Silhouette Intimate Moments, love stories with that extra something, books written especially for you by today's top authors.

Leslie J. Wainger
Senior Editor and Editorial Coordinator

KATHLEEN KORBEL

Jake's Way

SILHOUETTE·INTIMATE·MOMENTS®

Published by Silhouette Books New York

America's Publisher of Contemporary Romance

SILHOUETTE BOOKS
300 East 42nd St., New York, N.Y. 10017

JAKE'S WAY

KATHLEEN KORBEL

lives in St. Louis with her husband and two children. She devotes her time to enjoying her family, writing, avoiding anyone who tries to explain the intricacies of the computer and searching for the fabled house-cleaning fairies. She's had her best luck with her writing—from which she's garnered a *Romantic Times* award for Best New Category Author of 1987, and the 1990 Romance Writers of America RITA awards for Best Romantic Suspense and Best Long Category Romance—and from her family, without whom she couldn't have managed any of the rest. She hasn't given up on those fairies, though.

Thanks to Ginny and Rebecca,
who acquainted me with their friends.
And to the Literacy Council of St. Louis
for the help.

Chapter 1

It was setting up to be a good day. The cold had finally broken in the Wyoming mountains, leaving the morning air soft and the sky pale. Clouds hid the jagged edges of the mountain peaks, and mist shrouded the high plain. The air was full of birds and the rivers swollen with snowmelt. Jake Kendall had waited out the whole winter for a day like this.

He didn't bother reining his horse. Buck knew the way through the high meadows better than any man. The big black animal carried Jake at an easy canter toward the stand of aspens and cottonwood that bordered the gurgling stream. Jake didn't need to be this far up. His horses weren't going to need the meadow for a while yet, and Jake never had time to hunt game. But Jake had waited out the snow again this year, pacing the house like a caged animal, and it was time to get out. The winter told him too strongly what he wasn't. The spring reminded him what he was.

They had almost reached the old place, when Buck's ears flicked forward. Jake's attention had been on the shadow of an elk he'd just spotted on the other side of the river. He felt Buck's hesitation and swung around, the saddle creaking beneath him. And he saw what his horse had seen before him.

"Damn it," he swore, pulling the horse to a sudden stop. "Not again."

Buck lifted his head and waited, dead still beneath his rider. After all these years, Jake didn't even notice. Buck had been the first horse he'd trained, fifteen years ago. By now, the two were like separate parts of a whole rather than man and animal. And both of them had their undivided attention on the stand of trees.

A car. Tucked into the snow shadows that still hid the cabin from sight. Jake would have had to ride another two or three minutes yet to see the corner of the roof beneath the branches, so well had his great-grandfather situated it. But red cars just didn't blend well in the snow.

"I'm gonna have to close off that access road," he snarled, urging Buck forward with no more than a twitch of his thighs.

Jake wasn't in the mood for interlopers—not on his land, not on his time, and not on his spring morning. Some strayed hunter or dude-ranch visitor was about to find out just what happened when he broke into the wrong cabin. Jake was ready for a fight.

He wasn't at all ready for what he found.

She was standing in the doorway. Jake saw her hair first, the color of a blood bay. The sun seemed to snake through all the bare tree limbs just to set fire to where it tumbled around her shoulders. She was holding a cup of coffee and had her face lifted to the sight of the clouds that still swirled around the snowcapped peaks. Her eyes seemed to be the first green of the season.

Jake had never been struck dumb by a woman. He'd never had the time, and certainly had known better than to give in to inclination, especially the way his life had gone. He was struck dumb now.

She was small, probably no bigger than his little sister, five-three or so. But she had the kind of grace a man only dreamed about, a quiet poise that looked out of place here. She should have been at the front door of a hotel or restaurant, not a hundred-year-old settler's cabin in the middle of nowhere. She even wore the wrong clothes. Tailored, of tweed and corduroy, as if she thought she were at an English estate for a shooting week-end.

Then she turned those eyes on Jake, and he let Buck falter to an uncertain halt.

"Good morning."

Even her voice was cultured. Soft and deep, nudging something deep in him he didn't want nudged. Ruining the morning he'd wanted by doing nothing more than standing there.

Jake battled a flash of anger as he swung from the saddle. "This is private property," he snapped, his expression hard.

She was elegant and classy, but that didn't make a difference. Or, more truthfully, it did. Which was why he wanted her gone.

She smiled at him. "I know," she admitted with a vague motion of her coffee cup. "I was hoping to get over to see Mr. Kendall this morning."

"You just did." When Jake Kendall wanted to stare a man down, he tilted his hat down, just a little, so the shadow fell over his eyes. He did that now. "Now, what are you doing here?"

She went very still for a minute. An answer seemed to depend on her finishing the coffee in her cup, so she did it. Jake did his best to keep his eyes from the way her throat worked. It was a classy throat, white and soft and slender.

But that didn't matter.

"You're Jake?" she asked, and he dragged his gaze back to those big eyes of hers.

"I'm Jake Kendall, and you're on the Diamond K Ranch. The cabin is not for rent, and this isn't a dude ranch. Try Jackson Hole. I'm sure there are a few open this early."

She was shaking her head even before he'd finished, making her hair dance and sway. "No, you don't understand. Lee sent me."

Jake had thought the day couldn't get worse. "What?"

She nodded this time. "She said she'd written to you to let you know I was coming. She gave me a key to the cabin and said that you wouldn't mind. I'm here to write a book."

Lee. Damn it, anyway. He'd been trying to curb his little sister's enthusiasm since her third birthday when she'd invited the entire town of Lost Ridge to the ranch for a barbecue. He'd survived wounded animals, heartsick girlfriends, an entire high school football team with no place to go for a homecoming party and any number of lost souls looking for work. He'd actually been counting on some peace and quiet now that she had gone east to school.

"You don't exactly look like one of her classmates," he retorted without any noticeable warmth.

"I'm not," she allowed with another of those friendly smiles that could kick a man right in the gut. "I'm a teacher. She was in my creative writing seminar this fall, and we got to be friends. I know she said she wrote you about it. My name's Amanda Marlow. When I told her I needed to do some research on western folklore and history for my next book, she suggested hiding out at the Diamond K." For a moment, her attention wavered toward the vista beyond the trees. "She didn't mention that this was just about the most beautiful place on earth."

The teacher. Jake remembered now, the nonstop talk around the holiday table about Lee's latest mentor, the award-winning author who seemed to understand all Lee's babble about plots and themes and symbolism. The Hollywood-bound wonder woman who could make little Lee's eyes glow like hot rocks and made Jake feel left out and alone, even with Lee.

"It's also a place without a phone and with electricity that isn't very reliable," Jake warned. "And a bathroom with a half moon on the door."

"I know." She grinned. "I got the chance to walk through the snow in my nightgown and boots last night. Quite an experience."

Jake desperately searched for another alternative. Anything rather than leave this woman on his property.

"Uh, would you like to come in?" she asked now, lifting her hand in a stiff movement toward the interior of the cabin. Then she smiled. "I feel a little silly inviting you into your own cabin. But I was going to talk to you, anyway, about interviewing the hands."

Jake stiffened. "I have to get back to the ranch. Write what you want, but it's foaling season. Don't interfere with the working of the ranch."

On the porch, Amanda Marlow took a step closer, her gleaming boots clacking on the old wood. "Oh, I wouldn't interfere. Lee said she thought you wouldn't mind...."

"Well, I would. You want to rough it, that's your business. Any problems, let Betty Engleman know. She's my secretary at the ranch."

With that, Jake turned on his heel to where Buck waited in perfect silence.

"Jake, wait."

But Jake was already swinging back up into the saddle, the bridle jangling and the leather creaking comfortably under his weight. Buck shifted a little and ducked his head. Familiar feelings, comfortable smells, a horse and leather and wool. Miss Marlow was the interloper here, the stranger. And yet Jake was the one who felt uncomfortable. He didn't say another word before spurring Buck into a hard gallop back across the meadow.

That was Lee Kendall's fussy, old-maid brother Jake? Amanda watched the horse and rider streak across the snow and shook her head. From the way Lee had described her older brother, Amanda had been expecting a cross between Roy Rogers and Johnny Appleseed. Lee had said her brother was shy and conscientious and honest. She'd often talked about how Jake had pampered and overprotected her, the baby in the family, as they were growing up. Lee wanted to write a book about what it had been like for a seventeen-year-old boy to raise his three younger siblings when his parents had died, and dedicate it to the man that boy had become.

Lee was never going to pass creative writing this way. Her description of Jake Kendall would never serve. But then again, Amanda couldn't quite come up with one that served, either.

Hard. It was the only word that came to mind. He sat his horse like a tower of granite, implacable and overwhelming. His face, all angles and shadows without so much as a dimple to soften them, was the kind of face women dream of and fear.

Amanda had just spent six weeks in Los Angeles working with the people who were going to transfer her latest book to the screen, and she'd seen a lot of handsome men. A lot of tall, sculpted men with faces made up of angles and shadows. She'd seen men who had spent their lives learning how to portray a character just like Jake Kendall. She'd never realized until meeting Jake that they didn't have a chance of accomplishing it.

It was the intangibles. The way he stood, square on both legs, as if measuring the earth beneath him. The way he talked, his words straightforward and uncompromising, the timbre of his voice like old, scarred wood. It was the way he carried his authority, like an aura, around him. It was the fact that all of these intangibles were his nature rather than any kind of pretension.

Honest. He had none of the small vanities most humans succumb to. Amanda saw it in his bearing, in his eyes, in the way he rode his horse and wore his clothes.

She thought his hair was light, maybe a chestnut color. With his hat pulled so low across his eyes, she couldn't quite tell. Those eyes, though, she'd seen. Crystals in the shadow, glittering lights in the gloom. A pale, gray-rimmed blue that stood out against the weathered-oak tan of his skin like high mountain lakes at dusk.

He'd taken her breath away, literally. There was a power about him, a natural sensuality she'd never experienced before—even amid some of the best-known beefcakes in the world. He had a quick, easy grace, a command that compelled. When he'd turned away from her, she'd come much too close to walking right off the porch after him. Even now she couldn't keep her eyes from where his figure sped along the swollen creek, black horse and dark man, his head bent low over the extended neck of the horse, body one with the fluid motion of the animal. She loved to watch a man ride a horse, and she'd just realized it.

Amanda watched until he was out of sight and then turned back into the cabin. Her suitcases were still on the couch, and the bed beyond was still rumpled. The walls were simple white with bright quilts as decorations. The windows were open to the meadow and the mountains beyond. In one corner, kitchen appliances had replaced the old wood stove, and at the other end a fireplace waited with cold ashes in the grate.

Lee had told her that this one-room building had been erected sometime around 1870 and renovated by that hard man out on horseback so that no one would lose the history of his ranch. Kept for family, if they needed someplace to escape, or friends, for hunting. Smelling faintly of coffee and dust and pipe tobacco. The floor was wood, and the furniture was simple. Amanda smiled at the feeling of home it gave her and walked over to punch the button on her tape recorder as she refilled her coffee cup.

"Note," she recited. "Don't forget to include how important clothing is on impressions of these characters. What they wear says more about them than what they say."

It was the boots. His attire had been regulation—flannel shirt and jeans and sheepskin jacket. Probably nothing much different from what his great-grandfather had worn to work this same land. Worn and faded and practical. But Amanda hadn't been able to help noticing those boots. Not shiny and squared and showy, like hers. Like all those hard men she'd just fended off in Los Angeles. These boots were as battered as Jake's features. Sturdy, solid boots with a good-sized heel and spurs and more wear and tear than the access road that had brought Amanda to this little cabin nestled at the edge of the meadow.

And that hat. Not typical, not like Amanda saw in the cigarette ads. A little wider, a bit taller, with a flat crown and a low brim beneath which he could gauge his opponent without being caught. Well worn, soft, sweat-stained. Just a little different, but beaten by use into as much of a statement as the boots and the torn kerchief he wore around his throat.

"I'll head over tomorrow to negotiate some interview time with the ranch hands," she mused aloud, taking a sip of her coffee, her gaze out to the snow. "But I think I have my character. Problem is, he doesn't want anything to do with me."

"What do you mean, you didn't get my letter?"

Jake pulled his hat off and tossed it at the rack by the door before easing down at the kitchen table. "I mean I didn't get a letter. Just this strange woman standing on the front porch of Bart Kendall's cabin. Why didn't you call me, dammit?''

He heard a heartfelt sigh and imagined Lee's eloquent young eyes rolling dramatically. "Because I sent the book along, too. I wanted to surprise you. I mean, I knew how much you'd enjoy Amanda's writing. She has a degree in world folklore, and instead of just compiling it into some dry text, she incorporates it into stories. She brings it to life. Oh, Jake, her writing is like poetry. It's lyrical. It's—"

"Not in my mail," he interrupted before she really got up a head of steam. "I'm warning you, little girl. I'm not babysitting this one. If she gets tired of taking a light out to the outhouse, she's just gonna have to camp on somebody else's living-room floor."

"Oh, she won't be any problem, Jake. Really. She just wanted to talk to Clovis and José and everybody. You know, get local color. Stories and traditions and songs and stuff."

Jake scowled heartily. "Well then, we'll have to get that Little Doggie Chorus in shape real quick, won't we?"

"Jake!"

"It's foaling season, Lee. I'm not going to have some college greenhorn interfering with the men. They have enough to do."

"Just for a few weeks," she pleaded. "I'm going to be there for spring break, so I can help out then. I promise she won't get in your way."

"Spring break?" He couldn't help a small grin. "I thought you were runnin' off to the beach with all your Ivy League buddies."

"Well, I...they..." Another sigh, but this one suspiciously quiet. "I miss home," she finally admitted. "Do you mind? I'm still getting used to this."

"I told you you should go someplace with mountains."

"Jake..."

He leaned back a little farther, stretching out a crick in his back from where he'd been wrestling with a stallion who didn't particularly like the vet. "Why didn't you tell me?" he asked, eyes closed as he massaged the offending muscles. "It's gonna cost an arm and a leg to fly you back now. Betty could have had the tickets in the mail three weeks ago.''

"Because I paid for these. You have enough on your hands right now without funding my homesickness.''

"Don't be ridiculous—''

"It's too late to argue. I have my tickets. I'll see you in a couple of weeks. In the meantime, take care of Amanda. I promise, you'll love her, Jake. She's really the greatest person on earth.''

"Ahem." An old joke, going back to the days when Lee had been a kindergartner and fallen in love with the little boy sitting next to her.

"Except for a certain brother I know," she gave in with a giggle, just like she always did.

"And don't forget it," he demanded on a growl. He knew she could hear his smile. He had another brother and sister, older than Lee, out in the world now in their professions. He was close to all three. But Lee was the baby. His kid sister. The dreamer and the poet and the will-o'-the-wisp that was sadly missing from the cold, hard ground outside and the empty rooms inside. Lee was his favorite, and there wasn't a damn thing he could do about it.

"Please be nice to her," his little sister begged, not knowing what she asked. "Just till I get there.''

Now Jake was rubbing at his eyes. He was tired, he was sore, and he was frustrated. But most of all, listening to the life in his little sister's voice, he was lonely. He'd spent his entire life working for the day when his family could successfully escape the ranch, and now he missed them with a hard ache that just wouldn't ease.

"I'll be nice to her.''

Ten minutes later he found himself standing at the front window, a beer in hand and his gaze out to the fences and buildings that stretched out across the high mountain plain nestled amid the Wind River Mountains. José was loading the tractor with feed for a run to the pasture, and Clovis was grooming his horse, a solid little paint named Montana. The other hands were out seeing to fences, and his cook, Maria, was humming out in the kitchen.

The buildings were clean and neat, the fences solid and the work areas open and uncluttered. A few horses clustered in the breaking pen and another group could be seen grazing in the near pasture, all sleek and fast and bright-eyed.

Jake knew the place looked prosperous. It should. He'd busted his butt to make it look that way. People driving through the gates of the Diamond K gaped at the magnificent vistas, the tidy red outbuildings and the long, low stone-and-wood ranch house with the smoke that always curled above a roaring fireplace. The new ones marveled at Jake's luck to be able to live where he did, and the old ones shook their heads in wonder that he'd been able to hang on to it the way he had. Not one of them saw what Jake did when he looked out this front window.

Jake didn't see the smooth beauty of a well-run ranch or count the money on the hoof that roamed his pastures. He didn't see the ragged clutter of the mountains or the vast Wyoming sky. All Jake Kendall could see when he looked out his window was the prison those mountains had become.

The ranch was a success. His sisters and brother were grown, happily exploring their new lives beyond the borders of the Diamond K. And Jake, who had worked so very hard for just that, was left behind. He was trapped by his own success, and couldn't see a way out anymore. And now, like a bad joke, he was going to have to face Lee's newest mentor, who was everything that was missing from his life.

Everything he couldn't have.

Downing the rest of his beer in one slug, Jake took one last look out to where the sun glittered off the distant snowy peaks. He was going to have to talk to Amanda Marlow. But he wasn't going to have to do it just yet. Turning away from the window, he tossed the can into the trash and picked his hat back up. There was work to do. It was spring again. He should have been in a better mood.

Instead, his past had come back to haunt him.

Chapter 2

Amanda had always believed in the adage about the best defense being a good offense. With that in mind she set out bright and early the next morning for the Diamond K proper. Since there was no direct road good enough even for the four-wheeler she'd rented in Jackson Hole, she was forced to take two miles of uncleared gravel track and six miles of mountain road that twisted and turned through stands of pine and aspen, past precipitous drops, and over a couple of one-lane bridges. She eventually reached the old-fashioned wooden entryway proclaiming the Diamond K, where another mile of gravel road led to the main compound.

Horses and a few cattle grazed in the pastures. Well-kept fences stretched for miles. The same stream that sang to her at night meandered along the broad meadows where the grass was beginning to appear beneath the melting snow. The ranch seemed a vast place, with more sky than the entire state of New York and the embrace of mountains for grandeur. Clustered into a fold in the land were a group of long, low barns, corrals, outbuildings and the main house, a long ranch that seemed as much a part of the land as the stream and mountains.

Amanda pulled the car to a stop alongside another vehicle parked by the main house and climbed out. The air was crisp and dry, the early morning mist already burned off. From the barns Amanda could hear human and equine voices raised in some kind of dispute, and from the house she could hear the twang of country-western music. She smiled as she reached for her purse with the ubiquitous tape recorder in it, and headed for the Kendall stronghold itself.

"Heard you were comin'." The woman who answered the door greeted her with a hint of dry humor.

Amanda grinned in return. "Betty?"

She nodded and held the screen door open.

As Amanda stepped past, she took in the impressions of starch and rosewater. She bet Betty had doilies on her furniture and wore a hat to church. And that she knew exactly what went on all around the Lost Ridge community, but wouldn't ever say a word about it.

"My name's Amanda Marlow."

Betty seemed to know. "Jake's down at the barn right now," she said crisply as she led the way into the kitchen. "The vet's seein' to one of the stallions."

"Not with much success, from the sounds of it."

Betty huffed indignantly. "Bill Nelson's beast, no doubt. He sent him to Jake too late, ya ask me. Coffee?"

Amanda figured she had only one answer, since they seemed to be headed for the kitchen, anyway. "Thanks."

She didn't miss any of the living room as she passed. Some of it she recognized from listening to Lee's stories. The big front window that looked out over the sunset, the old upright piano Lee had learned to play on, the worn, overstuffed furniture Jake refused to replace. A filled bookshelf took up one entire wall by the stone fireplace, and the hardwood floors were covered in handwoven Indian rugs. All neat, clean and looking unlived in. No pictures, no mementos, no life.

"I heard you were teaching little Lee?" Betty asked, turning into the big, bright room hung with pots and herbs, where the radio seemed to live. It was giving forth Dolly Parton at the moment.

"She took a creative writing seminar I taught," Amanda allowed, as she scanned the almost surgically clean room, obviously well run and orderly like the rest of the operation.

Betty sighed like a maternal aunt. "I miss her. Hasn't been any fun in this house to speak of since she left."

Amanda could well imagine. Jake Kendall hadn't struck her as the type of man to waste his time on frivolous pursuits. Betty must have made up the difference in affection and attention. Jake Kendall might be an honorable man, and the most respected horseman this side of the Mississippi, but Amanda couldn't exactly imagine him tying the bow on a little girl's dress or cushioning the heartbreak of a first lost love.

"Jake says Lee's coming home in a couple of weeks," Betty was saying as she poured out two mugs of coffee for them both. "I didn't figure she'd last very long out among strangers before she had to come home."

Amanda couldn't help grinning. The last time she'd seen Lee, the fresh-faced young blonde had been on stage in a very liberated interpretation of *The Madwoman of Chaillot,* and bringing down the house. Lee was doing just fine. "It is pretty far away for her," Amanda agreed instead.

Betty nodded judiciously. "She's a bright young thing."

Amanda paused midsip for a definite nod. "A force to be reckoned with. It was a real pleasure teaching her."

Betty must have heard the sincerity in Amanda's voice and judged her by it, because suddenly there was a real smile on those tight, middle-aged features.

"Don't think badly of Jake for being a little brusque with you yesterday."

Amanda looked up, surprised. Betty waved her hand.

"He told me he'd found you at the cabin, and I took it from there. He's real touchy about that place. And he really didn't know you were coming. I found Lee's package at the bottom of all the correspondence when I got back this morning. Been out with a bad back." She shook her head as she tasted her own coffee. "It's gotten to the point over the years where Jake doesn't even know the mail's there if I'm not wavin' it in his face."

"He's that busy?"

Betty laughed, a short, sharp sound. "Sometimes I wonder how he ever got the chance to get to church on Sundays. He's worked mighty hard for this place."

Amanda took a symbolic look around. "It really shows. Lee thinks he walks on water."

"Well, she was only a baby when her mama died. Five or six. Jake's been everything to her since."

"And their father?"

Amanda didn't get her answer. Just then a door slammed at the back of the house and boots clattered across the floor.

"Betty!"

Betty's face folded into wry patience. "I'm in the kitchen, mister. Not in Casper."

Amanda turned toward the sound of the voice, her hands unconsciously clenched around the mug. She didn't exactly know what to expect this time, no matter Betty's explanation. She didn't know what she wanted. A different Jake Kendall? The same one? Would he seem smaller in this house than he had out in the soft mountain morning? Would he seem less distinct, more normal?

He seemed none of those things. Jake Kendall filled the doorway, his size undiminished, his strength and sensuality pervading the room. Amanda felt it in her chest like a slow sizzle; felt it in her fingertips and the base of her scalp. Jake Kendall was the most overwhelming man she'd ever known. And he didn't even consider it.

He was scowling at her again. "I see you showed up."

Amanda tried a faint smile. "One of my most infuriating habits. I can't take no for an answer."

His hat was still on, still pulled low over his eyes so Amanda could see no more than a glint of silver, like polished mirrors. Something deep inside those mirrors, though, sent little frissons down her back. He didn't wear his coat today, and his flannel shirtsleeves were rolled almost to his elbows. Amanda saw the power in those forearms and wondered briefly what the rest of him looked like. It didn't make her any more comfortable.

He didn't move. "Work out a schedule with Betty, then. And remember—"

"Don't get in the way," she answered with him and nodded. "I tried to tell you yesterday, but you didn't...uh, have the time. I've done this before. You won't even know I'm here."

He didn't need to voice his disbelief.

The sudden static in the room even set Betty to fidgeting. "Did you have a reason for yelling at me?" she demanded of her boss. "Or are you just in another ornery mood?"

Jake considered his secretary. There was no perceptible softening of his features, but somehow he softened. "Maria back from town yet?" he asked, his voice just as gruff, just as short.

"Is her car in the driveway?"

Amanda could have sworn that the corner of his mouth crooked just a little. "See if you can catch her at the store and have her stop by the feed store on the way back. They're supposed to hold some liniment for me."

"You gonna eat a real lunch?"

"You gonna fix it?"

Betty nodded briskly. "Peanut butter and jelly it is."

They didn't seem to need any more than that. Jake turned on his heel and walked back out the door, and Betty gave her head another slow shake and her coffee her undivided attention.

"He always that talkative?" Amanda asked.

"Only around company. Usually he's *real* quiet."

Jake didn't even notice the clattering from the stallion barn as he strode back from the house. He didn't hear José's hair-curling Spanish response or the laughter from Clovis. His mind was on the woman he'd just left. On what she was going to do to his life if he let her.

Maybe it was because Lee was gone that he was suddenly so restless. Maybe it was the spring, his time to get out and reacquaint himself with the Wyoming mountains, when the foals were born and the wildflowers returned and he could forget about how empty that house had gotten all of a sudden.

Maybe it was past time to settle down, just like Betty kept telling him. He couldn't honestly say he wouldn't mind walking back into the house at night to a home-cooked meal from his wife instead of the housekeeper. He'd like to share the day with someone. He couldn't even say he didn't ache hard along about the middle of the night when that bed got so damn empty he'd be willing to trade almost anything to fill it.

But even flirting with the idea of filling it with that woman who sat up in his house right now was pure lunacy. She wouldn't understand him. She wouldn't fit into his life and help him the way a wife would. Hell, she probably thought a good time was a night out at the opera or theater or something. Not small talk about how the mares were faring or what it took to get a good horse to be a great cutting horse.

She wasn't a farm girl, dressed in those tailored clothes. She was sleek and classy and expensive. She was the kind of person Lee wanted to become—smart and sophisticated and rich in ways he'd never get to taste. And aching for her wouldn't do him a damn bit of good. He was just going to have to get through her time here at the ranch and then go on with his life just the way it had been.

"Hey, boss, you listenin' to me?"

Startled, Jake looked up to find that he'd walked right into the stallion barn without even noticing it. In front of him stood Clovis and José, both dusty and disgruntled. The clattering continued from the general direction of the stall of the stallion Bill Nelson had asked him to handle. If the last two days were any indication, it was already too late. But that wasn't what Jake was thinking about as he faced his foreman.

Jake lifted his hat and took a swipe at his forehead with his arm. "What, Clovis?"

Clovis smiled with all ten of his remaining teeth, his leathery skin disintegrating into a field of wrinkles. "Distracted, huh, boss? Can't rightly blame ya. She's the sweetest lookin' lady I've seen in these parts since that Hollywood actress got lost from the dude ranch up over Jackson Hole way."

Jake gave the balding, bandy-legged man one of his best glares, knowing perfectly well that it wouldn't make any difference. "Well, comb your hair. She's gonna want to talk to you."

That earned a whistle of appreciation from both men.

"She's researching some book she's doing. And if I catch either of you slacking off on your work, you can just go on back to Massachusetts or wherever the hell she's from with her and try and find a job wrangling there.''

Both men bobbed their heads and grinned identical grins. ''Yes, boss.''

That did nothing to improve his temper. ''Now, what did you want to say?''

''Besides the fact that that palomino of Bill Nelson's should have his tail clipped right behind his ears?'' Clovis asked with a wry glance over his shoulder to where the stallion continued to voice his displeasure with the worming he'd received. ''Sweetpea's gonna drop that foal tonight. And I'd put money on the fact that Mistral's about to follow.''

Jake sighed. Another sleepless night. Clovis was a magician with the mares, sensing with amazing precision when they would foal, when they'd receive a stallion and when they were in any kind of trouble. But foaling wasn't something that was done alone on this ranch.

''All right,'' he decided, gazing down toward the shadowy recesses of the long barn where more than one equine nose peaked over the stalls. ''José, let's just work Filbert, Denver Lady and Joker today, then. I don't think I'm gonna have the energy to do a full load and then play midwife.''

''Maybe that nice Mizz Marlow'd like to watch tonight,'' José suggested with suspicious diffidence.

''She would not,'' Jake snarled, turning away again. ''We're not running a dude ranch here.''

She'd be gone soon, he kept thinking. Bored with the emptiness of the high plain, the silence of the mountain nights, the stories of men grown old wandering from ranch to ranch. There couldn't be anything here to interest her. There couldn't.

Bart Kendall had settled the Diamond K to raise cattle. Two wives, twelve children, three droughts and innumerable Indian raids and range wars later, he had died in his bed and left the place to his eldest and only surviving son, Ezekial.

Amanda had come out to Wyoming to steep herself in the local history, the culture that had evolved over the years since the mountain men and Indians hosted the fur-trading rendez-vous back in the 1830s. The book she intended to do would encompass both sides of western history, that of the settlers, the trappers and cattle drovers, and that of the Indians, who had been slowly pushed from their ancestral hunting grounds. A book of contrasts, of a culture growing and one almost withered away.

In a few weeks when the weather was warm enough and the mountains free enough of snow, she'd head up to the Wind River Reservation and meet with the historians and storytellers there. But for now, she wanted to know how the ranches had grown, how the people had survived horrific winters and dry summers. How they'd entertained themselves, and about the legends they'd left behind.

Unbelievably she'd hit paydirt right here at the Diamond K. Records from those first Kendalls. Letters, deeds, diaries, all hoarded away in the attic for posterity and mostly forgotten until Amanda's request had brought them to the ever-efficient Betty's mind.

Bart's first wife, Hattie Simpson Kendall, had been a schoolteacher back East. She'd taught her children and written down her thoughts during those long winters when her husband was gone and her children asleep. She'd recounted stories about lost children, long rainless summers and blizzards, doubts and dreams that, even written by guttering lamplight in a snowbound cabin in the lonely mountains of Wyoming, were universal and unchanging.

Amanda knew her, knew her dreams and her doubts and the private hurts and sorrows that every woman hoards away. She knew that Hattie, who had died at the age of thirty-one in childbirth, was the everywoman of her book. Carefully turning those precious, brittle pages alone in the dining room of the Kendall ranch, Amanda was flooded with the adrenaline of discovery, of insight. For the first time in almost a year, she felt excited.

"What are you doing?"

Still lost in the century-old world of Hattie's words, Amanda took a moment to even hear the abrupt question. It took her another to look up.

She wondered if Bart had looked anything like his great-grandson did now. Had he been big, powerful, strong enough to cut out his place in a wild land? Had he stunned his wife to silence every time he showed up in the doorway?

"Betty got these down for me," she finally managed to say, straightening away from the pages. "She said you wouldn't mind."

Jake shifted his weight and glared at her, his expression unreadable. He reached up and lifted his hat off his head to brush a forearm back over his forehead. Amanda had been right. His hair was light, a darker blond than his sister's, thick and just a little curly, creased beneath the constant pressure of the hat.

She shouldn't stare. She couldn't help it. She should get up or speak or smile, as she usually did if confronted by a problem. She couldn't. He seemed to hold her in place with only the force of his eyes.

His shirt was sweat-stained, and his boots muddy. Amanda could smell horses, leather and liniment on him, and thought them the most honest aromas she'd encountered in a very long time. The seductive scents of honest work and accomplishment. The silence between them threatened to stretch into discomfort.

"You have a real treasure here," Amanda suggested, gesturing to the papers scattered around her on the table. "Most people aren't lucky enough to have their history so carefully preserved for them."

He stiffened a little. Hardened. Again, she couldn't quite read his reaction. He'd resettled his hat so that it protected his eyes. But for the briefest of moments Amanda thought what that hat was hiding was a flash of pain in those chiseled features, a raw grief that had no place in Jake Kendall's expression. But as quickly as she caught it, it was gone behind the shifting of a jaw, the squint of his eyes.

It didn't make any sense. And yet, it made Amanda want to stand up, to go to him. She held her place. "With your permission, I'd like to incorporate some of Hattie's story in my work."

"You said you did folklore," he said. "What does that have to do with the ranch?"

Just the tone of his voice overcame her good sense. He didn't understand, and Amanda had to make him. The possibilities those words had created were already burning in her, and that wasn't something she could forfeit again.

"I do," she allowed, meeting those mesmerizing crystal eyes with her own. "But I prefer to incorporate real folklore into accounts of fictional lives. How the folklore grew in the culture, who passed it on, who kept it. People seem to enjoy it more that way than when I just put everything in an anthology. If Lee didn't send you one of my books, I can get one for you if it would help. I have one on the Appalachians, *Simple Gifts,* and another on the Mississippi called—"

He waved her off even before she finished. "I have a ranch to run, Miss Marlow. That leaves me precious little time for anything else."

Amanda stepped forward again, afraid of losing her link to the past, the spark that would ignite an entire book. Hattie was a gift, and Amanda wasn't the kind of author to simply give a gift back.

"Hattie was so eloquent," she protested, her hand instinctively out to him, to stop him, to convince him, to make him understand the fire that had been missing for so long. "She deserves to be heard. If you don't read me, read her. Read what your great-grandmother said about your home, because I promise you'll see this place in a whole new light."

"I don't need a new light," he snapped, turning on her, standing so close Amanda could see the stubble of new beard on his chin. She could feel the brush of his breath on her cheek and the curious, curling heat of his gaze. "I see this place every day, and there isn't a damn thing that's romantic about it."

Amanda faced him, unflinching, mesmerized by the glint of those eyes, unnerved by the harsh cant of his voice, the steely control of some emotion that churned just below the surface.

"Take the damn things," he snarled, bearing down on her. "Take whatever the hell you want. Just get out of my hair."

Amanda backed up, his ferocity frightening her. She bumped up against the dining chair and reached back to balance herself. He was scaring her. He was compelling her. His nearness sizzled along her nerve endings like imminent lightning. His eyes smoldered. His hands clenched at his sides, and Amanda could see the pulse jumping in his throat.

How could one man take the strength from her knees? How could he make her ache just by glaring at her? By letting his gaze slip from her face down to where the top button of her blouse lay open. Down to the corduroy slacks she'd worn and the boots that would survive snow and pasture. She thought she saw derision in his gaze, frustration. She thought she saw the sudden smolder of desire, and it frightened her even more.

By the time his gaze returned to hers, there was only cold ferocity left. "People like you can't leave well enough alone," he accused her on a growl.

Amanda didn't know what he meant. She wasn't sure he did. She straightened, fought for composure. For sanity when her heart was thudding and her palms were damp with anticipation. "You don't understand...."

His laughter was as harsh as his expression. "Oh, I understand all right." He lifted a hand. It was all Amanda could do to keep from flinching. But he didn't mean to strike her. He reached out to test her skin with his finger. Amanda caught her breath. She couldn't quite pull a thought together past the sudden churn of electricity just the brush of a callused finger could ignite. She couldn't understand the sudden softening in those haunted blue eyes.

"I understand just fine," he murmured. His hand slid past her cheek to her hair, and his fingers curled along her throat, holding her, freezing her with the scorching intensity of his touch.

His eyes met hers, enigmatic, hypnotic eyes, eyes that glinted with ferocity and yet melted with a sudden, inexplicable yearning. Amanda was certain he meant to kiss her. She trembled with it, battered by the onslaught to her senses, suddenly hungry and afraid. She met his gaze with more courage than she had, with more composure than that hot, hard blue left her. Her chest burned for air. Her legs threatened to buckle. For a brief breath of a moment, they stood poised on the brink of something neither understood, and it shook Amanda to her very core.

Just as suddenly, Jake let go. "Take the papers," he said, straightening. "Talk to the hands. Buy a horse if you want. Just stay clear of me."

And with no more than that, he turned and walked back out of the house. It took Amanda another solid five minutes before she could manage a coordinated movement.

Dear Lord, what had just happened? She'd been frozen like a frog in the glare of a flashlight, thought and action thrown into sudden immobility by just the touch of one man. That had never happened before. She'd been engaged, so close to the altar that she could hear the organ music, and she'd never felt so shattered by the loss of her fiancé's touch as she felt now. She'd never had to reach around and support herself on a chair just to keep from puddling right down on the floor where she stood.

Jake was sexy, there was no doubt about that. Sexy in a way she'd never experienced before, earthy and raw and sensual. But more than that had brought her down. The ferocity in his eyes hadn't been simple desire. It had been conflict and longing.

What was it she'd seen in his eyes? What history? What loss? Amanda had come to the Diamond K in the hopes she could cull stories and gather jokes and songs and riddles from the hands. But it was the boss who haunted her. She wanted to understand this man whose sister adored him, who commanded respect and yet treated her with a kind of harsh anger that didn't make sense.

What had hurt him? Who had hurt him? Because Amanda was sure that that was what had been lying beneath his curious words and actions. A hurt so deep that it scarred him. A hurt that had been buried more deeply than the papers in that attic.

For a long few minutes she stood where she was, her fingers lingering over the place Jake Kendall had touched. She could still feel his hand on her, the rasp of work-hardened fingers, the almost painful gentleness of the contact. The stunning impact of his ambivalence. Contrasts and questions. Chemistry and confusion.

He was the most potent, troubling, fascinating man she'd ever met. He'd just told her to stay away from him. Amanda looked out the front window at the far end of the room to where Jake Kendall was swinging up onto a paint horse in the corral, and all she could think of was what she could do to get around his edict.

Because she wouldn't stay away from him. It was a stupid decision for her to make. Unproductive, unwise, certainly unpopular. The last thing she needed right now was the enigma of Jake Kendall. The last thing she wanted was conflict. She'd had enough of that in the last three years. She'd had fame and fortune and the double-edged sword of adulation. She'd come to Wyoming to recover her peace, to rediscover the joys of being a hermit. And her second day here, she was trying her best to figure out a way to give it away again.

Stupid.

She smiled anyway, a tremulous, nervous smile that was equal parts exhilaration and terror. Amanda might be a folklore writer, but what she really liked was mysteries. And Jake Kendall was the most intriguing mystery she'd ever come across. A mystery that still crackled across her fingertips like an electrical storm. He'd unwittingly challenged her with his silence, and now she had no choice but to answer. It was probably the most dangerous thing she'd ever done in her life, but she was going to get to the bottom of Jake Kendall, whether he liked it or not.

Chapter 3

Bart's a good man. He tries real hard to make this place something, but it just seems the weather and such conspire against him. We been on this land nigh on eight year and still can't seem to get ahead. If he weren't so fierce proud of this little bit of the mountains, we might have long since left. But I guess it's in his blood.

Amanda put down Hattie's diary and looked out across the meadow. The sun was setting, washing the snow in a soft rose light. The mountains beyond were mauve, and the sky a startling deep blue that was reflected in the stream. Overhead a flock of birds broke the late-afternoon silence, and the trees rustled. The stream gurgled and chattered in never-ending refrain. Amanda listened hard, but she couldn't hear anything else. Not a thing. This vast, open space, these magnificent mountains, were silent.

It had been so long since she'd been able to enjoy silence. Since she'd been able to take in a really deep breath without fighting the urge to cough. L.A. had been a cacophony of traffic and humanity, and before it her college campus had never seemed to sleep. In the last seven years since leaving home, Amanda had lived in New York and Philadelphia and

Boston. And every day in those cities had drained her juices a little more. Every honk and curse and low-flying airplane that had interrupted her sleep had stolen her precious peace where the words were born.

Jake Kendall had been given a rare gift in this place. His ancestors had fought plagues and locusts and Indians and weather of all kinds to preserve it for him, never knowing quite what a precious commodity it was.

Jake said there was nothing romantic about it. Maybe so, but there was something awesome about it. Something magical and mysterious. Amanda had been so long away from the special silence of the mountains that she could see it. She could smell it, taste it, hear it. And until she'd sat on this old porch with the ghosts of Bart and Hattie Kendall to keep her company, she hadn't even known she'd missed it quite so much.

"God, I hope you cherish this place," she murmured to the absent Jake as she watched the sun set over his land. "I hope you know just what it is your great-grandparents fought so hard to preserve for you."

"Jake's tied to the Diamond K the way a baby's tucked into a mama's teat," Clovis said with a nod of certainty. "He don't see no reason to go more'n twenty miles from home."

They were sitting in Stilwell's, the Lost Ridge claim to diner fame, where Amanda was treating Clovis to an early dinner. It was technically his day off, but as there was a mare overdue for foaling, he wanted to be back in the barn by dark, when mares preferred to do their birthing.

Amanda took a sip of her iced tea and initialed the tape she'd just recorded of Clovis's memories of his daddy's days on the trail. "Jake doesn't even go to the horse auctions or anything?"

"Don't need to. People come to him. Ranchers, outfitters, some of the top competition riders in the business. They all know where Jake Kendall lives. They want a good cuttin' horse, stock horse of any kind, that's the place to go."

"You've been with him for a while."

Clovis nodded and took another big slug of steaming coffee. "Got tired of hirin' out. One bunkhouse looks pretty much like another, and I ain't got family left to speak of."

"Isn't his ranch a little smaller than you were used to?"

"Sure. I used to ride range in Montana, Utah, New Mexico. Started in Texas when there was still some room down there, but it's all fencin' now. Not many places left you can spend a couple of months in the saddle without seein' anything but cowboys. Not like in my grandaddy's day when a mustang really had to cut cattle for a living and a man spent his nights singin' a herd to sleep."

Amanda nodded. "I want to get some of your songs on tape later, if you don't mind."

"Got no voice to speak of," he demurred, his complexion coloring a little. "But I'll give you the words."

"Clovis," the waitress demanded, swooping in on them wearing jeans that looked spray painted on and a pink ruffled blouse over much of her well-endowed frame. "You gonna have some pie today, or you just gonna make me broke on coffee refills?"

Clovis grinned with every one of his remaining teeth, his face wrinkling up like old tissue paper at her approach. "Can't I just sit here watchin' you sashay around, Lila?"

Her answering smile transformed her makeup-ladened face into sweet affection as she took a pat at what Amanda's mother would have called her chosen-blond coiffure. "Sure you can. You just gotta pay for it, like everybody else."

Clovis nodded. "Apple. With cheese."

Amanda considered the row of half-consumed pies in the case behind the counter and wondered if they'd sit half as heavy as the blue plate special. "Apple," she conceded with a half-hearted smile.

Lila tip-tapped back along the worn linoleum floor to the matching counter with its red swivel stools and donut plate and thirty-year-old cash register. People spent a fortune in Los Angeles to copy decor like this for trendy burger joints and upscale bars. This was pure small town, from the red Naugahyde booths to the flickering neon sign in the window that proselytized Eat, to the surly short-order cook who thought grease was an herb. The combination didn't seem to bother the town of Lost Ridge, because the place was full.

Amanda hadn't been surprised to see every head turn as she followed Clovis into the restaurant. She knew about small towns and strangers. Clovis had taken great delight in setting everybody straight the minute Lila had first shown up by introducing Amanda as a writer-lady friend of Lee's who'd come to Lost Ridge to learn about the real West. Lee's recommendation had gone a long way to turn the slightly closed expressions into ones of welcome.

"Doesn't he see his family?" Amanda demanded suddenly.

Clovis looked up in some confusion. "Who?"

She grinned sheepishly. "Jake. I'm sorry, I was just thinking about what you said about Jake's not leaving the ranch. His sisters and brother aren't here anymore. When does he see them?"

"They come here. Ever' one of 'em knows better than to ask Jake to set foot on a plane. Jake just ain't one for travelin'." The grizzled little man huffed a couple of times, which was evidently his version of a laugh, and smoothed his well-slicked graying hair back yet again. "Why, last time Jake even left town was for Gen's graduation from doctor school. Kids chipped in to get him a ticket to Chicago, thinkin' how excited he'd be to see a big city. He derned near walked home, he hated it so much. I think he just made it through the ceremony before he found himself a plane to take."

Amanda couldn't help grinning, thinking of the acerbic, closemouthed Jake battling the hustle and bustle of Chicago. It would have been a picture to behold.

Amanda didn't really pay attention to the sound of the door opening behind her, or the tinkling of the bell that hung over it. She was thinking of what questions she could get away with asking Clovis about his boss. There was so much she wanted to know, and only a certain amount fell beneath the umbrella of research for her books.

"Well, there he is," Clovis said suddenly.

Amanda looked up from her last sips of iced tea to see him looking over her shoulder. "Who?" she asked and turned.

She didn't need an answer. She got one, anyway.

"The boss."

She couldn't take her eyes off him. She couldn't close her mouth or form words. He'd taken off his hat and stood at the other end of the diner ironing out the brim with his hand, giving the diner a quick look around. His hair was tousled and his face clean-shaven and his jacket exchanged for an old gray rag wool sweater that had a little hole up by the shoulder. Same boots, though. Hard, battered and solid as their owner. As he stood there, several people in booths and at tables called out greetings.

Amanda was thinking that she should have turned back to Clovis. She should have remembered the value of discretion, or at least attempted to hide the flush that was slowly creeping up her neck at the sight of him. Then he responded to the townspeople and Amanda was frozen all over again.

He smiled. A real smile, warm and friendly and just a little shy, so that it crinkled up his eyes and showed the stark white of his teeth against his tanned features. He held out his hand again and again, greeting this neighbor and that with questions about relatives or animals or occupations.

Amanda could see that each person he greeted was truly glad to see him. The men showed respect, and the women showed the kind of maternal pride that tends to bloom around a local boy who's done well. No wonder Jake Kendall didn't need to leave town. He'd made it his own.

That smile, though. That crooked cant that said so much but betrayed so little. He was comfortable here. He belonged. He spoke the common language and knew he held the respect and affection of the people he met. Which made Amanda wonder what he felt every time he saw her.

She was about to get the chance to find out.

"Hey, boss," Clovis called out with an upraised hand. "Over here."

Finally the urge to hide surfaced, but it was too late. He was turning their way. Amanda saw his expression stumble over her presence as surely as if he'd been a runner hitting a pothole. The pleasure dimmed; the certainty froze.

She was an alien. An interloper. Amanda could see it all the way across the room and resented it. She resented even more the loss of his smile. It had metamorphosed him completely, melting the rigid loner into a bright, open neighbor with just a trace of vulnerability peeking through. In other words, the man Lee had described all semester long.

But that wasn't something he was willing to give Amanda just yet. She wasn't someone he really knew. Someone he could trust. No matter what electricity the two of them kindled when they met, this was his place, and it was her job to accommodate. She might not have been from Lost Ridge, but her hometown wasn't all that different. She knew from experience that she was going to have to earn that smile back.

Well, she decided, manufacturing what she hoped was an easy smile of greeting for him, I've earned everything I have so far. How hard could a simple smile be in comparison?

She almost laughed out loud. Every publisher and educator along the East Coast put together couldn't match the determination in this one man. She was in trouble.

"Come over and sit down," Clovis was inviting, even as Jake greeted a few more people on his way down the narrow aisle. "We was just talkin' about you."

Amanda turned on Clovis, wishing she could stop him or warn him or something and knowing there wasn't anything she could say.

"About me?" Jake asked, coming to a stop at the booth.

He seemed to tower above Amanda. He did it on purpose, too, his eyes dark and suddenly a bit flat.

"The ranch," Amanda amended quickly. "Clovis has been talking a little about his work, and that naturally led to what he's doing now."

"He tell you a lot, did he?"

His eyes seemed so hot, so cold at once, boring into hers. Leaving her no room for thought or deception. "Oh, yes," she agreed, wondering why she felt like a speeder who'd just spotted a cop. "He remembered a lot of stories and riddles and songs his father and grandfather used on the trail. I even heard some new Jim Bridger stories I hadn't come across yet."

Slowly Jake nodded, his hat still in both hands, although his knuckles were a little taut. "Clovis has been known to tell some great stories."

Clovis didn't seem to notice the sudden tension. "Have you eaten yet, boss? Sit on down."

Jake seemed to startle a little at the sound of his foreman's voice. "Oh . . . uh, no. You're busy, Clovis."

"Heck, no," the little man challenged, scooting over to give him room. "We're just jawin', now. Mizz Marlow here was sharin' some weather signs with me. You know, like as how bees don't get wet and the birds wash in the dust when it's about to rain. That kinda thing."

Jake didn't take his eyes off Amanda. Turning his hat once in his hands, he abruptly nodded. "All right."

Amanda wasn't sure whether she felt better or worse when he sat down. She certainly didn't feel any more relaxed. His proximity danced along her nerve endings like static electricity. His distrust set her teeth on edge. His eyes drew her gaze like a hypnotist's watch.

Once again, she thought she caught something unreadable in their depths, something that tugged at her. Confusion, ambivalence. Not contempt or anger, but frustration. Dislocation, as if he suddenly weren't sure of himself.

Again it disappeared quickly beneath the hard glitter of challenge. Again it bothered her, because she knew from too long experience that it was that brief glimpse deep inside him that was important.

Clovis didn't seem to notice. He kept right on discussing Amanda's information as he resettled his hat and jacket further along the booth. "Y'know, we was talkin' about how pigs can see the wind. Why, I ain't heard that one fer years. Just years. My mama's favorite was 'when the dew's on the grass, rain will never come to pass.'"

"That right?" Jake answered absently, still faced off with Amanda, his gaze still hot and hard as he set his hat down alongside his place.

Clovis nodded from behind his coffee mug. "Ask her," he insisted. "She's really got some good ones. Maybe we should collect 'em so's we can predict the weather better, ya think?"

He huffed again, his face reddening in delight.

Amanda had nothing to disappear behind. She felt naked and unsettled. She wanted to ask Jake what was troubling him so much. "I'm quite the expert on predicting harsh winters by vegetable," she admitted, trying for levity, wishing her chest didn't hurt with the tension. "If you'd like, I'll do a free check on your onion skins next fall for you."

"And here I've been relying on the weather service."

She tried another small smile. "Give me a good onion and a woolly worm any day."

Jake dropped his gaze to where he was fingering the edges of his hat. Amanda retreated briefly to her glass of iced tea, and then remembered that she was in need of a refill. He caught her looking for Lila.

"How do you like the local choice in restaurants?" he asked, just a little edge to his voice.

Now Amanda's smile was sincere. "It reminds me a lot of home."

Jake gave her a good look up and down. "I thought Boston had a better reputation than that."

Amanda never got the chance to set him straight. Just then Lila returned balancing two slices of pie, the coffeepot and another cup and saucer, which she set in front of Jake.

"Saw you come in," she greeted him, pouring for him even before setting down the pies. "Heard Bill Nelson finally gave in and sent you Sidewinder."

Clovis snorted unkindly. "Day late, as usual. Only good use for that animal is stickin' pictures in a book."

"He'll come around," was all Jake said as he picked up his cup for his first drink.

"Menu?" Amanda asked, offering him the battered laminated page that had been amended with grease pencil and then stuck next to her side of the booth.

Lila thought that was so funny she almost dropped Amanda's pie. "Menu?" she demanded with a hoot. "You kiddin'? Jake here hasn't surprised me a day in his life. What'll it be, Jake?" she demanded, hand on plump denim-clad bottom. "Steak or steak?"

Jake's smile was a little tight. "Make it steak this time, Lila."

She nodded with satisfaction. "Bleedin' and burnt," she pronounced, then turned to Amanda. "Cook threw that steak on the grill the minute Jake walked in. He hasn't had anything else in the ten years I've worked here, have you, Jake?''

"Guess not, Lila."

Amanda didn't know what to do. For the first time in years she felt completely at a loss with another human being. Jake sat in stony silence drinking his coffee while noise continued unabated around him in the rest of the diner. Clovis dug into his pie with a gusto Amanda couldn't quite muster, and Amanda was left with silence.

"Hey, Jake," a man from a nearby table called out. "Saw old Nate Thompson other day, said to tell you that as soon as he moved to summer pasture, he's comin' by for those trail horses you promised."

Jake turned to answer, and Amanda was struck by the strength of his profile. Clean, hard lines, his nose just a little hooked, his chin strong and solid, his jaw like granite. His eyes pale as memories. Honest, rough-hewn features that gnawed at her composure in a way no others had before. She quelled an urge to run her fingers through the tumble of his thick hair and smooth it back off his forehead. She turned away to keep from falling headfirst into the icy waters of his eyes that seemed to thaw for anybody but her.

"I'll be lookin' for him," he said, his expression easing. "Got some real hardy little things this year should be perfect for the Tetons."

"Did I also hear that Tommy's gonna be in town again?"

Jake nodded, sipping his coffee. "He's comin' to take a look at that cutting horse he wants."

"That pony as good as I've been hearing?"

Then Amanda saw something in Jake she hadn't seen yet, a deep, quiet glow of satisfaction. Pride. Nothing that anyone could take offense at, simply the pleasure of something good.

"Maybe, Ed," he said with just a hint of a smile. "Maybe."

"Maybe?" Clovis demanded in outrage. "Hell, son. That pony can cut the flour out of a biscuit and not break the crust."

Ed nodded his lean balding head. "Well, everybody's sure looking for another Grayboy."

Jake nodded, obviously knowing what the man was talking about. "Well, he may just get him this time. I've always had good luck with Grayghost get, and this one looks to be no different.''

Amanda waited for the rest of the discussion on horse lineage to pass before asking the obvious.

"Grayboy?"

Jake was turning back to her as Clovis jumped in. "Best damn cuttin' horse in the U.S. He's won more money for riders on circuit than any other horse in the last decade. Foaled right at the Diamond K."

"Circuit," Amanda echoed. "Rodeo?"

"Cutting horse competitions," Clovis said. "The National Cutting Horse Association Futurity and World Championships for the last three years runnin' were won on Diamond K horses."

Jake lifted an eyebrow at her. "You're not familiar with cutting horses?"

"I'm not familiar with the species at all," she admitted. "I've been on a mule, but I have a feeling it's a little different."

Jake's expression was one of disbelief. Clovis put it into words.

"You don't know horses? Then what are you doin' a book on the West for?"

Amanda grinned at the outraged little man. "I'm doing folklore," she admitted. "Not a dictionary."

"But all your good stories is about horses," Clovis protested. "Wouldn't be no West without 'em. Would there, boss?"

Jake hadn't taken his eyes off her. Amanda could feel them like a brand, an accusation, and it unsettled her. She didn't know what Jake was thinking, what he suspected or expected. She just knew that she was making him unhappier by the minute.

"Is this how you do your research?" he asked quietly. "Just show up someplace and try and figure out what's going on?"

Amanda's first reaction was to bristle. She had a dual master's degree. If there was only one thing she'd come away from higher education with, it was the ability to research. And no rancher who'd been never farther from home than the local diner had any right to question her.

But then she realized that she hadn't been allowed yet to present her case. Jake had judged her on sight for some reason, and left the rest to supposition. It was high time to set him right.

"I came to the Diamond K," she allowed, "for a chance to do my research and writing in peace. My schedule has been a bit hectic the last few years, and I was having trouble getting into this new book. As for research, I have enough books, journals, maps and tapes back at that cabin to sink a good-size ship. I usually start there and then go out in the field. In fact, I'm due up at the Wind River Reservation in about six weeks."

"Then why are you trompin' all over my ranch?"

Clovis stiffened at his employer's words, even more his tone. If Amanda's reasons had been a little more altruistic, she would have stiffened right alongside her new friend. But she had to admit, at least to herself, that it was more than research that was bringing her over to the other side of that long, silent meadow.

"I came," she said with great control, "to introduce myself, just like Lee said. When Betty found those papers for me, I couldn't help reading through them. They're just what I want. More than anything I already have." She looked down at her pie, still whole and fragrant before her, before braving Jake's expression again. "And, I guess, I'm not quite used to all the quiet yet. I miss voices. I figured I'd try doing my on-site and existing research simultaneously."

Jake seemed to be making some kind of judgment. "That outdoor john a little too realistic, after all?"

Amanda couldn't help a short bark of laughter. "Mr. Kendall, I grew up with one of those things in my backyard. Don't patronize me."

"Here you are, Jake," Lila announced, bringing the table to a sudden silence as she slapped down a plate brimming with a slab of charcoaled meat, French fries and cole slaw. "Eat up. I've already got your pie out."

Amanda looked away from the raw surprise in Jake's eyes and finally attacked her pie before either of them had a chance to say anything more.

The pie surprised her. After that leaden lump of meat somebody called meatloaf, the delicate crust and delicious crisp apple filling didn't seem to be possible. Amanda took a bite and looked up at her dinner companion where he was knifing into a steak that was thick, juicy and as red as blood on the inside. He must have noticed the look on her face. He immediately turned to Clovis.

"She had the blue plate, didn't she?" he demanded.

Clovis looked a bit confused. He looked to Amanda for verification.

She nodded.

Jake shook his head and turned back to her with the first betrayal of friendliness in his eyes. "Clovis should have warned you. The blue plate here is leftovers from at least two dinners and three school lunches, but Clovis never notices. He can't taste food. Never get the blue plate."

Amanda swallowed the pie in a gulp. "I take it the steak is a pretty safe bet?"

His sudden grin was almost wolfish as he speared a piece of meat into his mouth and promptly dispatched it. "Haven't been disappointed yet."

By the time Jake made it back out of Stilwell's, the sky was deepening to night and the air was cold. He shouldn't have stayed that long. He never had before, preferring to eat his meal quickly and take quick care of the type of business he tended to find among the crowded tables at the diner, so he could head home before the sun set.

Tonight he'd arranged an extra load of hay from Wilbur Potts and set a date for Steve Bennett's wife to come out and look over the herd for a speed horse for her daughter's first foray into barrel racing. He'd evened accounts with Doc Marks for the time he'd spent wrestling with Sidewinder, and promised Bill Evans a first look at the new crop of foals. But he'd also wasted too much time sitting with Amanda Marlow.

Jake stopped out on the sidewalk and settled his hat back onto his head. He could smell woodsmoke from somebody's house and the yeasty fragrance of baking bread from the back of the diner. The feed store was open, and there was a card game going on over at the volunteer fire station. The movie showing at the Halcyon was about four weeks old and too boring even for an excuse to neck. Life walked along at its normal Saturday night pace in Lost Ridge.

Last Saturday when Jake had walked out of the diner, he hadn't even noticed how routine it all was. He'd slipped a toothpick between his teeth, just like he always did, waved a greeting to the people he knew on the streets, climbed behind the wheel of his truck and turned back for home. Tonight his gut ached with a hard frustration he hadn't allowed in years.

He strolled along the sidewalk, hands in back pockets, head down. Pacing familiar territory, giving motion to unfamiliar feelings.

Resentment. Who was she to come into his life and set him on his ear? Who was she to set foot in his town and remind him just how small and provincial it was? How predictable and dull?

Hadn't she noticed how she stood out in that little diner, like a star among streetlights? Hadn't she felt the least bit uncomfortable with her sophistication and style among people who shopped at the local thrift store and yearned for nothing more than a Sunday go-to-meeting outfit? The room had been full of Stetsons and feed hats, and she'd strolled in there with her wool slacks and cashmere turtleneck, a swan sitting in a pond of ducks.

And then she'd made him sit with her. She'd made him smell the soft hint of summer that hovered over her hair, and look into the pine forest of her eyes. She'd smiled at him and turned his gut into a brushfire.

Betty had been telling him for years that he needed a woman. He couldn't argue with her. But he sure as hell didn't need *this* one. He could still feel the silk of her hair in his hands, could see the smoke of surprising desire in her eyes. He could hear the sharp intake of her breath as he'd held her still, inches from kissing her, from giving in to the clamorings of his body over the warnings from his head.

He knew better. Uncomfortable jeans were never enough of an excuse to lose your sense of direction. And Jake had never had a doubt about the direction his life would take from the moment his daddy had dropped dead in front of him. He'd never veered the slightest from the course he'd set himself that day, knowing that his mother was too sick to take over the ranch and knowing that the ranch, such as it was, was all that kept all five of them off welfare. It was only now, with both his parents long since in their graves and Zeke, Gen and Lee safely out in the world, that the life he'd built for himself seemed empty.

It was only Amanda Marlow, with her hot eyes and her soft mouth, with her gut-wrenching fire of enthusiasm that could break a man's heart if he let it, who could make him feel so bad. He'd seen the way her face had lit up when she'd held Hattie Kendall's diary. He'd seen the hunger in her, and it had twisted in him like barbed wire until he'd wanted to hurt her. Until he'd wanted to hold her.

"Jake Kendall? That you?"

Startled, Jake looked up to see Millie Eberhart walking his way with an armful of books from the library she'd probably just closed up for the day.

"Miss Eberhart," he nodded, forefinger to his hat, just like he always did to the tiny old woman.

She stopped to smile up at him. "Haven't seen you in a while. How's little Lee doing out in the big world?"

"Just fine. She's coming back for the spring holidays in a couple of weeks."

The fragile-looking white head bobbed decidedly in the soft light of the street lamp and dying sun. "You tell her to come see me when she does. I miss having her pester me."

Jake smiled, even though he didn't feel like it. "I'll do that."

He was about to walk on, as if he had someplace to go, when she leaned forward in confidence. "Somebody said you have Amanda Marlow stayin' at your place. That right?"

Jake fought back a sigh of frustration. "Up at the old cabin."

Miss Eberhart's eyes got big, and she shook her head with awe. "Imagine that. You must be thrilled to death to have someone so special up there. Why, I was just reading *Simple Gifts* again the other day. It reminded me so much of my own family back in Virginia, don't you know. The purity of her language, her descriptive power. It's no wonder they gave her those awards. Mark my words, she's going to be one of the country's leading writers. Another Twain, in her own way. And to think, you're there to see those magnificent words born."

Jake couldn't manage much more than a vague nod of the head to the little woman's exuberance. He fought the rage her unknowing enthusiasm kindled in him. Blind, dark rage born of shame and fed with frustration. The kind of rage that Bill Nelson's palomino put into those flying kicks of his. Sometimes Jake Kendall wished he could kick out like that, too, blindly destroying everything in sight.

Instead, he stood stock still, his head down toward the little librarian, his mind filled not with marvelous words, but images of soft lips and hungry, questing eyes.

"How were you ever so lucky?"

Jake all but shook his head. "Pardon?"

"To get her at the Diamond K."

Jake straightened, fought the urge to wipe at his forehead. "Oh. She taught Lee a course, and you know Lee. She gave her a key to the cabin. I don't care, long as she doesn't spook the horses."

Miss Eberhart laughed, a high, tinkly sound that went with the crocheted collars she wore on her dresses and the orthopedic shoes. "You scamp," she scolded. "I'll have to find a way to come up to your place and see her, now, won't I?"

Miss Eberhart suddenly had Jake's undivided attention. "Oh, I'm not so sure right now, Miss Eberhart. It's pretty wild out there, what with foaling season and all. How 'bout if I ask her to visit at the library? She might even . . . sign something . . . or . . . something."

The librarian, who had served the town since the first book had been slipped onto the old schoolhouse shelves in 1944, nodded her head vigorously. "Lovely, dear. You tell her that. I have all her books. But then, I imagine you do, too."

Jake fingered his hat one more time. "Nice seein' you, Miss Eberhart. Time to get back, though."

Before she could think of anything else, he spun around and headed for his truck. A couple of people waved as they walked toward the firehouse, and another called from Ed Deever's food store. Jake didn't even notice.

Amanda shouldn't be here. She was going to change everything. She was going to bring everything he'd built down around him. Somehow he had to convince his guest and his little sister that it would be better if that old cabin back up in the meadow stayed empty. Then he could sleep again. He could walk the streets and sit in the diner without having to face her, think of her, worry about her.

He could have his self-esteem back. At least maybe he could get his peace of mind back. Without Amanda Marlow there, day after day, to taunt him with the difference between them, he could once again forget who he wasn't and just get on with making a living.

After all, most days that was all he had time to do, anyway.

Jake had never been able to convince himself of that before. It was a cinch he wasn't going to be able to now.

Chapter 4

"She wants to *what?*"

Clovis twisted his hat a little tighter in his hands. "Well, I didn't think it was such a awful idea, boss."

Jake took a step toward his foreman and thought better of it. If he killed him, he'd never get the rest of the foals safely born or breed the mares for next year's crop.

"Of all the harebrained, addle-minded—"

The little man straightened to his full height, bristling with good intentions. "Well, it makes sense. She's writin' a book about the West. How's she supposed to do that if she can't even sit a horse proper?"

"The same way you talk about all those women you say you've known over the years," Jake snarled. "She makes it up."

Clovis's face crumpled noticeably. If Jake had been feeling any more charitable—or had managed more than fifteen minutes' solid sleep the night before—he might have regretted his outburst. As it was, he'd been spending all his free time trying to figure out a way to get Amanda Marlow away from him, and Clovis was sabotaging him behind his back.

"And just when were you planning on doing this?" he demanded, glaring down at his foreman. "We have ten horses ready for heavy training, seven more mares just about ready to drop and a couple already back in season. We have a herd that's just about ready to be moved out into spring pasture and fences that need to be mended. You want me to go on?"

"I get some time off every day," Clovis defended himself. "Or were you gonna take that away, just so you ain't bothered? And what are you gonna tell Lee when she comes home, expectin' us to have been taking care of her friend?"

"That she should know better this time of year."

Clovis faced his boss with impunity. "Any time of year, more likely," he snapped and turned away.

Jake sighed in frustration. "Just don't let those mares suffer," he said.

Clovis almost came to another halt. It had been a peace offering. Unfortunately it smacked as the deadliest of insults. Clovis would have starved himself rather than let his mares suffer so much as an inconvenience, and Jake knew it.

The little man spun around, his voice echoing along the barn. "What do you have against that girl, anyway?"

Jake had been all set to lead Joker out for exercising. Clovis's words brought him to a halt. They loosened the sick shame and dread that he'd been fighting to keep at bay for so long.

"I think she's a pampered rich girl without enough to do," Jake snapped instinctively to cover his real reasons, the real fears and loathings.

Clovis snorted. "Shows you what you know. She didn't even wear shoes till she was eight."

And without another word, he stalked off.

Jake couldn't quite turn back to his work. Suddenly, on top of everything else, he was fighting jealousy. What right did Clovis have to that kind of information? Why should Amanda feel so comfortable with him that she'd offer up something so personal? No woman decked out in cashmere and tweed could possibly be proud of the fact that she'd spent her childhood barefoot.

Or could she?

Jake spun on his heel then, spooking the buckskin alongside him. Joker shied and snorted, his ears flattening at the sudden movement. Instinctively Jake scratched his withers and murmured to him. But he didn't realize that what he was murmuring was, "Doesn't make any difference. Doesn't make any damn difference, at all."

Amanda had lied. Well, she hadn't told the entire truth. She'd said that she wasn't used to the silence just yet, which was why she kept showing up at the Diamond K's front door. The truth of the matter was that she *was* used to it. Not the sweet, free silence of the mountains that could almost refresh a soul single-handedly. The kind of silence that was born of isolation. The kind that sounded the same whether you were sitting alone in a wide open meadow with no more company than a hawk, or a fourth-floor efficiency in the middle of the busiest city on earth.

Amanda was lonely. Desperately and definitely, isolated at first by her upbringing and then by her sudden, surprising fame. Fawned over when all she needed to be was incorporated. Examined and critiqued when she'd needed to be introduced.

Amanda had reached college on a scholarship, uncertain of herself, of her experience and worth, a country girl from the deepest backwoods of the Appalachians fired with curiosity and purpose. She'd worked three jobs to bring in enough money to spend the rest of her time in libraries and classrooms satiating the greatest addiction known to man, the thirst for knowledge. But somewhere in those cluttered, noisy halls of campus, sometime during those long, hard hours of struggle, she'd disappeared so neatly into the fabric of the school that no one had really known her....

Until her first book had been a surprise, runaway bestseller. Suddenly interviewers dug up professors who glowed about their special student and fellow students who had been privileged enough to sit in on rap sessions with her.

Still, no one had come forward to get to know *her*. They'd only shown up on her doorstep to be known *by* her. And so, writing had become her escape and her prison. Colleges, competing to add her name to their rosters, had courted her. And Amanda, so far away from home and forever cut off from it, a changeling caught between two worlds, had traveled from one college to another in the hopes of finding some kind of place she could feel comfortable.

The Diamond K was the closest she'd ever felt to that. No one cared who she was or what film stars were fighting to play the lead in the movie based on her book. The people of Lost Ridge saw her as Lee's friend, and that was enough. Betty offered coffee and conversation, Clovis offered horseback riding lessons, and Jake...Jake offered something even an award-winning author couldn't quite give words to yet. A new restlessness, a heightened physical awareness, a gnawing deep inside where the memories of her family lived and all their dreams still lay implanted. Deeper where her own dreams had struggled to survive amid all the noise and confusion.

Jake Kendall pulled at her in a way no one and nothing had in her life. He had what her Uncle Mick had called grit and gumption. Jake stalked her dreams and haunted her days, the feel of his callused hand against her cheek, the steel of his eyes and the uncompromising individuality of his stance.

And yet, hidden where no one who knew Jake Kendall thought to look, lay ghosts that looked a lot like Amanda's. Ghosts of loneliness, of frustration and need. Imprisoned there behind that steel-trap jaw and laconic attitude was a hunger that could well have frightened her if she let it, because it was a hunger that made hers pale in comparison.

It was a hunger that so bothered Jake Kendall that he denied it by lashing out at Amanda.

"I'm afraid I didn't bring real work clothes," she apologized to Clovis.

The leathery little foreman, who had adopted her on nothing more than Lee Kendall's recommendation, grinned like a jack-o'-lantern and handed her a bridle. "Don't matter. We can get these just as dirty as jeans and a sweatshirt."

Amanda smiled back at him and closed her hand around the leather-and-metal apparatus, making it jingle faintly. Two equine heads turned in their stalls at the sounds. "If you really don't mind, Clovis. I know how busy you are."

Clovis let fly with a stream of tobacco juice that decorated a corner pile of sawdust on the floor of the barn,. "Man's got a right to spend his lunch hour any way he sees fit. I choose to teach you about horses. You said something about buyin' one, didn't you?"

Amanda blinked in a bit of confusion. "Did I?"

Clovis hit his target again in a way that seemed like judgment. "'Course, you might not find anything you like. Even with a fine herd like the Diamond K's got, can't please everybody. But ridin's the first step to buyin', I'd say."

Amanda's grin was brighter than her co-conspirator's. "My thought exactly." Lifting the bridle, she gave it another rattle. "Where do I start?"

"Fourth stall from the end," Clovis informed her with a definite shake of the head. "A real sweet mare who's a year or two past any real excitement. I brought her in from the pasture this morning just for you."

Amanda followed him down the row of stalls, past a beautiful gray horse and a dirty-looking brown one and a pinto who kept nodding as if making judgments of her own.

"These are all mares?" she asked.

"All ladies," he nodded. "Can't expect anybody to get any work done in a coed dormitory. Geldings are in on the other side, and stallions in a different barn. They're just a little touchier to get along with sometimes."

"Like Bill Nelson's horse?"

Clovis shook his head. "That ain't a horse. It's a disaster on four legs. I can't imagine what that man thinks is gonna come out of an animal like that."

"Why did Jake agree to train him?"

"'Cause Jake has this strange idea that there ain't a horse he can't work with. And until that one, I'd 'a' said he was right. I never seen anybody better on a horse than Jake Kendall . . . here she is. Pokey."

Amanda scowled, beset by the same feeling she had on her first day of undergraduate school. Pokey. Next Clovis would offer to lead her around on a rope so her parents could take her picture.

Pokey was a pretty horse, anyway. She was big and dark brown, with a star on her forehead and immense liquid brown eyes.

"I read in the original papers that the Diamond K started out raising cattle," Amanda said as Clovis unlatched the stall door and swung it open. Pokey watched with placid interest. "When did they decide to go with horses instead?"

"That'd be Jake," Clovis allowed, stepping on into the big, airy stall. "His daddy was a good man. Tried his best and all, but I just don't think he was meant to be a rancher. And, truth be told, this ain't real cow country. Too high up, mostly. Cattle's down more toward Pinedale."

"Then how could Jake raise horses?"

"Knack. Pure cussedness. There's somethin' about Kendall men and this piece of land that don't always make sense. They can't seem to leave, even if it's good for 'em. 'Course, the first thing he did was invest in an indoor ring so he could work all winter on a horse if he wanted. All right, now, walk up alongside of her here and make her acquaintance, just like this."

Pokey seemed perturbed that Clovis would sidle up alongside her and begin rubbing her neck. She butted him right in the chest, as if to say, we know each other too well. However, she lifted her head to inspect Amanda when she did the same.

"You're a pretty girl," Amanda crooned, breathing in the age-old perfume of horses and hay, of leather and old wood. The sunlight streamed in the gaps in the wall, milky and dancing with dust motes, and the other denizens rustled around in their quarters. The sights and sounds and smells calmed Amanda, quieted her in a way nothing had since she'd been a child standing in her Uncle Mick's barn with the cows. There was something solid and real about the place, earthy in a way that centered a person.

"When I was a girl," she found herself saying a few minutes later as she helped Clovis bridle and saddle the big mare outside by the corral, "we used to ride this mule bareback up the mountain to go blackberry picking. Mule's name was Martha, and she could hold six of us at a time. Uncle Mick used to throw us right up on her back like we were sacks of flour. He was a huge man."

"Mules are fine animals," Clovis assured her. "But they ain't horses. There, that's right. Tighten the cinch just one more time before you get atop her."

Amanda took a look up at the very high back of her mount, at the stirrup she'd measured beneath her armpit to match the length of her leg. It was somewhere just south of her belt line, which made her wonder how she was supposed to reach it.

"I'm sure this was a wonderful idea when I thought of it," she murmured, more to herself than her teacher as she gave the cinch one more careful tug and readjusted the ends. Considering just how foolish she had a feeling she was about to look, she heartily wished they could have done this back inside the barn.

"Now, Pokey, she'll hold real still for you," Clovis assured her. "All you have to do is slip your foot into the stirrup, bend that other leg a little and vault right into the saddle."

Amanda bent her leg higher than should have been possible and managed to wedge her foot into the stirrup before it sprang back into place. That left the rest of her in an uncomfortable physical relationship.

"Bend now," Clovis urged.

Amanda stared diligently at her kneecap caught between her face and the stamped leather of the saddle. She thought of the patient attention Pokey was paying her, her head turned around to watch Amanda's progress. She thought about what she was doing to her tendons and ligaments. She tried to bend.

She tried to vault.

She made it just about up as far as Pokey's rib cage.

"I'm . . . too short," she panted, trying desperately to lever herself higher by clutching at the saddle horn. Pokey stood there. Amanda was afraid the saddle that she had tightened would slip right down to the horse's belly, and she'd end up in a little heap in the dirt. Then she remembered that anyone in a ten-mile radius could be privileged to see her ignominious position.

Clovis made the most interesting choking sounds, but he stayed right by Pokey's head to make sure she wouldn't move.

Amanda closed her eyes and prayed they didn't have an audience. She must not have been sincere enough. Suddenly a set of strong, impatient hands grabbed her around the waist and lifted her right up into the saddle.

"Is that how your uncle did it?" Jake asked, his voice very dry.

Amanda faced him. "Thank you," she acknowledged, her voice sounding just a little more breathless than she'd actually been, her cheeks growing rosy. She could still feel the dig of his fingers into her skin, the easy, fluid power of his muscles as he'd lifted her. She saw the glint of suspicious humor in those steely blue eyes beneath the rim of his hat.

"I hope you don't have this much trouble getting into your books," he retorted dryly.

Amanda proffered a wry smile. "Heck, no. I only have to climb those one chapter at a time."

Still he didn't take his gaze from her. "Clovis," he said. "Didn't it occur to you that Pokey might be a little much for her first lesson?"

Clovis seemed to find that scratching behind an ear helped him answer. "Pokey's the sweetest mare we got, boss."

"She's also the biggest. Next time, let her have Sweet William."

Clovis started at the periphery of Amanda's vision. "You sure?"

Jake nodded. "He's more her size." Then he turned his conversation as well as his attention to her, and Amanda felt it like the brush of a warm breeze. "Unless you got something against geldings."

Amanda saw frank appraisal in those eyes. Arousal, hard challenge. It lit a small, very hot fire in her belly that made sitting in a saddle a little uncomfortable. "I understand they're easier to control than stallions."

The corner of Jake's mouth crooked just a little. "Takes a real rider to handle a stallion," he admitted, his voice low and almost intimate, his thumbs hooked in his back pockets, which made a person want to look closer at his front.

Amanda almost looked over at Clovis to see whether he was hearing what she was. She couldn't pull her gaze from Jake's, couldn't break free of that freezing, burning blue. She couldn't shake herself of the feeling that his invitation was more challenge than attraction. A game of dare by which he would judge her. Whatever it was, it was snaking along her limbs and setting up the most unnerving static dance along the back of her neck. Her chest felt uncomfortably tight inside her Aran knit sweater, and her palms were damp.

"From what I understand," she countered, her voice as intent as his, her own hands clenched around the reins, "most stallions are all bluster. All you have to do is call their bluff and they back right down."

Jake's eyes sparked dangerously. Amanda kept reminding herself that she was situated above him. She shouldn't have felt so intimidated. Still, there was something so overwhelmingly male about his stance, his expression. Something so dominant.

He shrugged. "It could be real dangerous finding out, though, couldn't it?"

Amanda couldn't quite come up with an answer.

He tipped a finger to the brim of his hat to Amanda, his mouth quirked. "Hope the rest of your first lesson in the Wild West goes a little better."

Amanda fought to control her rebellious body. It took a second to find breath and unscramble words from the puddle Jake left her in, but she did. "I doubt it," she managed to say, still breathless, wishing she could somehow get Jake Kendall to stay and talk to her a little longer. "I have a feeling you're dying to see me make an ass of myself again."

Jake allowed a brief, smug grin. "Whatever you say, ma'am."

And he turned toward the barn.

Behind him, Clovis had taken to staring. "Hey, boss!" he yelled as Jake opened the big wooden door, "Sweet William? You sure?"

Jake never turned around. "I don't think I stuttered, Clovis."

Amanda watched Jake disappear into the darkness of the building and thought how suddenly cool the spring wind was here.

"Is there a problem with Sweet William?" she asked the top of Clovis's head.

Clovis didn't quite look up. "No-o-o..." He was still watching the closed door.

Amanda didn't like the sound of that hesitation at all. Shifting just a little in the saddle so that it creaked beneath her, she turned to follow Clovis's line of sight. "He bucks, right? Tries to rub people off against trees? Bites chunks out of your leg?"

Finally Clovis startled to attention and lifted his head to address her. "Oh, no," he disagreed. "He's more a gentleman than Pokey here's a lady. He's a real fine horse. Purebred quarter out of Impossible, and that's a real calm line."

Amanda looked down at the bemused brown eyes. "Then what's the problem?"

"He's the boss's horse."

Amanda looked back toward the door. "That huge black thing I've seen him ride?"

"Oh, no. That's Buck. Sweet William is his trainin' horse. When he wants to show another horse good manners, he demonstrates on old Bill."

"Then why the concern about letting me ride him?"

Clovis's face bunched up with intensity. "Because he's the boss's horse," he repeated as if it shouldn't have been necessary.

"Clovis," Amanda retorted gently. "They're *all* his horses."

That produced a belated grin, albeit still halfhearted. "No, ma'am. You see, Sweet William and Buck and Alabaster, they're the boss's personal string. And nobody rides 'em but him. That's just the way it's done."

Now it was Amanda's turn to stare at the closed door as if she could conjure up the vision beyond it. The impact of Clovis's astonishment was beginning to sink in. The foreman was surprised because of Jake's generosity. And he didn't even suspect the kind of animosity Jake seemed to hold toward Amanda.

She didn't know what to do. She didn't even know what to think. All she could remember was the hot ambivalence in Jake's eyes when he'd caught hold of her face back in the house, the pure sexual power of him no more than five minutes ago, and it made her shudder.

"You want, we can saddle him up now," Clovis offered.

It took Amanda a minute to remember what Clovis was referring to. "Next time," she offered with a small smile. "After all the trouble I had getting up here, I'm not getting back off this animal until we're finished."

Clovis's grin was broad and untroubled. Amanda wished she could feel the same.

"Okay, then, missy, we'll start our lesson."

She was going to be sore. She was going to be *very* sore. Amanda knew that because by the time she got back off Pokey again—this time sliding down her side like a very thick brown banister—she couldn't quite get her legs to hold her up. Clovis had been a wonderful teacher, gentle and persistent, not once laughing about her mistakes or chiding her when she pulled too sharply on Pokey's sensitive mouth. They had walked and trotted and cantered, and Amanda's only trip back to earth was the one she made at the end of the lesson. Even so, she wondered just how cowboys had survived—and then managed to populate—the West. It was the one question she didn't have the guts to ask Clovis.

"Did'ya like it?" Betty asked, holding out a cup of coffee when Amanda reached the front door of the house.

Amanda straightened carefully, already cataloguing places that were stiffening, and surprised herself with a smile. "Yes," she admitted, stepping inside. "Next time I want to go really fast."

Betty laughed. "Hadn't figured you for a hot-rodder."

"Jake offered to let me practice on Sweet William," Amanda said offhandedly as she accepted the coffee. "Thanks."

Betty didn't let her down. The woman's plain, round face folded neatly into astonishment. "You're kidding."

Amanda shrugged. "That's what Clovis said."

Betty's attention veered right out toward the corrals. "Well, what do you know?"

Amanda turned with her, but there was nothing to see except the visiting Bronco she'd seen parked next to hers. "This western hospitality has me all confused," she admitted, sipping her coffee. "I mean, back home, it's as easy as inviting a person to the table and to join in when the music starts. If what

I hear is true, the western code is that a cowboy's horse is sacred. Inviting you to use it is like giving an engagement ring. I'm not sure how to take that after being yelled at for four days."

"Maybe he's finally decided not to hurt Lee's feelings, after all," Betty suggested, almost to herself, as if she were having as much trouble unraveling the problem as Amanda.

"Oh, thank heavens," Amanda retorted. "For a minute there I thought he wanted to be friends."

Betty's answering smile was swift and wry. "Don't get me wrong. He's a good man."

Amanda nodded. "So I hear."

"He's just a little . . ."

"Hard to live with sometimes."

"Private. He doesn't like surprises. Never did. I always figured it was 'cause of the fact that he had to deal with so many when he was young, that was the only way he could cope."

Amanda couldn't help nodding along with her. It wouldn't hurt, she thought, to remember just how different their childhoods had been. Hers had been graced with music and words and a close, boisterous family to offset the troubles. He had had to create his own stability. It had to do something to a person.

"Well," she conceded, knowing that the words she really wanted wouldn't be accepted here. "He's lucky to have you and Clovis."

Betty shook her head. "Luck has nothin' to do with it."

Amanda was thinking of going back to the little cabin and trying to squeeze into the three-by-three shower stall and coax some hot water out of the solar tank when the stallion barn door opened. She knew it was Jake even before she saw him. Alongside strode a wiry, graceful young man in regulation jeans, flannel shirt and a five-gallon hat that looked like he'd used it to beat out fires. Jake led a pale gray horse behind him.

"You see Jake work a cutting horse yet?" Betty asked.

Amanda shook her head, watching the easy rapport between the two men, the flashing grins and natural swaggers. Jake had his spurs on again, and it tickled something in her.

Betty was already turning toward the door. "Come on."

Amanda wasn't exactly sure how Jake would take her appearance. He was still conversing with the man alongside him as she and Betty approached. Across the way two men who were digging fence posts stopped and leaned on their post-hole diggers. Clovis stepped from the mares' barn. Amanda and Betty walked up to the corral fence, Amanda admittedly a bit more slowly than Betty.

"You know anything about cutting horses?" Betty asked, standing against the fence as if she were waiting to go into church, her coffee cup still held steadily in both hands.

"Just that a good one can cut the flour from a biscuit without breaking the crust."

Betty grinned. "Then you probably heard it from Clovis. A cutting horse is used to cut cattle out of the herd. Best ones are bred just for that. They have cow sense. Know what a cow's gonna do before he does it. They don't need 'em as much now, what with fencing and smaller spreads and such. Only real range left is up Montana, Idaho way. But the competitions are getting tougher. It's pure poetry to watch one in action."

"Are those the horses they use in rodeos?" Amanda asked.

Betty shook her head. "Those are calf-roping horses. He trains those, too. But the cutting horses are his pride and joy."

"Does he always have an audience like this?"

Betty took a considering look around. "I've seen people come in from town to watch him work a horse. You just don't see anything prettier."

Jake led the horse into the bigger corral, an oversized rectangle that held a herd of about twenty head of cattle. The man with him proceeded to unhook the gate and wait for Jake. Amanda leaned against the fence and prepared to watch.

He was talking to the horse. Amanda couldn't hear what he was saying, but the horse's ears were flicking, first forward, then backward, as if keeping track of both Jake and the cattle. He was a pretty gray with black stockings, mane and tail, small and well proportioned, with the well-developed hindquarters of a quarter horse and the face of a mustang. He had a sweet eye, as Clovis called it, big and liquid and friendly. As Jake swung into the saddle, the gray came alert.

Amanda had seen ballet. She'd seen almost every team and single sport known to the North American continent and a few Olympic events. She had never seen anything with the grace and power and precision of Jake working that horse. They spun, they danced, they moved with the grace of figure skaters, whirling and backing and sidestepping across the corral as if it were a dance floor. Jake faced the horse toward one of the cows, and the horse went after him. Anticipated him, tracked him, faced him down. They tracked the animal, face to face and movement for movement, until the cow finally tired and headed away from the herd. Then they did it with the second, third and fourth, all picked out by some minute signal from Jake.

She couldn't take her eyes from them, a Remington statue in action, power and muscle and intelligence. She soaked in the calm, quiet command in Jake's riding, the fluid sensuality of the way he sat that horse, working him with his hands and his legs and his feet, and sometimes just letting the reins drop from his hands and letting the horse work on his own. The horse never surprised him. He never out-thought him. Man and horse were one, and suddenly Amanda understood why it was such a powerful sexual symbol.

"He's something, isn't he?"

Amanda startled at the masculine voice alongside her. She'd forgotten everyone else in the place, so mesmerized had she been by Jake's performance.

The man Jake had been talking to now addressed her. Mid-thirties, same tan as Jake's, same laconic style. Brown eyes, thin lips, hawkish nose. His face was calm, but his eyes were alight as they watched Jake and the horse.

"I've never seen anything like it," Amanda admitted. "Is the horse for you?" she asked.

He nodded, still watching. "I came a little early. Jake's been tellin' me about that little hoss, and I couldn't stand the suspense. Jake Kendall doesn't give away a Grayghost get very easily. I wanted to be here before he changed his mind. Impressive Gray there is going to be another world-class winner."

Jake ran the last animal down to a standstill and suddenly lifted the reins, placing his hand gently on the horse's neck. The animal settled back into an easy stand, his gray coat gleaming with sweat, his sides heaving.

"Oh, yeah," the visitor breathed in awe. "That's a Grayghost get all right."

"You always get your horses from Jake?" Amanda asked, her attention still where Jake sat, quietly stroking and praising the horse.

"When I can. Most of the ones I ride Jake owns. This is a real special treat for me."

"But Jake doesn't compete himself. Why?"

The man looked over with a broad grin. "Do me a favor," he pleaded. "Don't put any ideas in his head. I got enough competition. If Jake ever got it in his head to try the circuit, I'd go broke."

"This is Tommy Wilson, Amanda," Betty introduced them. "World Champion last two years on Grayboy. Tommy, Amanda Marlow."

Tommy was in the process of tipping his hat when he caught Amanda's name. "Amanda Marlow?" he demanded. "The one who wrote that book about life on the Mississippi River? You're kiddin' me."

Amanda caught her breath, terrified that her bubble of normalcy would evaporate beneath this man's bright eyes. Even so, she shrugged in concession. "I'm here to do a book about the West."

But Tommy simply nodded and looked back to where Jake was turning the gray back away from the herd. "Well, you couldn't be in a better place. What Jake does is a dyin' art. Type of man he is is dyin' out, too."

Jake walked the sweating, heaving horse toward them, his eyes hidden beneath the brim of that hat, his posture more relaxed than Amanda had ever seen it. A man in charge, in his element. She envied him unspeakably. She couldn't take her eyes from him.

"He's still a little rusty from winterin'," Jake drawled.

Tommy grinned like a pirate. "Yeah, pure pitiful specimen of animal, ya ask me."

Jake's mouth crooked in that faint, telling grin. "I'll let you take him off my hands, I guess. Long as you don't work him too hard."

Tommy laughed. "I got the money in the car."

From somewhere José loped into the corral and took the gray from Jake as he swung down. Amanda could see the sweat along Jake's neck, the new stain around his hatband. He'd worked hard, and it seemed to make him taller, somehow. More potent, more distant. She smelled it on him, heard the faint jingle of his spurs, and fought a rush of exhilaration.

Jake didn't bother with the gate. He climbed the corral and hopped outside right alongside Betty and Amanda.

"So, that's what a cutting horse does," Amanda commented, wishing her throat didn't sound so dry. "Sweet William won't do that if I get up on him, will he?"

Jake's grin grew a little, but Amanda could see the difference. The command, the presence that she hadn't even felt in town.

"Not unless you ask," he assured her.

Tommy Wilson loped back over with a very thick envelope in his hand. "I'll pick him up first of May, Jake. That okay with you?"

Jake nodded. "Give me time to work the rest of his kinks out."

Tommy smiled and handed Jake the envelope. Then he gave him his hand. Jake shook it.

"See you in May," Tommy acknowledged.

"May," Jake echoed.

Tommy was ready to turn away when the situation finally overcame him. "I'm real glad I didn't bring Farley with me," he crowed. "He would 'a' done his best to outbid me."

Jake shook his head. "We shook on it, Tommy. Tell him he can come look for himself sometime."

Tommy turned to Amanda with a wide, triumphant grin. "See what I mean? There aren't any businessmen like Jake anymore. Don't make him too famous or I'll have to stand in line for my next hoss."

Tommy headed on down for his car, and Jake handed Betty the envelope.

"I'd better put this away," Betty said.

Jake just nodded. "Gettin' a load of hay in today. Save some for it."

And then, without another word, he walked away. Amanda couldn't take her eyes from him, wishing she could think of something to keep him there, to find out more about him, to stand close enough to him to bask in that damn aura of his.

"A handshake and cash, huh?" she said to Betty. "What about the paperwork?"

Betty shrugged. "Handshake's all Jake needs. He's built his business on it."

Amanda finally turned to her, amazed. "But this isn't Dodge City, Betty. What about all those lawyers waiting in the wings?"

Betty didn't seem terribly anxious about it. "Oh, I finally made up a bill of sale with all that stuff on it. I'll get both of 'em to sign it when Tommy comes back in May. But the deal was done two years ago when Jake promised Tommy that horse when he started training Impressive Gray. Besides, nobody'd ever think to doubt Jake's word."

Amanda caught herself smiling. "Uncle Mick," she murmured. "He was a farmer, the only man in the family not down in the mines. He never understood anything but cash and a bible promise."

The two women headed back toward the house together.

"He's the Uncle Mick you dedicated that book to? The one who was the storyteller back home?"

Amanda looked over, surprised.

Betty's expression never changed. "Well, it seemed so important to Lee and all, I thought I might just read a little of it, especially since Jake was never gonna get the time to do it. I liked the Jack stories the best, the ones like Jack and the beanstalk, and all. Those from your Uncle Mick?"

Amanda spoke thoughtfully. "He was one of the few people who still told 'em."

"You miss him."

Amanda saw Jake walk back out of the barn, a saddle thrown over his shoulder, another horse waiting by the hitching post. She thought of honesty and trust and the kind of simple values that she'd been looking for ever since her Uncle Mick's funeral.

"I escaped the Appalachians to discover the rest of the world and ended up making a career of going home. I guess it's the best way I can keep Uncle Mick's memory alive. There aren't many like him anymore."

Betty came to a halt by the front door, her own attention on Jake, too. "Don't let that boy put you off. I'd like to see a book about this place, too."

"What does he have against me, Betty?" Amanda asked, seeing another flash of white as Jake grinned down at José before turning the new horse out into the corral to work. One smile, that was all she wanted.

It wasn't. She admitted it. But it would do for starters.

But Betty couldn't do much more than shake her head. "I've never seen Jake Kendall deliberately hurtful to anyone in my life. Never seen him this out of sorts, not since the day I first met him and he was handling this entire ranch almost completely on his own at the age of thirteen."

Amanda turned her head. "Thirteen? But his mother didn't die until he was seventeen."

"His daddy died when he was twelve. Just keeled over one day, when it was always his mama who was so frail and all. It was Jake who single-handedly turned this ranch around from a near-bankrupt, scrub-and-clapboard cattle ranch into one of the most successful horse ranches in the state. And he did it all by his twentieth birthday, with those little ones to raise." Betty turned on Amanda, fierce pride in her eyes, daring Amanda to argue. It was the most emotion Amanda had ever seen on the woman. "He's a good man," she repeated definitely.

"I know," Amanda agreed. "But for some reason, he doesn't like me. And I just can't figure out why, Betty."

But she would. And when she did, she'd figure out what to do about it, because the more time Amanda spent at the Diamond K, the less she wanted to leave. And it wasn't only the mountains and fresh air that were attracting her.

Chapter 5

He couldn't stay away from her. Jake had spent the last week working himself into unconsciousness, blistering his hands on the fences and his feet on the floor of his house. He'd spent all night helping foal two colts and then spent all day in the saddle working the horses.

And still he stood at his window watching the moon spill out over the valley and thinking that Amanda Marlow slept no more than two miles away.

Damn her and her soft, sweet hair, her inquisitive, knowing eyes and her gentle grace. Damn the way she laughed when she learned something new on a horse and the way she made the men stop and take notice when she walked or talked or rode. Damn him for taking notice, too.

He ached for her. He dreamed of her. He taunted her, knowing full well that he was the one walking away burning. She was everything he could dream of in a woman, gentle and bright and compassionate. She was tougher than he'd given her credit for, suffering his tongue with amazing humor and doggedly climbing back up on Sweet William the last four days to master the basic art of horsemanship.

He'd stood just inside the barn door this afternoon, surreptitiously watching her like a lovesick teenager sneaking a look into the girls' locker room. She'd been up on the gelding cantering around the outside ring with an ease that was well beyond most people, no matter how long they had ridden. The little dun had taken right to her, until Jake couldn't imagine himself on its back anymore.

Jake could still see the way her hair had rippled in the sunlight, a rich banner in the breeze. The way her whole face lit up with discovery. He could almost hear the music of her laughter.

He wanted to get to know her. He wanted to have her in his hands. He wanted to hear her stories and share some of his own, and then sink into the darkness together.

He couldn't. If he let her too close, she'd find out. And he couldn't do that. He'd hidden his whole life, and no beautiful, sassy woman with college degrees and a house back East was going to change it.

It was too late. It had been too late for a long time.

But it didn't stop him from aching.

She couldn't seem to get his attention. Amanda had done everything but handstands on that horse trying to get some kind of reaction out of Jake Kendall, and all she'd managed since that first foray into double entendre was the grudging admission that she wasn't embarrassing herself in the saddle.

It was driving her crazy. She should have been catching up on her sleep. She should have been poring over the texts of western lore she'd brought with her that were even now spread out over the bright yellow down comforter that covered the old brass bed behind her. She could have at least spent some time practicing on the dulcimer that rested on the battered wooden table.

She should have been sensible.

Instead, she was fascinated. She was driven. She was—God help her—she was fantasizing. She'd shown up on the Diamond K hoping to find a quiet corner where she could pry open the past on a grizzled veteran or two, maybe roam over the landscape to get a feel of its scope, its demand and reward.

Taste a small town again and reacquaint herself with its rhythms and characters. And all she'd been able to concentrate on had been one character. One silent, hard, enigmatic character with the most intriguing smile she'd ever seen short of the Mona Lisa and a diamond-hard pride as compelling as the West itself.

She should have been concentrating on the work at hand. Instead she stood at the window that overlooked the wide meadow, the mountain stream, the black press of mountains, and thought of what Jake Kendall would look like in the moonlight that silvered the tumbling stream and glimmered over the undulating grasses. She, who had given up romantic notions right after her brief and disastrous engagement, was thinking what a waste all this moonlight was when Jake Kendall was asleep no more than two miles away.

Amanda sighed and turned away, her flannel nightgown brushing her bare feet. She surveyed the tiny cabin where so much struggle, pain and joy still whispered from the walls, and thought of how long it had been since she'd had such company. Since she'd stood on land a man had fought to hand down and was still cherished as deeply by the inheritors.

It had been that way with her Uncle Mick's place, the original Sullivan homestead. But his son hadn't kept faith with the land, such as it was, and had sold it for the money to get to Houston. Now Amanda had no home, not the one her parents had sweated to provide and lost to the mines, not the one her Uncle Mick had grafted her to. Certainly not the one she inhabited back in Boston, so impersonal it should have listed "occupant" on the mailbox.

Jake Kendall had the Diamond K. And it was obvious in every callus on his hands, every crease in his weatherbeaten face, every scar on his face and hands, that he knew what he had. He'd fought just as hard as every one of his ancestors just to hold on to it, and that was something that drew Amanda like a moth to an open flame. A dangerous flame. Because no matter what she wanted, Jake Kendall wanted nothing to do with her.

"What do you have against me?"
Amanda saw her presence impact on Jake as surely as if she'd

struck him. Bent over an old tractor, the engine in several pieces in his hands, his own shirt off in the unusually warm afternoon, he stiffened. Still he went on working.

"Don't you have anything better to do than bother somebody who's busy?"

Amanda walked around to get a better view and wished suddenly she hadn't. His hat was off and his face was grimy. She wanted to wipe at it with the handkerchief that trailed out of his back jeans pocket. His chest was bare and glistening with sweat. She wanted to...well, it didn't bear to think what she wanted to do. She'd lain awake all the night before watching the moon pour into her window and thinking about what she'd like to do to Jake Kendall.

He was simply too potent. Too overwhelmingly male. And it had been a very long time since Amanda Marlow had enjoyed the pleasure of someone with those attributes. The fact that he was an enigma only added to the frustration. The fact that he was, for some reason, by turns irritated and aroused by her, made her want to take a handful of hair and...she was wandering again.

"I have plenty to do," she assured him. "But I've spent the last week at this ranch and managed to get about three sentences out of you without pulling teeth. It's beginning to annoy me."

Finally Jake straightened. Amanda restrained herself from stepping back. His eyes glinted with an odd, flat light. His upright chest was inches from her nose.

If only he'd had a smooth chest. She could concentrate on the matter at hand, because she'd never cared for smooth chests. But that sweat was glistening like dew on the dark gold hair that curled over some pretty impressive pectorals and an absolutely riveting abdominal wall.

She wondered what it would feel like against her palm, would taste like on her tongue. She lifted her eyes to his, blushing furiously at getting caught and hoping he didn't notice her rubbing her hands along her pants legs.

She seemed to be in luck.

"I didn't invite you here," he reminded her, pulling out the handkerchief and giving his face a swipe with it.

"You missed a spot," Amanda instinctively offered.

He stopped. "What?"

She didn't know why she did it. She certainly couldn't excuse her action, simply because she'd been fantasizing about it. Grabbing his handkerchief out of his hand, she reached up and wiped away the last trace of grease from his jaw.

What she'd done seemed to cause a reflexive tightening in him. In her, it provoked a delicious chill that was dangerous.

She did her best to smile past both their discomfort. "I straighten pictures on walls, too," she apologized, handing back his cloth with fingers that trembled just a little. "Sorry."

He smelled like work. Like fuel and exertion and sunshine. Warm sunshine. Amanda fought to keep her eyes up and swore she'd never give in to impulse again.

"You were saying," she said with a small smile, unable to keep from thinking that faded jeans were an absolute work of art. Faded, soft, well-worn jeans that fit like a tight hug. A very tight hug.

It took him a minute to speak. "I said, you showed up at the worst time of the year expecting to be baby-sat, and that's just not going to happen. Besides, you got Clovis to fetch and carry for you."

She tilted her head, just a little. "Jealous?"

Amanda wasn't sure what kind of reaction she'd expected. Jake glared at her, his posture rigid, his jaw like steel. Amanda saw fury, frustration and something else—something even darker.

That something passed before she could even name it, and Jake whirled back around on the engine he was dismantling.

"I'm busy," he snarled.

Amanda shook her head and looked around her. They were out behind one of the outbuildings, and she could see a corner of one of the fields where some of the horses were gathered. She could see the stretch of plain that carried the stream. There were wildflowers peeking out this morning. The aspen would soon be budding. On the ranch, the new cycle of life had already started. Jake and his men spent their days working hard with their hands, building something intangible, something precious that no trendsetter or analyst or company CEO could take away from them. They worked with integrity and trust and loyalty, and Amanda had been too long away from those qualities not to taste them again like the first honey of spring. She yearned for them almost as much as she yearned for the man who didn't seem to see anything unusual about his adherence to them.

And she, the writer, the award winner, didn't know how to tell him. So she told him a story instead.

"My daddy worked in the mines," she said. "Him and his two brothers, Earl and Ralph, and my brother William Paul. Got up every morning at four to get to the mine for his shift, and came home so tired all he could do was eat dinner and fall asleep in his chair. My mama would take us little ones over to her brother Mick's, who scraped a living out on a dirt farm nearby. Only man in the family that didn't trust to the mines. He died without a dime, just like my daddy and his brothers, and my brother William Paul. But Uncle Mick had his stories, the ones his father and grandfather before him had handed down. He had something that nobody from Washington or the bank or the state capital could take away from him. And when he died, he had so many people in the chapel at Salt Lick, that you couldn't get in. It didn't matter that he never knew what indoor plumbing was, or electricity. He was a great man. And you don't get many people like that in your life. . . ."

Amanda faced Jake now, her expression gentle. Jake straightened again, stiff and uncomfortable with the picture she'd painted, as if he'd just been caught trespassing.

"All I've heard about from Lee is her big brother," she continued carefully. "Now, I've heard a lot of little sisters boast on big brothers, but this was something different. If you want the truth, it was one of the reasons I took her up on her offer. I wanted to see if Jake Kendall could really remind me of my Uncle Mick so much. If he really did have all that honor and honesty and integrity that you just can't buy with a three-piece suit." Amanda was trying so hard, knowing that she wasn't saying it correctly. It was something so deep in her, so ingrained, that she'd only put it into manuscripts before. "Well, you make me miss him all over again. I just thought you should know that."

Amanda's heart thudded. She wrapped her hands into fists and hugged them to her, protecting her from the raw emotion in Jake's eyes. She'd meant to bridge the gap between them, and somehow had driven them further apart. Something in her words had ravaged him, and she wasn't sure what. Something ignited a harsh reaction that smelled like grief. He stood before her, the wrench clenched in his hand almost like a weapon, and didn't answer. And Amanda didn't know what to do.

"I'm sorry," she conceded. "I was hoping we could be friends. Maybe noncombatants, anyway. I'll try and stay out of your way."

She was turning to go when she heard him move, an abrupt sound, as if he were stumbling to life.

"Where the hell's Salt Lick?" he demanded.

Amanda didn't turn back. "West Virginia," she acknowledged. "It's just about as big as Lost Ridge, but poorer. Nobody would have been able to afford Stilwell's."

"Aren't you just a little out of place when you go home looking like that?"

Now it was Amanda's turn. She stopped, lifted her head to the glorious blue of a mountain sky and battled the old pains. "I don't go home anymore."

"Ashamed of them?"

She turned on him, but it was pain she saw in his eyes, not challenge.

"They're all dead," she said. "And I've changed too much for everybody else to be comfortable with me." She didn't realize how lonely her smile looked. "They don't think they can talk to me anymore, now that I've left."

"I can see why," he countered, "if you show up looking like you do here."

"I don't apologize for what I am, Jake. I can't go back to being barefoot even if I wanted to."

"What *do* you want?" he asked, and suddenly all pretense died between them.

The air crackled with unspoken emotions. Amanda saw his eyes darken, saw his knuckles whiten over that wrench. She felt the gnaw of pain in her chest that had been her only answer all these years when she'd asked that same question.

"I want to go home the way I am," she admitted. "And I can never do that. So I guess I'll try and make it where I am. What do *you* want?"

She could touch the tension between them, winnow her fingers through it like a field of static, curling over her and brushing her skin. She could see the cost of his control.

"I want..."

Amanda held her breath. She felt her heart skid and right itself. She saw the last word in his eyes, felt it in the way he stood, heard it in the rasp of his breath.

And she almost answered.

"I want to get this engine repaired by suppertime," he grated. "And I'd appreciate it if visitors would ask me when they intend to disrupt my schedule."

For a minute Amanda couldn't answer. She still couldn't breathe, Jake's near brush with the truth still skittering through her. She raked her trembling fingers through her hair and hoped he didn't realize how shaken she was.

"Of course," she acknowledged. "After all, this is your ranch."

"That's right," he retorted. "It is my ranch. You might want to remember that a little more often."

Amanda managed a smile. "By the way, I never thanked you for lending me Sweet William. He's a wonderful horse."

Jake shrugged, as if to say that even that much gratitude was too much a burden.

"Would there be a chance I could... rent or lease a horse while I'm here? So I can ride back and forth to the cabin instead of taking those damned roads?"

Jake lifted the wrench. "Use Bill. He won't mind."

Amanda immediately shook her head. "No," she disagreed. "Not your work horse. I'm enough of a bother as it is. You let me know when you get a chance. I'll keep practicing in the meantime. And... and I'll stay away from you, if that's what you want."

He didn't answer. Amanda saw the ambivalence and understood it perfectly. She felt the draw and fought it as hard. She prayed for reprieve and yet wasn't sure she was brave enough for it.

All she got was another shrug. "I'll let you know," he said and turned back to his tractor. And Amanda returned to her car and the cabin that had begun to echo with more than ghosts during the long spring nights.

She was halfway across the drive before he spoke.

"Amanda—"

Amanda turned, unsure what she'd heard in his voice. He was standing as stiffly as a man about to be sentenced to death, and his eyes were dark, hooded in the bright sunlight. She couldn't quite see what he hid there, but she felt the discomfort, the ambivalence.

"Yes?"

He opened his mouth to speak, still holding tight to that wrench, still as rigid as pain. "I'm . . . don't pay any attention to me. It's been busy around here, and I've been in a bad mood. I meant it about Sweet William. You're comfortable on him, and he likes that upper pasture. Go ahead and take him."

Amanda knew better than to argue a second time. She knew, too, what Jake was offering. The least she could do was be gracious enough to accept, even if she was still no closer to understanding.

"Thank you," she answered with a smile. "And next time, I'll ask you first. Since it's your ranch and all."

She wished he'd at least smile. He just nodded and turned back to his tractor. And Amanda turned back to her book, knowing full well that she couldn't even think to investigate it until she'd unraveled the mystery in Jake Kendall's eyes.

It *was* his ranch. His world. The only place he knew he belonged on this earth, where he knew what he was worth. Jake looked out the window on this spring evening watching the shadows melt and pool out across the meadow, and thought of how Amanda Marlow threatened to change his life. How she thought to impact on it.

But she had the entire damn world to make her impact on. She could fly to Boston or Beirut or Beijing to lay claim to a piece of earth. Jake had here. He had these mountains and meadows and rivers to call his. He had men who understood him and horses who worked for him, friends to call on and neighbors he could depend on and who could depend on him. He had sense in his life and he had control. And nowhere else did he have that.

No matter what she did, she couldn't take that away from him. She couldn't lay claim to his land, to his place. He never needed to be lonely here; he never felt like an outsider. And to Jake, who had given up so much over the years, that was something he simply couldn't sacrifice.

The lights were on at Clovis's side of the cabin he shared with José. Jake decided that he'd go on down and get Clovis and check on the mares. Grabbing his hat from the rack, he strode across the hardwood floor and banged open the screen door.

Even across the yard he could hear the music floating from Clovis's cabin. Sounded like bluegrass. Probably one of the local stations. Clovis did like his music. He played a mean mouth organ when he wanted. Jake crossed the yard and headed for the lights, a half smile already on his face. They'd just serenade the mares with that little tune.

His boots clacked on the wooden porch as he raised his hand to knock on the door. Just then the music stopped.

"That's real pretty," he heard Clovis say. "What else do you know on that thing?"

Jake's hand dropped. He moved enough to see in the window.

"Try this, Clovis."

Jake froze. The clear, waterfall notes of a dulcimer spilled from inside the room. The melody was sad, soft and sweet, the playing delicate. Clovis's harmonica joined in, and then José's fiddle. Jake could see the three of them through the curtains, each bent over their instrument, eyes closed, their music binding them together, shutting him out.

He stood there for a long time, through that song and into the next, as Amanda offered Appalachian melodies in exchange for Clovis's western versions. They never heard him on the porch while they laughed and played.

Finally Jake turned and walked back through the darkness to his house. Closing the house up in darkness, he stood at the front window, alone in his own house, on his land, aching for something he couldn't have. Hurting for something that was too old to atone for. Looking out from the prison he didn't know how to escape, the prison that had no bars. A prison that Amanda Marlow reinforced with every step she took.

"Is Jake taking good care of you?"

Amanda instinctively laughed. She'd spent another night doing research on her bed since she obviously wasn't supposed to get any sleep there anymore. She'd come home from the impromptu concert at Clovis's to find that the moon had washed the valley and mountains in the most mystical glow, robbing her of every ounce of pragmatism she'd fought so hard to accumulate. Again all she could think of was what Jake Kendall might look like under it. How his eyes would look, silver blue, with the moon softening his skin into a whisper beneath her fingers.

The moon made her mad. But Jake Kendall was making her ache, and that had kept her from sleeping.

Now she was at the ranch, speaking to Lee on the telephone.

"He's been a real gentleman," Amanda assured his little sister. "I've talked to the hands, and Clovis is teaching me to ride."

"And Jake? What's he doing?"

"Well, he's letting me hang around during his busiest time of the year. A girl can't ask much more than that."

Amanda heard the heartfelt sigh on the other end of the line and diagnosed it as the frustration of a very romantic little sister whose ideas about what she'd had in mind for her big brother and her favorite teacher weren't panning out. She tried very hard not to laugh again.

"Has he at least read your book?"

There was some kind of commotion outside. Amanda switched ears and turned to try to see it. "No," she said, attention only half on the call. "He's much too busy right now. Betty read it, though. She liked it."

"Of course she did. It's wonderful. How's the new book coming?"

Men were gathering over by the corrals again. Amanda heard Betty come out of the den and approach the front door. She tried to stretch the kitchen cord a little farther, but it just wouldn't go.

"Damn fool," Betty muttered, shaking her head.

"Book's fine," Amanda assured Lee. "Listen, kid, you're spending a fortune on this call. I'll see you in a couple of weeks, right?"

"Seventeen days. Take care of Jake till I get there."

Once again, Amanda fought her instinctive reaction. "I will," she promised. She hung up the phone in time to hear Betty gasp.

"What's going on?" Amanda demanded, trotting for the front door.

"Jake's been in a temper all morning," Betty answered, never taking her eyes from the corral area. "Guess he's going to take it out on Sidewinder."

Amanda reached the woman's side just in time to see Jake reach over from where he sat astride the big palomino and pull the blindfold from the horse's eyes. The result was instantaneous, breathtaking and terrifying. With a shrill whinny, the animal went straight up in the air. Every hand on the place, and probably a few from neighboring spreads, crowded atop the corral fence, cheering Jake on as he clung to the horse's back. Amanda stopped breathing completely, certain that any minute she was going to see Jake airborne.

"Oh, my God."

Betty gave her head a sharp little shake. "It is somethin' to see, isn't it?" Amanda noticed, though, that her hand was clenched around the pen she'd carried out with her, and her eyes never strayed from the action outside.

"Is that really the way a horse is broken?"

"Not normally. Jake raises his the right way, trainin' 'em from the minute they drop. Bill was just pure neglectful with this animal, and now he wants Jake to cure his problems for him."

Another ragged cheer went up as the horse reared and then kicked, still not displacing Jake. Amanda's chest was beginning to hurt.

"He's going to kill himself," she whispered.

It was an even more impressive spectacle than Jake on the gray. Man and animal battled this time, and the look on Jake's face was fierce. His hat was crammed low as he bent his head toward the horse. His expression was pure steel, the line of his jaw rigid, his eyes focused like lasers on the animal beneath him, as if he could communicate with the animal telepathically, beating him into submission with just the force of his mind. One hand gripped the reins and the other flailed free.

"Don't go to leather, Jake!" somebody crowed.

Amanda reached for the door without even thinking. Betty grabbed her hand.

"Stay here," she suggested in a tone that brooked no comment. "Nothing you can do out there you can't do here."

Amanda looked over at the woman in surprise.

"Jake knows what he's doing," Betty assured her without looking her way.

But even Betty didn't sound like she believed it. She'd said Jake had been in a temper that morning. Why? Why was he so determined suddenly to risk at least injury on a horse that looked at least three-fourths frothing crazy? Why did he look more driven up there than determined? Amanda didn't go out the door. But she turned back to watch with her heart in her throat, sure somehow that she was responsible.

For a minute, it looked like Jake was going to win. The big palomino slowed a little, trotting around the corral and only launching into the air on every third step or so. Amanda could hear the surprised chatter from the hands. She could see the cautious straightening in Jake's posture. Her own stomach eased far enough out of her throat to allow a decent breath, and even Betty seemed on the verge of a smile.

Then, suddenly, the horse bolted. Amanda wasn't exactly sure what happened. It seemed almost as if he'd had a seizure. He lifted straight in the air and twisted at the same time, screaming in fury. Jake stayed with him until he hit the ground and tumbled over his own feet. Jake sailed right over the horse's head. The palomino rolled after him.

Amanda made a convulsive move for the door. Betty held her back.

"He's fine," she chanted as the men jumped off the fence and began trying to restrain the horse and get to Jake. "He's fine."

But he wasn't. He didn't move when Clovis bent over him. Amanda could see his boot-clad legs and nothing else stretched out in the mud. Three men crowded around, all frowning and murmuring. Clovis lifted a very worried face toward the ranch house, and Betty let go of Amanda's hand.

"All right," she snapped. "Now go on out. Tell Clovis I'm callin'."

Amanda ran. Now that he'd freed himself of his rider, the palomino followed quietly to the next corral. Clovis and José bent over the crumpled form in the mud, frozen and uncertain. Amanda made it to the corral and squeezed in through the railings.

"Don't move him," she panted, terror squeezing her throat.

"Wasn't about to," Clovis assured her. "Is Betty calling?"

Amanda nodded as she crouched down beside him. Jake was on his back, his hat off, his legs twisted a little beneath him. His face was ashen, and blood streamed from a cut over his eye.

"I think ole Sidewinder nailed him with a shoe on the way by," Clovis commented, still crouched, his hands fluttering a little in impotence.

Amanda opened the top buttons of Jake's shirt and yanked out his own handkerchief to stem the blood. He was breathing, she could see it. His pulse was thready. It suddenly infuriated her that she didn't know enough to help him—that nobody on the ranch knew enough to help him. She was an author, not a paramedic, for heaven's sake. She shouldn't be the only one capable of action.

"Don't any of you know first aid?" she demanded, shaking at the pallor of Jake's skin.

Clovis offered a very weak smile. "Sight o' blood makes me sick."

José seemed to find the need to retreat to his mother language for solace. Amanda turned back to Jake, not sure whether to chafe his wrists or wring her own hands. "Well, I hope it was the paramedics Betty was calling in there."

"Better not be," Jake grated between clenched teeth.

He still hadn't opened his eyes, and his color certainly didn't look any better, but Amanda was damn near reduced to tears of relief.

"Are you all right?" she asked, thinking that it was the most stupid thing she'd ever said.

"Kind of a dumb question," he answered, his voice faint and strained, his eyes still closed. "I just . . . fell off a horse."

She wanted to grin. She wanted to touch him and couldn't. "You hit the ground doing about sixty, I think. Betty called for help."

"Get me up."

He opened his eyes then, and Amanda could see just how all right he was. Pain scored creases in his forehead, tautened his eyes and reduced his breathing to careful pants.

"I will not," she argued. "You could have hurt your back."

"I didn't hurt . . . my back. I hurt my ribs. Now, get . . . me . . . up."

"Jake, I don't . . ."

He must have figured it was a waste of time glaring at her. He glared at Clovis instead, who seemed to take that kind of thing more seriously. Between him and José, they managed to wrestle Jake back up to his feet.

"Damn," Jake gasped, sagging just a little in their support, eyes closing briefly. "I'm gonna have to shoot that animal."

Clovis laughed. "Either that or recommend him as a bronc."

Amanda felt foolish trailing behind as Jake, Clovis and José walked very gingerly toward the house. She could see him splinting his side as he walked and wanted to hit him again for even getting up. She saw the flash in his eyes when she challenged him and thanked God he was all right. She thought of how stupid it was for a man to prove himself by wrestling half a ton of animal into submission.

At any other time or place, she would have immediately pictured that scene in terms of her book. She would have taken it, dissected it, transcribed it into the time period. Dispassionately, distanced. Standing in the middle of the present, she'd already be lost in the past.

As Amanda trailed along behind the three men, Jake's hat in her hand, her own eyes riveted to the slow, very careful way he walked, the way he weaved every once in a while as if the ground weren't quite steady beneath him, the last thing on her mind was her book.

Chapter 6

"Damn fool."

"Shut up, Betty."

The woman bristled in outrage. "You're my boss," she snapped. "Not my father. Talk to me like that again and you can do your own books."

Jake's answering smile was at best grim. "I'm sorry. I'm...a little..."

"Stupid," the woman finished for him, slamming a cup of coffee down before him so hard the liquid sloshed over the rim. "I've seen you mad before. Scared, drunk, delirious and dumbstruck. This is the first time I've ever seen you stupid."

He seemed more used to the diatribe than Amanda, who sat along openmouthed. "Thanks."

Amanda wasn't sure whether she was more amazed or frustrated to see him sitting at the kitchen table. He didn't look appreciably better than when they'd stood him up out in the corral. Only a little cleaner, with a row of not-too-neat stitches marching along the crescent-shaped laceration along the left side of his forehead.

"Well, look there," Doc McPherson had marveled while sewing his patient up in the living room. "Right down to the bone. You're lucky you're not seein' double."

"I *am* seein' double," Jake had answered evenly, eyes closed, hands clenched.

The doctor had simply nodded with some kind of professional satisfaction and gone on stitching. "Not surprisin' at all." Amanda had spent the time looking out the window.

Betty had called the doc, not the paramedics. It seemed that this hadn't been the first time there had been a medical emergency of some kind or another out at the ranch, and the doc, an old friend of the family's, usually had a better response time—and didn't insist that the patient be transported all the way to Jackson Hole for treatment, which none of the men liked, anyway. A short, thin man with less hair than Clovis and more wrinkles, he peered at the world through half lenses and seemed to consider the human condition an endlessly amusing situation. Much more composed by the time he showed up, Amanda had immediately cast him in the part of the small-town doctor trying to bring medicine to the untamed West.

The doc was gone within about fifteen minutes, and Maria dispatched to town to pick up prescriptions for antibiotics and pain medicine for Jake's "most probably busted" ribs. Clovis had gone back out at Jake's insistence to keep working Sidewinder on a lungeing line just so the horse understood that bucking a rider off did not win him some time off from training. That left Amanda and Betty for nursing duty. Amanda didn't think now was the time to admit to a queasy stomach.

"Are you still seeing double?" she asked tentatively, wondering what they were supposed to do if that got worse—or what worse was.

Jake took an exploratory sip of coffee. "I'm fine. I keep saying that, but nobody believes me."

"That's 'cause they're lookin' at you," Betty challenged from where she stood over by the sink, arms crossed and forehead pursed. "What are we gonna do tonight, I ask ya?"

"Nothing," Jake assured her yet again, even though not as heartily as he obviously intended. "I told you, I'm fine."

"No, you're not," she argued. "You're—"

He lifted a hand. "Stupid. Yeah, Betty. I heard."

Amanda squirmed a little in her chair across from him. Her own coffee was going cold in her hands as she did her best not to stare at the strain on his hard face, the careful way he breathed and talked so his chest wouldn't work too much.

She hurt for him, and it made her angry. He didn't want her to. He didn't ask her to. He'd probably be mad if he knew. But she couldn't help the notion that somehow she was responsible for this . . . stupidity. He'd been so intense on that horse. She could still see the glint in his eyes, as if what he'd been doing had been more than a contest or a job; it had been a battle. A proving ground of some kind. And Amanda simply couldn't imagine what Jake Kendall had to prove to anyone.

"I'm talkin' about keepin' an eye on you tonight," Betty insisted. "Last time you hurt yourself, the kids were home. I can't stay, and Clovis doesn't know what to do for anything with less than four legs and a tail."

Jake's scowl was pretty impressive considering the fact that he still didn't move much. "Leave me alone, Betty, or I will get somebody else to do my books."

She snorted. "In a pig's eye. Nobody else knows your system. Now, you figure somebody to stay and wake you up, or I'll do it for you. I'm sure Lila'd be happy to help out in a mission of mercy."

Jake actually stiffened in outrage. Then he thought better of protesting and dropped his head into his hands. "You're tryin' my patience."

"Why does he need to be watched?" Amanda asked quietly, certain she didn't want the answer or the responsibility Betty was inexorably shoving her way.

"His head," Betty sighed. "Has to be wakened every so often, make sure he makes sense—as much sense as he ever makes—and can see and the like. Make sure he isn't bleeding in there, though how he could in that thick head of his, I don't know."

"Which means I won't need a baby-sitter," Jake insisted yet again from behind his hands.

"Which means you need a caretaker if you ever try and get on that horse again."

"Betty, you're makin' my head hurt."

She snorted again.

"I'll do it," Amanda offered.

Jake's head came up fast. It went back down even faster.

"No," he snapped on the end of a stifled groan. "I don't need you."

"I know you don't," she acknowledged with a grin she knew he wouldn't see. "But I'm a bigger sucker for missions of mercy than Lila is."

"Go find a pagan baby or something. Leave me alone."

But Betty was already moving. "I'll show you the girls' old room," she said. "You want one of the boys to get you some stuff from the cabin?"

Amanda shook her head, wishing that her chest didn't feel quite so tight. "I'll get it before you leave."

"Nobody's staying!" Jake yelled without moving.

"Pay no attention to him," Betty suggested. "He's bein' stupid again."

He'd had better days. He'd had worse ones, too, but that was usually hard to remember at two in the morning. His ribs scraped every time he moved. His head was pounding like a brass band, churning up his stomach and playing havoc with his balance.

Jake had been kicked in the head before, knew what a concussion felt like. Just because he did, didn't mean he liked it any better. All he had to do was get through the night and back on his feet tomorrow, and the worst would be over. He'd be back on schedule, back in control.

He'd have Amanda back out of his house again.

He wouldn't smell her faint perfume as she walked by or hear the throaty music of her humming as she clattered away on that computer of hers out in the kitchen. He wouldn't have to let her pace his room and acquaint herself with his life. He wouldn't open his eyes to see her smiling at him.

The moon was out, hovering in the sky right outside his window, like an insistent visitor. A quiet reminder of everything he had in his life, the mountains, the pastures, the silent Wyoming sky—and of everything he didn't have.

"Jake?"

Her whisper was like the breeze through the grass. Even aching and sore and sick, Jake couldn't help reacting to it. He turned from the moonlight to see her standing next to his bed, her hair tumbling wild and gleaming around her shoulder, her nightgown as white as moonlight in the dim room. He couldn't quite see her eyes, though. He had to imagine the quick life there, the hungry intelligence that was so like Lee's, but more formidable. More mesmerizing. More threatening.

"I'm awake," he said.

"What day is it?"

His smile was wry. Not the question he wanted from a beautiful woman at two o'clock on a moonlit morning.

"The same day I lost that argument with Sidewinder," he said, rubbing a little at the stitches that still burned across his forehead. It was that or clench his hands together. She moved a little, and her hair drifted like smoke around her pale face. It made him want to winnow his fingers through it, to test the softest skin there at the back of her neck and see what he found when he brushed that pale flannel from her shoulders.

"Where are you?" she asked, just as she had the last two times she'd been in, right on the schedule Betty had seen fit to set up. Time, place and person, something he'd forgotten completely for a minute lying out there on the ground. Amanda had stopped asking who was president along about midnight when Jake had assured her that he didn't care enough to remember. He wasn't any more patient this time.

He might have had a lot more success in fighting their little plan if he'd been able to get back up from that table this afternoon without immediately falling into Amanda's arms. He might have even succeeded then if when they'd asked him what was wrong, he hadn't been too distracted to answer.

God, her hair had smelled so good.

"At the Beverly Hills Hotel, having drinks by the pool."

"Jake—"

"Aren't you a little overdressed for a swim?"

She scowled at him. "I'm the poolside bartender."

Jake couldn't help a grin. "Then make mine a double."

"How are you feeling?"

"Like a horse sat on me. You?"

"Like I'm baby-sitting a six-year-old."

He tried to chuckle, but that hurt. "That'll teach you to listen to Betty."

That was when Jake noticed that her hands were clenched, too, right in front of her, as if she were holding herself together. Her fingers were long and graceful, ringless. They looked like sculpture in the moonlight that washed her. Jake wanted to taste one of those fingers. He wanted to feel them on his skin. He wanted to find himself so immersed in her that he could forget everything, everyone, who he was and who she was.

But he knew better. He'd known better all along.

Amanda started. "What's wrong?"

Jake hadn't even known he'd groaned out loud. Amanda's eyes widened, dark pools in the shadows. Deadly, deep water that looked far too inviting. Jake fought a sudden yearning that made the pain from his ribs pale in comparison.

Amanda took an instinctive step forward, unclenching one hand. Jake was afraid she was going to reach out to him. He couldn't let her, because if she touched him, he'd lose control. Even sick, even battered like an old suitcase. He'd been alone too long, and he knew that that wasn't going to change.

He'd never forgive Betty for doing this to him.

Ignoring the shriek of pain from his chest, he pulled himself up to a sitting position. "I needed to stretch out a little," he lied, turning back to the window. The scene outside faded and swam a little before settling back into place. "Go on back to bed. I'm fine."

"Are you going to take your medicine?"

"No."

He could hear her huff of impatience. "Jake, don't be stubborn. Dr. McPherson said that you could have the pain medicine if you hurt. And you need that antibiotic."

"No, I don't. He's just trying to support the town's economy."

"Would you tell me something?" she demanded. "Why'd you spend all that money on the drugs if you weren't going to take them?"

Jake turned back on her, irritated, frustrated, furious. "Because it's easier sometimes to let people think they're going to get their way. Now, would you go back to bed so I can get some sleep?"

Amanda glared right back at him, just as frustrated. "I'll be back at four," she informed him, hands on hips. "Just so you know."

Jake knew his expression was inhospitable. "Try not to wake me."

By four o'clock Amanda was the one seeing double. She'd really tried to catch some sleep during the hours in between the checks, but it hadn't happened. She'd seen too much today, felt too much, leaving her raw and unsettled. Caffeine thrummed through her, and the silence propelled her. She'd written, but the words had had nothing to do with her book, with any book. She'd stretched out on Lee's bed and closed her eyes, only to see Jake's eyes.

As the world outside slept on past moonset, when even the birds hadn't quite decided to rise, she crept back into his room, hoping this time that he would be asleep. The last three times she'd walked in, he'd been waiting for her, as if afraid to let her sneak up on him. Not exactly the way to get over injuries, she would have guessed from the careful way he moved. Certainly not the way to regain your good humor, she knew for certain from his attitude.

His room had been a shock. Not the furniture. It had been his parents', she knew from Lee. Simple pine furniture, well used and loved, a big double bed with a hunter-green-and-cream comforter, a dresser and nightstand, a big, overstuffed chair by the window that overlooked the pastures. All that she had expected. It was the same kind of furniture that populated the rest of the house, functional and worn. Lived in.

What had surprised her had been the decorations. With the exception of the girls' bedroom, every other room Amanda had seen in the Kendalls' home had a spare, almost spartan decor. Every time she'd walked into the house, Amanda had looked for some sign that three other children had grown up amid these walls, that those children had once had parents. Usually pictures were grouped on living room walls, or atop pianos. The walls held one Navajo rug, and the piano had a fine layer of dust.

The rooms, for all their comfort, had no life.

That had been reserved for Jake's bedroom. Every surface was crowded with frames, every wall hung in childish art and portraits. Amanda finally saw Jake's parents, an earnest-looking young couple who shared responsibility for their children's looks. Lee, from infancy to graduation, school pictures and candid shots on horseback or at play or in the kitchen. Genevieve, she guessed, whose last picture was with stethoscope and lab coat, her arm around a very uncomfortable-looking Jake in his city best, her rich brown hair and eyes the antithesis of her brother's. Ezekial, who shared Genevieve's darker looks, in various sports uniforms graduating into mortarboard and then down vest and pickax. A handsome, open young man with an impish smile.

It was as if Jake fortified himself with his family every morning and night, as if they were something so private and special to him that he couldn't share them with everyone who tracked through his house on the way to a horse sale.

It was, Amanda knew, a reflection of how private a man Jake Kendall was. Lee might be able to wax eloquent about her family, collecting them into stories much as Amanda had always sought to do, but Jake would measure his bond alone and in silence.

Amanda looked again at the shadowy geometrics atop Jake's dresser, saw in her mind the forest of pictures, and ached to ask him about each one, knowing full well that he would never think of sharing them with her. Knowing just how bad he'd been feeling if he'd let her breach this stronghold at all.

"Jake?"

He was asleep this time. The light from the bathroom washed across him, betraying a jumble of bedclothes from his attempts to get comfortable. He lay on his back, his head to the side, one hand across his belly. The comforter reached his chest. Amanda stood at the bottom of his bed for a moment longer, watching him, thinking of how powerful those shoulders were, how the sun had glided across that chest. Wishing suddenly that she could explore the same terrain the sun had, could warm it as thoroughly. She pressed her fingers against her lips, as if she could contain the hunger she'd never allowed before.

She tried to take a step back, and ended up faltering. Then she tried to walk over to him again, steeling herself to do the job she'd offered to do and no more. She'd taken exactly one step when her bare foot came down on something soft.

A towel. Amanda looked down, as if it would explain how it got from the bathroom to the floor halfway to the bed. Then she looked up and realized that sometime in the last two hours Jake had carried himself into the bathroom and back again. Maybe he'd actually taken some of his medicine. Obeying well-honed instincts, she bent over to retrieve the towel and return it to its proper place.

The bathroom was early functional, and all male. Amanda was sure that no cleaning lady saw the inside of any part of Jake's private inner sanctum, but especially the bathroom. It was clean, and fairly neat, with white tile and basic fixtures. But no professional hand arranged its contents. No one had bothered to dilute the male setting with frilly touches of silk flowers. There was toothpaste and a razor on the sink, and a pair of jeans thrown over the towel rack. Shampoo in the shower and a full bottle of cologne that she bet one of his family had given him for Christmas and remained as unopened as those antibiotics. It made her smile. Jake Kendall didn't wear artificial scent. He didn't need it.

Brushing the jeans aside with hands that strayed just a little over the soft denim, Amanda folded the towel and rehung it. She was turning back to leave when she saw the trash can. More importantly, she saw what was in the trash can.

Most trash cans have trash. This little wicker basket that sat next to the door to the bedroom was stuffed with magazines. Old magazines, well thumbed and tattered like well-loved stuffed animals. Amanda took a guilty look out to where Jake still slept undisturbed, and bent to satisfy her curiosity.

She frowned and then crouched down and fingered more slowly through them.

Travel magazines. Every one of them, with bright, evocative pictures of exotic cities and countries: Venice, Paris, Hong

Kong, Thailand, the moors of Scotland and the Great Barrier Reef of Australia.

Amanda couldn't understand. Wasn't Jake the one who Clovis said didn't like to go anywhere? The man who considered all life to exist within twenty miles of the Diamond K? What had that trip to Chicago been all about?

Amanda's father had never had a desire to leave West Virginia, but he'd never even bothered to open the cover of the *National Geographic*. He'd never hidden in his room where he thought no one else could see and pored over old magazines with stories of the places he never wanted to see, anyway.

Amanda caught herself looking out into the darkened bedroom again, the *Travel and Leisure* magazine still in her hands where it had fallen open by itself to a spread on New York.

New York. Even bigger and noisier and more impersonal than Chicago. And Jake had obviously been reading about it all alone, for a long time.

It didn't make sense.

Carefully she replaced the magazines back where they belonged and straightened. She took a second more to compose herself, because suddenly she hurt in a whole new way for Jake Kendall. She hurt for someone who kept his dreams in a wastepaper basket.

Did he, though? Could Clovis have been mistaken? Could this man who was so successful, so self-contained and well respected, have hidden dreams that he thought he wouldn't be able to fulfill? Had he wanted the ranch, or simply been handed it without chance of refusal?

She'd seen what he was like up on his horses. There was a compelling life to him, a magnificent power that infected her in a way no other human had. He couldn't possibly hate the animals he trained.

But could he want something more and know he couldn't have it? Was this what he'd given up for his sisters and brother?

Was this, then, part of the pain that licked at the edges of those crystal-blue eyes? Part of the reason he resented Amanda so much?

And if so, why? She had to find out, somehow. But she knew she wasn't going to do it now. Carefully stepping out of the bathroom, Amanda walked around to the foot of Jake's bed so it looked as if she'd just entered from the hallway.

"Jake?" she called, a little louder this time.

He started at the sound of her voice, and Amanda regretted waking him. Grunting, he rubbed at his chest with his hand. Amanda fought the urge to take that hand in hers, to smooth her other hand over his injuries. *All* his injuries.

Jake Kendall didn't need her compassion. He had a family, he had friends, he had people work for him.

But who was here with him now? Who did he let close enough to be compassionate for him? Who did he tell his dreams to? He had friends who had paced outside the house until they'd known he was all right, who badgered him into taking care of himself, and carried his reputation far and wide simply for the privilege of working with him. And yet there were things Jake hid from those people.

"Wake up, Jake," she almost begged, her gaze on the twin prescription bottles by the bed she could see hadn't yet been breached, after all. "I need to go through the routine."

He never opened his eyes. "My name is Bonaparte," he growled. "I live in France, and if you don't leave me alone, I'm going to have a field marshal blow you to hell."

She chuckled. "Oh, good," she allowed. "You're feeling better."

"I'm feeling like hell," he corrected her, finally getting his eyes open. "But nothing you can do can change that."

Somehow the hall light managed to reach the blue of his eyes and Amanda could have sworn she read something totally different there. Something that looked an awful lot like that challenge out by the barn.

For a minute, she was afraid he'd really been awake all along, had seen her sneaking around in his bathroom. She clamped her hands to her legs and prayed for insight.

"I imagine that means that the pain prescription's still out of the question."

"It does."

She nodded, trying her best to deflect his intensity. "I'd be more than happy to offer some of the folk remedies I've picked up," she suggested. "But there just aren't a lot of cures out there for broken ribs and concussion. On the other hand, I'm a whiz at warts."

She almost thought she saw a smile as he resettled on the bed. "Warts."

Amanda nodded, warming to her subject, relaxing a bit. "Oh, yes. Warts are very high on the folklore pop charts. You can cure them by holding them up to a full moon or burying something that rots, or washing them in the rainwater from the stump of a white oak tree. Do you have any warts?"

"Sorry."

She shrugged. "Not much call for that anymore, anyway. How 'bout a fever? I do a great fever."

"A fever. No," he admitted. "I think that's the only thing I don't have."

"Of course, if you don't take your antibiotics, I might get lucky. I've always wanted to tie soap to the bottoms of somebody's feet. Or better yet, mackerels."

He actually seemed to choke on that. "I don't suppose plain old aspirin would work?"

Amanda grinned at him, encouraged by the crook at the corner of his mouth. "Not nearly imaginative enough."

"Or aromatic, I'm sure."

"Of course, the question is where to get a good mackerel in Wyoming."

"Something that's troubled me for a long time."

He wasn't laughing, not quite. Amanda was sure that he rarely laughed outright. But for the first time he really seemed to be enjoying himself around her. It made her wonder. It made her hurt in a funny way that had to do with the empty cabin she inhabited and the cautious softening of Jake's eyes and the secrets he kept in his room.

"You should probably get back to sleep," she demurred, shoving her hands into her pockets.

"Probably."

"Especially since I'll be back in at six to wake you again."

"You're not in your nightgown anymore," he said.

Amanda looked up to see that thaw still holding. She shot off a hesitant grin. "I gave up and got dressed," she admitted with a shrug. "I'm not getting any sleep, anyway. It seems to be a full-time job checking in on French generals."

"You don't have to come in anymore," he insisted. "I'm not even seeing double now."

"And risk incurring Betty's wrath?" she demanded. "Don't be silly."

Jake scowled mightily. "Silly is not something I'm often called."

Amanda had to concede the point. "I'm sure. I'll see you at six, then."

His humor was fading fast. "I told you. Not on my account."

"Not yours. Mine. By six you might have worked up a fever from the infection you're going to get from that huge cut with all the horse stuff in it. I mean, as it is, I'll just have time to scare up some fish."

"The door's going to be locked," he informed her and sat up.

She yanked her hands out of her pockets and slapped them on her hips. "Are you this pleasant with everybody?" she demanded. "Or do I bring out the best in you?"

"Amanda," he protested, swinging his legs over the side of the bed. "Leave it be."

"No, I mean it. I'm trying my damnedest to get along with you, and so far you've acted as if I were trying to sabotage the ranch."

"Me," he snapped, turning to impale her with his sudden anger. "You're trying to sabotage me."

Amanda could only stare at him. He was climbing to his feet, those long, hard legs encased in nothing more than undershorts, his chest bare and gleaming softly from the bathroom light. She knew she should get the hell out of his room, but she was frozen to the spot. No woman should see this much of Jake Kendall. No woman should have to face both his wrath and the sight of his near-naked body at once.

Even if he was weaving around like a punch-drunk fighter as he stood. Even if he was bruised and churlish. She was suddenly breathless; and she hadn't run anywhere. She was sweating, and she was still standing across the room.

"What are you doing?" she demanded, instinctively stepping toward him, anyway. "And what do you mean I'm sabotaging you?"

He pushed her away and held onto the bedpost for support, his head down a little so that his hair fell across his eyes. Amanda came perilously close to sweeping it back with her hands.

"I'm getting . . . up," he grated, taking a careful breath. "Alone."

"Why? Just so you can fall on your nose?"

He turned on her then, and Amanda saw that the dizziness had passed. His eyes were sharp and clear and deadly. He was angry. He was ambivalent. He was intimidating her again when he shouldn't possibly have been.

"I'm going to the bathroom," he informed her in a steely voice. "Do you want to help?"

"What do you mean," she repeated instead, "that I'm sabotaging you?"

"That's why you make me mad," he told her, straightening by inches, one hand loose from the bedpost, his height crowding her, his body mesmerizing her, his expression stunning her. His eyes were smoldering. "You won't let go. Not with the ranch, not with the hands, not with me. Did it ever occur to you that I don't want you here?"

She should have been angry. She was hurt instead. "Why?" she asked, her voice soft with confusion.

Jake cursed. He cursed violently. "Never mind, Amanda. Just go."

"I don't think so," she persisted. "This is the the closest I've gotten to the truth with you, and I don't think I'm going to get another chance. Why?"

His head shot up, his eyes blazing. "Because I want you," he said. "That's why."

Amanda felt battered, by his words, his emotions, his power. He was the one without clothes on, yet she felt naked. Exposed and vulnerable. She struggled to stand her ground, to keep her head up, to pull words free of the whirling emotions his words had unleashed. "That's so bad?" she wanted to know, her voice now very small, the truth escaping before she realized it. "Wanting someone?"

He glared at her, and suddenly Amanda saw all the pain she'd only guessed at before. It tore at him like barbed wire, leaving those beautiful, proud eyes raw and sore. Leaving Amanda in shreds, because she knew he wouldn't let her reach out to him.

"I've made some mistakes in my life, lady," he snarled, a cornered, injured animal. "But I'm not about to make that one."

"Why?" she demanded, not even coherent enough to understand why she was protesting. Running on instinct, fueled by loneliness and attraction, by emotions she couldn't even label yet. "What have I done to you?"

"You don't belong here."

Amanda shook her head. "Who says? Hell, Jake, this place is more like where I grew up than anywhere else I've ever lived."

Jake pulled himself together and away from her, his eyes hardening. "You left, Amanda," he said simply. "And I didn't. Now, I'd appreciate it if you'd close the door on your way out."

He didn't wait for an answer. Not protest or agreement or argument. Pushing himself away from the bed, he walked into the bathroom and closed the door. When Amanda heard the lock click, she turned from the room and didn't come back.

Chapter 7

Amanda stalked the early morning hours like a caged animal, her bare feet padding across the hardwood, her one hand holding coffee, the other hand spiking through her hair. The radio was giving out farm reports, and the horses were beginning to wander toward breakfast. It was going to be another beautiful morning, the sky softened with low clouds and the snow line creeping back toward the mountains. It was the kind of morning she liked to stand by a window and watch the world come alive, to wake slowly, like the mist clearing off the meadow.

This morning she had no patience for the mist or the snow. She had no thought for the wonder of nature. This morning she was still awake from last night. She was still locked out of Jake's room. She was still reeling from the admissions he'd made in the dim, dark hours before dawn.

He wanted her.

Should she have been so surprised? She'd sensed it in him the minute they'd met, that dark desire, like liquid smoke in his eyes, that crackle of tension that leapt between them the minute they got closer than a corral apart. She'd felt it in her chest,

like an inflating balloon. She'd felt it in her belly, a slow fire
that never quite banked.

She'd admitted it herself. Even now her palms sweated with
it. Her heart stumbled, and her thoughts skittered out of control, harassed by images of Jake threatening to kiss her, his
fingers in her hair. Jake battling that horse into submission, his
body taut, his eyes sparking fire. Jake standing before her in the
darkness, his body draped in shadow, his fury sounding too
much like anguish, his hands trembling.

Even so, Amanda still couldn't quite believe that Jake had
said it. Amanda had only known him a matter of days, but she
knew the kind of control he kept. Jake was a man who held his
thoughts to himself, who held his most special memories locked
in his room. He was a man who let his actions speak for him,
who had friends and neighbors who respected and liked him,
but didn't really know him.

She'd left. She'd left, and he hadn't. God, Amanda wished
she knew what he'd meant by that. Did he think she'd sold out,
somehow? That she wasn't good enough because she'd tried her
best to make her way in the world away from the Appalachians?

How could he? He'd sent his own sisters and brother away.
He'd badgered them and bullied them and financed them
through the best schools, so that now they were spread over the
country.

Amanda was so tired. She was so confused. If only she had
somebody to talk to, someone she could trust. But it was another legacy of the traveling years. The closest she'd come to a
friendship had been with Lee, and she certainly didn't want to
talk to Jake's sister about her less than cerebral problem.

If only it were glands, she thought miserably, it might be
easier. But it wasn't. It had gone way past that the moment Jake
had first reined in in front of that cabin.

If it were just glands, she would have spent far fewer nights
alone in her hotel room in Los Angeles, where the offers hadn't
come with conditions. No, she thought, with a sad shake of her
head as she dumped sugar into her latest cup of coffee, there
had been conditions. In Los Angeles men had wanted to bed

her because of the person she'd become. Jake refused for the same reason.

Sometimes you simply couldn't win. She couldn't change, and he undoubtedly wouldn't, and suddenly Amanda wasn't at all sure she'd get any more of a chance to discover those secrets he buried beneath all that harsh discipline.

"Has he given you much trouble?"

Amanda shot up so fast she nearly hit her head on the range hood.

"Betty, don't do that," she protested, once she could breathe again.

The secretary stepped on into the kitchen, her crepe-soled shoes whispering over the tile. Hanging her coat up in the mud room, she turned for a cup of coffee to find only dregs left. She turned a quizzical eye on Amanda.

Amanda proffered a grimace. "He locked himself in his room about four. For all I know, he could have been dead since four-thirty.... No, I take that back. I did hear him cursing in there along about five. I think he was trying to turn over."

"You mean you haven't gotten any sleep?"

Amanda lifted her coffee to punctuate. "I was afraid of ambush. You forgot to mention how surly he gets."

Betty actually looked penitent as she rattled around starting another pot. "It's the only way I can get people to stay. Jake doesn't take to being an invalid well."

"You do have a way with an understatement, Betty. He does this often, does he?"

The taciturn woman shrugged. "He works with horses that weigh half a ton and sometimes don't take much to humans. It's bound to happen once in a while."

"Well, I hope you have better luck with him than I did," Amanda retorted, taking a very large sip of coffee. "I couldn't talk him into taking his medicine or answering any of the questions or even admitting that he hurt."

"Did you check his pupils, like I said?"

"Don't be silly. I wasn't about to get that close." For more reasons than one, but Betty didn't need to know about that. Amanda hid her reaction behind another sip of coffee.

She was seeing Jake again, dark and ferocious and over-powering in the throbbing silence of his room. Jake, threatening her composure and invading her sleep. Jake, who didn't want her here.

Jake, who hid brightly colored magazines back where nobody should be able to find them.

"Y'know, I was thinking," she mused as nonchalantly as she could, "with Jake recovering and Lee coming in, maybe they could take some time off and visit Zeke out on that dig he's doing down at the Navajo reservation. Lee said she hadn't seen him since the spring."

Betty's laughter was a bark of surprise. "Not likely."

Amanda proffered an expression of bland curiosity. "He mad at Zeke or something? I thought they were all close."

Betty turned on Amanda with that look of the old hand about to break the greenhorn in. "Last time Jake Kendall left this place, he darn near busted his bank balance to get back. He'd rather be in traction with a back brace on than leave this ranch."

Amanda leaned her elbows back on the island counter and settled in, a look of amusement replacing the curiosity. "You're kidding. Why?"

Betty shrugged. "It's just Jake's way. He's got no desire to see anything but the Wyoming mountains, got no reason to ride anything but a horse and maybe, on occasion, a pickup truck."

Which wouldn't explain the long article on the gondolas of Venice that had looked so well perused.

Why?

Amanda couldn't imagine. Clovis, she might suspect of hyperbole. Betty, on the other hand, had to have information dragged out of her, and an adjective was almost beyond her scope of information.

Amanda shook her head, still sipping her coffee, her eyes more on questions than the scene in front of her. "I can't imagine he wouldn't even visit his family. I mean, they're all so far away."

It didn't seem to bother Betty any. She poured the first cup of coffee from the new pot and stirred in about a half cup of milk. "They know Jake well enough to visit here, if they need.

And it's not like none of 'em can afford to come home. Jake does well enough to get 'em here if they can't do it themselves, though now that Zeke and Gen are out of school, they're doin' fine by themselves. Those children just aren't tied to this piece of land, like Jake is."

"That seems to be a Kendall trait," Amanda offered.

Betty nodded. "As long as anybody can remember, there's been a Kendall here. One of the most beautiful spots on earth, and one of the hardest to turn into anything. But that's always been the Kendalls for you. Just hardheaded enough not to listen to anybody but themselves."

Amanda couldn't help laughing. "Well, now, that's a trait I've certainly seen in the last twenty-four hours. I guess Jake never considered turning the place into a dude ranch? There are so many nearby."

The shake of Betty's head was definite. "He's got no patience for that kind of thing. Didn't want to tie the children down to helpin' run it if it came to that. Besides, his real calling has always been horses. That's what he's good at, and that's what he does."

Clovis tried his best not to make any noise sneaking in the back door, but he didn't do very well.

"Boss awake yet, Betty?"

Betty turned on him like a mother hen. "You're not going to bother that boy when he's still laid up from that beast. Now, you just get back outa here."

Clovis's features crumpled into misery. "Oh, I wouldn't, you know that. Not normally. Not till he came stompin' out with you chasin' him, I wouldn't. But it's Alabaster."

"What about Alabaster?"

All three turned to find Jake in the kitchen door, struggling to get his arm into his shirt.

Betty went right on the offensive. "Don't you dare go out of this house, Jake Kendall. You just busted your ribs and stove in your head."

"Betty," he said, calming her with more patience than Amanda gave him credit for, especially considering the color of his skin and the lines of pain and weariness etched on his face. "Hush. What's wrong with Alabaster, Clovis?"

Clovis actually pulled off his hat and wrung it in his hands. "He's down, Jake. I think it's colic."

"Well, get him up," Jake barked, right back in command. "I'll be right out."

"You will not!" Betty protested, even though by now Amanda could tell that the woman knew it was useless.

Jake turned on her with calm consideration. "I'm not gonna feel any better in here," he told her, his breathing a little strained. His jeans were on, and his feet had socks on them. Amanda couldn't imagine what it had taken to get his undershirt on. "It's my horse. Now, help me with this sleeve."

He never even acknowledged that Amanda was in the room. Betty slammed down her coffee cup and walked over to him, easing his shirt around for him so that he didn't have to reach much with his ribs.

"I'll call the vet," she bit off, pulling the front closed with a tug so he could button it.

He smiled that crooked little-boy smile that made Amanda's knees weak and bent over to kiss the top of Betty's head. "Thanks," was all he said before he turned back to his room.

It took Amanda a minute to recover her senses.

"You were sayin' about hardheaded Kendalls?" she asked, her thoughts still whirling around the relief of seeing Jake on his feet, the concern that he was going out to hurt himself again, the misery of knowing that he hadn't even so much as turned her way while he'd stood there.

Betty gave a very unladylike snort and went back to her coffee. "The prime example, right there. We probably don't have to worry about another Kendall carryin' this place on. Jake's gonna kill himself before he ever gets a chance to settle down and have children."

Children. History, home, continuity. Amanda ached with the pictures that provoked, with the sudden, piercing yearning that she'd held tightly in check all these years. A place of her own, a piece of land to always come home to, to hand down with the stories of family, with the traditions of a place and a time, with the devotion of a person who knew the value of all those things.

Before Jake had a chance to wander back through, Amanda set down her cup and straightened to leave. "I think I'll head off now, Betty."

Betty nodded. "Thanks for puttin' up with him. I notice he wasn't gentleman enough to thank you himself."

Amanda shrugged and turned for her computer, where it lay packed and ready with her work on the dining-room table. "He was a little preoccupied."

"Will you be by again tomorrow?"

Amanda turned back to the woman just in time to see Jake appear in the living room, hat on, boots in hand, his one arm held close to his side, his gait slow and careful, his face harsh with the discomfort he thought nobody noticed. Amanda turned abruptly away and walked back into the kitchen. "No," she said. "I think I should probably spend a few days in the cabin. Besides . . ."

Betty scowled. "Don't let him scare you off here."

Amanda looked up in time to see that Betty's gaze was directed not at her, but the door in toward the living room. Amanda turned to see that Jake had arrived, his features now much more composed, his posture straight and his manner deceptively easy.

He turned his attention to Amanda, and she saw the embers left from last night in the icy blue of his eyes. It almost robbed her completely of the power of speech. She clutched the computer to her chest like a lifesaver.

"Did I scare you off?" Jake asked.

Amanda forced herself to smile. "Hardly. It's just that I have work to do today, too."

Betty didn't seem to feel the undercurrents in the room. She faced her boss with hands on hips. "Do I have to be your mama?" she demanded. "Remind you of your manners? Where I was brought up, it was proper to thank a person for stayin' up all night with me to make sure I was all right."

Jake allowed a smile then. Not the bright, winsome smile he'd given Betty before, but a tighter, slightly darker version. An expression of self-deprecation. "Did I forget to thank you?" he asked. "Thank you, Amanda. You were patient with me. Betty's right. I can be . . . a little irritable when I'm not feeling well.''

Amanda tilted her head a little and returned his smile, trying her best to answer him without considering the last exchange they'd had. ''The entire West seems to be a well-spring of understatement. You're welcome, Jake. I hope Alabaster's all right.''

A brief flash of surprise glinted in his eyes. ''You going back to the cabin now? You can take Bill, if you want.''

''Thanks, but I'm going to town. I have some stocking up to do.''

He nodded and turned away. At the last minute, he flashed her a grin over his shoulder. ''Don't forget those fish.''

After the night Amanda had spent, she'd never have imagined laughing as she left. Even so, she did.

Amanda loved small towns. There was a definite pace to them, a taste that you could roll around in your mouth like fine old wine, a little musty, a little dry, a little fruity. There was a closeness that defied petty jealousies and transient arguments. Lost Ridge was no different.

Basically a one-street town with two stoplights, one funeral home and two clothing stores specializing in denim and flannel, it had been originally built in the late 1800s, with some of its original brick buildings surviving intact.

The bank had a new drive-up window and the theater had added a video arcade, but other than that, Amanda imagined that this town beyond the fringe of high-tourist Wyoming hadn't changed appreciably in the last forty years. She wandered the stores and sidewalks like a traveler come home.

''Jake doin' all right?'' Ed Deevers asked as Amanda checked out at the market.

''Well,'' Amanda hedged, noticing that three other patrons turned for her answer, ''he's back up working today.''

Ed just grinned, showing a big silver tooth beneath his walrus mustache. ''Yep, that's Jake's way.''

''Hear you got elected to keep Jake in line yesterday,'' Lila said when Amanda stopped by for the steak at Stilwell's. ''How'd it go?''

Amanda grimaced. "Well, I still have all my fingernails and about half of my sanity."

Lila's laugh scraped like a nail file. "If all I had to do was look at him, I'd be happy to volunteer," she admitted. "But far as I know, he's been laid up four times since he took over that ranch. Any more than that, he probably wouldn't have anybody left workin' for him. He just doesn't take to vacations the way some of us do."

Amanda had to agree. "I guess not."

Over at the feed store, several of the old men who congregated around the old pot-bellied stove in the back turned in greeting.

"You that friend of Lee's, right?"

Amanda smiled. "Jake's fine. Surly as a cat in a roomful of rockers, but fine."

They all laughed. "A good boy," one of them acknowledged. "But he sure can't stand bein' away from his horses."

Another nodded. "It's his way."

Jake's way. Amanda heard it again and again as townfolk asked after him and shared little Jakeisms with her. How he handled all his business in cash, how everyone wished the government's word was as good as his, how Jake had always shown an uncanny knack with horses, even back when he was a little one and his daddy ran the ranch for cattle.

Amanda heard how tough things had been when he'd been a child, heard it in the careful choice of euphemisms his father's old friends used, how his father had struggled against weather and economic conditions and his own inability with animals until it had killed him. She heard how little Jake had always been wise beyond his years, a serious boy who had grown into a tough, respected young man.

His neighbors spoke of him like their adopted child, and accepted Amanda on sight because of her connection with the family. There were only a few looks that betrayed a curiosity over the single, young lady friend of Lee's baby-sitting handsome, eligible Jake Kendall, but evidently Betty's edict had already settled that score. In Los Angeles or Boston or New York, Amanda would have spent the day skirting lewd suggestions. In Lost Ridge she was safely protected behind the Kendall connection and Betty's recommendation.

By the time she made it back to the cabin, tired and stiff and satisfactorily full of the most delicious steak and french fries she'd ever had, Amanda found herself wondering how the town would view her continued presence. Would they be as neighborly, as hospitable, when the outsider actually moved in? Would they understand if she bought land and returned to their little town every time she had free time to write? Or would they consider that presumptuous? Visitors were one thing, she knew. Interlopers quite another.

Amanda caught herself toying with another scenario, one with more permanence, one that addressed much more than her homesickness. Stepping out of her car, she saw herself riding up to the cabin on a spring morning, to write—knowing that she'd be going home in time to cook supper for Jake. Knowing that the place she could call home was more than a house or a piece of property.

Filling her arms with bags of groceries, she shook off the thought, fought the stab of hunger it provoked, and walked on up to the porch to let herself in. She had a good three days' worth of material she had to get down on floppy disc. She had more research to do, more material from the early Kendall ranch to go over. She had to stay away from the ranch house for a while to get her perspective back.

And that's just what she did. For the next two days, Amanda holed herself up in the cabin, clad in nothing but a flannel nightgown or the new denim-and-flannel wardrobe she'd bought in town, and pounded on the keys. She sat on the porch when the weather warmed to an unseasonable sixty and watched the ice break off and tumble down the stream. She sat at the little handmade oak table in the kitchen and listened to the coyotes serenade the moon at night. And slowly, surely, she began to regain her focus on the book. She strayed into the territory of the Old West and didn't try so hard to find her way out. She channeled the fire and steel of a modern man into the cattle drover who actually made his dream come true and bought a little piece of scrub and mountain in Wyoming. Singing the old cow lullabies and retelling the tall tales that had been swapped by the camp fires, she almost forgot the rest of the world around her.

That is, she did until the blizzard hit.

At first the weather didn't concern her at all. She awoke the third morning to hear the wind moaning around the cabin like a woman in labor. The snow hadn't started yet, but the sky was heavy with it, a dark, gunmetal gray that completely ate away the tops of the mountains. The world shrank into that single meadow. The trees around the cabin bent to the wind and the grass whistled.

Amanda got dressed and sat down to work, sorry that the warm respite was over. It would have been nice to sit out on the porch and watch the mule deer edge across to the stream. But bad weather was a blessing to an author. You didn't pay as much attention to the world around you as to the one inside. So, for a while, Amanda escaped there and was happy.

About noon, she noticed she was getting cold. The light was getting bad, so she figured it was time to turn the lights on. She probably needed to change batteries in the computer, too. When she got up from the table, she was surprised to see that the wind carried snow. Lots of snow, so thick and big that it was hard to make out the stream. The mountains were gone completely. Amanda smiled. So this was what it was like to be really alone in this cabin. It would be good to recreate the feelings Hattie Kendall had written of.

Amanda was glad that she had no place to go today. The cabin would be cozy enough, and she certainly had enough food on hand for a good couple of weeks. The road would probably be horrible for the next few hours until the snow settled down a little.

It did occur to Amanda, not for the first time, that she should have brought a radio out with her to keep abreast of things. But considering her background and the minimal scope of her demands, there wasn't much she couldn't handle. Stretching out the kinks she'd accumulated from riding a chair all morning, she walked over to turn on the lights, impatient to be back to work. Nothing happened. Amanda took a look down to the battery charger she'd left plugged in. The red charging light was off.

"Fine," she said with a sigh. "My batteries are shot."

The temperature was dropping fast, and the small furnace that served the cabin was electric. And it looked like the electricity had just been lost to the storm. Amanda decided that she'd talk to Jake about investing in some propane. In the meantime, she'd settle for a big fire in the fireplace. Apparently, she was really meant to rough it. It had been a very long time since she'd written anything longhand by firelight.

She took the time to turn off her computer and pack it away before facing the task of building a good fire. Not one of those wimpy fires for a romantic evening that petered out in about an hour. She needed a real log burner that would see her through the worst of the snow. Luckily she had one pile of wood inside and another protected beneath an overhang outside. Nothing to worry about.

Taking the precaution of adding a few more layers of clothing against the quickly dropping temperature, Amanda went to work on the fire. This had been something her Uncle Mick had taught her to do. He'd kept a fire lit twenty-four hours a day in his wood stove back home that cooked his food and heated his house. A big stone fireplace, in comparison, was child's play.

It took her thirty-eight verses of "The Old Chisum Trail" to lay the fire just the way she wanted, and another four to find matches. By that time she was not only cranky, but chilly. It would have been nice if she'd remembered to bring her gloves. She'd left them on her hall table back home when she'd run for the airport.

"'Cum-a ti yi yippy, I, yippy ay...' Come on, damn it, you're not supposed to smoke like that . . . where's the flue? 'Cum-a ti yi yippy, I, yippy ay . . .' No, no, don't do that! No!"

Amanda had started a great fire. A jim-cracker of a fire, as Uncle Mick would have said. It flared with impressive heat and deep orange flame that any other time would have been deeply satisfying. The only problem was that evidently somebody hadn't cleared last year's nests out of the chimney yet, because all the smoke Amanda generated poured right back into the room.

"Now you're in trouble, Kendall," she cursed, coughing and spitting as the thick black smoke surrounded her.

Amanda ran right for the window and threw it open. Snow blew in and the temperature fell another ten degrees. She threw open the door and realized that she was really in trouble now. She couldn't even see the stream. The cabin was frigid, she had no heat, and the fireplace wasn't working. And there was no way she was going to be able to find her way back out to a road in this snow.

Well, she thought, she had a full tank of gas. She was just going to have to crawl into the Jeep and hope the heater would keep working until the snow stopped.

That was when she saw it. Or she thought she saw it, a shadow in the snow. She thought she heard a faint breath of sound through the howling that sounded like a whinny.

"You're losing it," she muttered, turning back to get into her coat and collect her things. "You're seeing the ghost riders in the sky. It's a blizzard, you idiot, not the desert."

She'd pulled everything she was afraid would be ruined by the cold to the door and had just turned to open it again when it slammed in on itself. Amanda jumped and screamed. Then she let out an oath.

"Damn wind."

"Amanda, what are you doing?"

She spun around and looked, and she still didn't believe her eyes.

"What the hell are you doing here?" she demanded before thinking.

Jake didn't think she was particularly funny. "Saving you, looks like. Come on."

"Jake, you shouldn't be out in this. Your ribs."

"A little too late now." He reached out and grabbed her. "I didn't think you'd be able to build a fire. Now, let's go. Get what you need and I'll get you back to the ranch."

"What do you mean, I can't build a fire?" she retorted, pulling away. It took her a second to finish, because the smoke was stinging her eyes and making her cough. "Somebody didn't clean the chimney. I make a *great* fire! How'd you know I was having problems?"

"Ranch electricity's out. We'll talk later, Amanda. We're not going to be able to get through this much longer. Now, come on!"

They took long enough to kick out the fire, shut the windows again and turn off the water before heading back out onto the porch. Amanda had been expecting his truck, maybe another four-wheel vehicle. Instead, Buck was waiting for them, the snow already a white blanket on his neck and withers. She shivered deeper inside her coat and wished again for her gloves.

"A horse?" she demanded incredulously, looking out on the snow. "Jake, you shouldn't be on a horse."

"Get up on him."

She looked way up. "Oh, God."

Jake cupped his hands right by Buck's front legs. "Come on, we don't have time to argue. I'll give you a boost."

Amanda didn't want him to have to lift her. He'd hurt himself again.

"Wait, I know. Bring him by the porch."

"What?"

She scrambled back over, picked up her things and climbed the porch railing, teetering on the ice, in the wind.

"Amanda!"

But he brought Buck over, and the big black waited patiently for her as she slid her leg over his back.

"This wouldn't have been a problem if you'd kept Bill like I told you," Jake growled as he carefully swung into the saddle behind her.

"But Alabaster was sick," Amanda protested, trying to fit into the saddle with him. He fitted his arms right around her and gathered up the reins.

"What's this?" he demanded when the computer case bumped into his knee.

"My computer."

He didn't say a word. He just grabbed it from her and swung it onto the front porch.

"No!" Amanda screamed, seeing two thousand dollars disintegrating before her eyes as the case slammed into the front wall and skittered across the porch.

"Too much to carry," was all he said. "What's this?"

"Touch my dulcimer," she warned with every ounce of venom in her, "and you'll find yourself facedown in a snow-bank."

She thought she heard him chuckle, deep in his throat, as he turned Buck toward home.

"Hang on," he warned.

Amanda grabbed the saddle horn, even though there wasn't any way she could have slid off, cushioned as she was by Jake's body. The snow stung her cheeks. The cold numbed her fingers. But she had to close her eyes against the surprising warmth in her belly, the tight pleasure in her chest at the feeling of Jake hard against her.

"Why didn't you drive a four-wheel up here?" she asked. The wind whipped her words away until she could hardly hear them. She should have thought more about wearing a hat, too. Her ears were red.

"Because a truck can't smell the barn," Jake informed her, his lips only millimeters from her left ear. His hat brushed her hair. Amanda could almost feel his stubbled jaw alongside hers.

She turned to challenge him. "He can't smell the barn in this stuff."

"Never been lost on him, yet," he assured her. "Where are your gloves?"

She grimaced. "Boston."

"Fine place for 'em to be when the blizzard's in Wyoming."

"A blizzard?" she asked, her voice very small. "Really?"

Amanda could feel the force of his glare. "Good thing I thought to come for you. We would have found you along about Fourth of July with all the other dumb greenhorns."

"I'm not a dumb greenhorn," she protested, trying to hold on to the saddle horn, her dulcimer and the waterproof bag with her notes, floppy discs and underwear without bumping into Jake. "I can handle myself just fine. We just don't have blizzards in West Virginia."

"No kidding."

They bumped along as Buck picked his way through the blinding snow.

"Here."

He was tugging off his gloves, thick, leather gloves as beaten and worn as his boots.

Amanda closed her free hand over his. "No. Leave them on."

"Don't be stupid, Amanda. You'll get frostbite."

"And you're immune? This is your horse, bud. Not mine. You can't feel your hands anymore, and you're not going to be able to steer. And then both of us'll be found on the Fourth of July."

"Buck knows the way better than I do. Now, take the gloves."

"Is all your livestock in?"

He didn't answer right away. The wind battered them, and the snow slithered down exposed collars to dampen shirts. Amanda had never been so miserable in her life. She would have sold rights to her next manuscript for those gloves. But she damn well wasn't taking them from Jake Kendall.

"No," she answered for him. "They're not. So when we get back—" she couldn't even say what she was thinking, *if* we get back "—I doubt sincerely that Clovis is going to want to see me out there herding cattle."

"Horses."

"Whatever. Keep the damn gloves."

"What about your hat?"

"I'm not taking that, either, so shut up."

"Are you always this pleasant to people who rescue you?"

Amanda couldn't help a grin even as she did her best to bury herself more deeply into a wool coat that was much better suited for hailing taxis in New York than crossing frigid meadows in Wyoming. "Only if they were just as pleasant when I made sure they weren't hurt too badly."

He chuckled again, a rumble that felt almost like a purr against Amanda's back. "Touché." She felt him moving against her again. "All right, do this. At least take my scarf and wrap it around your head. My hat'll protect me. Tie your bags to the saddle horn and stuff your hands up your sleeves. Don't worry about holding on, I'll hold on to you."

"But your ribs—"

"Amanda, stop arguing. We've got to work together, or we aren't getting back."

She did as she was told. Amanda could smell Jake on that scarf, leather and wool and warm male as she wrapped it up over her nose and ears. She fought the urge to sink right into his hold like a frightened child seeking her parent during a storm. His arms were so sure and strong, his chest warm against her back. She thought she could feel the steady thud of his heartbeat, but knew it was just wishful thinking. The world around them was disintegrating, but Jake cushioned her like a fragile gift.

"Jake?"

"Yeah?"

"Do you really know what you're doing?"

"Yeah."

"So how long is it going to take us to get back?"

Another pause that made Amanda nervous all over again. "Don't know. I've never had to find my way back from the cabin in a blizzard before."

Amanda lifted her head a little and tried to see through the snow. All she saw was white. No trees, no landmarks, no nothing. Just howling, burning snow. Buck plodded on, setting one foot carefully in front of another, and Jake was wrapped around her. But even so, there was no way for sure to know if they were heading in the right direction, or farther into the snow. And for the first time since she'd stood by a mine shaft with a cluster of other women waiting for news she didn't want, she was truly afraid.

Chapter 8

Amanda's watch stopped an hour later. After that she lost track of the time they spent trying to get back to the ranch. Her toes were on fire inside those thick socks and expensive boots, and her clothes were soaked through. Her fingers had hurt for a long time, but she couldn't quite feel them anymore. She was shivering and scared and desperately trying to stay warm.

Jake never faltered. He cupped her body right into his, shielding her from the worst of the wind with his back and sharing his hat by bending right alongside her head. His arms were wrapped so tightly around her that she couldn't move, much less fall, and he kept talking to her.

But he couldn't quite take away her terror. It had been a very long time since Amanda had been completely in another person's care, and she wasn't sure how to surrender to that. She wasn't sure how to trust Buck as much as Jake did, even though the horse never so much as stumbled in the snow. She wasn't sure she could keep the tears down. She was tired and frozen and frightened, and only Jake was keeping her together.

"So how come you didn't know this was going to happen?" he asked in her ear, his voice as calm and deliberate as it had been when they'd set out.

"I don't have a radio. Did you know?" Amanda had to clench her jaw to keep her teeth from chattering, because if they did Jake would try to sacrifice more articles of clothing.

She could barely feel the pressure of his jaw against hers as he shook his head. "Surprised everybody. It was supposed to be flurries."

"Uh-huh."

"You're the folklore expert. Don't you predict weather with chicken entrails or something?"

"Actually there isn't much lore on snow. Except that there are going to be as many snows in a winter as the moon is days old when the first snow comes."

"Not much help to us now."

"There's also the one about the north wind bringing the worst blizzards. I don't suppose this one's out of the east."

"Sorry."

"Jake?"

"Uh-huh?"

"Thanks for coming for me."

She thought he might have smiled then. She couldn't lift her head enough to look anymore. "That's okay. Thanks for staying with me after I got kicked."

"You already thanked me for that."

"Yeah, but this time I mean it."

His words almost did her in. Squeezing her eyes shut again, Amanda fought the swell of tears, the nudge of panic that kept tickling at the back of her throat. Finally all she could do was let out a shivering sigh.

"I hate being scared," she admitted miserably.

Jake tightened his grip on her until it felt like an embrace. "I know," he said. It should have helped. It brought the tears even closer.

"I wish," she said, "that I could understand why you think so little of me."

His reaction was abrupt. "Why I what?"

Amanda shook her head. "Nothing. I'm sorry." She shouldn't have said it. She didn't know why she did.

But Jake had heard her. He turned his head just a little so that she could feel those fierce eyes on her. Amanda squeezed hers even more tightly shut against the invasion, against his words.

"You think that I—"

But she never found out what he was going to say. Just then Buck came to a shuddering halt. Jake's head whipped around and he stiffened.

"Hey, boy," he crooned, his voice hesitant, his attention on the swirling snow before them, his hand stroking the horse.

But Buck wasn't listening to him. His head was up, his ears flicking forward. Suddenly the big horse let out a long, shrill whinny. Beyond the howling white there must have been a reply, because he repeated the call and abruptly broke into a trot. If Jake hadn't been holding on, Amanda would have fallen right off. As it was, she barely avoided hurting herself on her dulcimer.

"That's it," Jake praised the animal, leaning into the gait. That was all the encouragement Buck needed to leap almost straight into a full-out gallop.

"Are we here?" Amanda tried to ask, her heart suddenly in her throat.

"We're someplace," Jake assured her. Then it was all he could do to concentrate on his riding, because even they could hear the answering horses this time.

Amanda couldn't stop shivering. She was inside the ranch house, seated in front of the most delicious fire she'd ever seen in her life, and she couldn't even feel it. She couldn't feel her fingers or her toes or most of her thighs.

"I'll tell ya, boss, we was gettin' real nervous," Clovis babbled, all but hopping from one foot to the other in excitement. "We barely got what stock in we did. The rest we're just gonna have to get food out to in the mornin'."

"It's real bad out there," José agreed. "Coffee's comin' soon, Mizz Marlow. Okay?"

Amanda did her best to nod. All she could do was cry and shiver. She felt like an idiot. She felt like she was shaking apart, and still she couldn't feel her hands. The blanket slipped off her shoulders again.

"Amanda, you have to get those clothes off," Jake commanded, pulling it back up.

She nodded again, never taking her eyes off the life-giving fire.

Jake bent down on a knee in front of her. "Amanda..."

She lifted tear-swollen eyes to him. "I didn't think you could do it, Jake. I—I'm sorry. I thought..." The rest of the confession was swallowed in a gulping sob.

Jake didn't answer. He just straightened and reached out to pull her to her feet. "Come on. We're going to get you warmed up."

Clovis came to immediate attention, pulling on gloves and hat. "We'll make another round down in the barn, boss."

Jake nodded. Amanda felt his arm around her shoulder and knew he was leading her into Lee's room. It didn't seem that she had the energy to do more than follow. She didn't even think to say goodbye to Clovis and José, even after the two of them had appeared out of that snow like delivering angels on horseback, whooping and shouting welcome as they personally guided Buck the rest of the way to the stables. That made her cry, too.

Jake left Amanda standing in the center of Lee's room as he rummaged through drawers. "I know she's got some warm stuff in here. Get your clothes off, Amanda, now. You're getting hypothermic."

Amanda tried. She let the blanket fall again and began to fumble with the hem of her sweater. Her fingers wouldn't work. She couldn't get them to hook beneath the heavy knitting and pull. And underneath that was her new flannel shirt with all the buttons. And those denim jeans with the snap and zipper.

She was close to dissolving again when Jake turned around with an armful of nightgown and robe.

"Here," he commanded, already out of his coat, his jeans just as wet as Amanda's. For some reason, though, he wasn't shivering. Amanda couldn't understand it. Slinging his cache over his shoulder, Jake reached for her sweater and yanked it unceremoniously over her head. "I'll do it."

Amanda stiffened abruptly, the thought of Jake doing something so intimate worming right through all that inertia.

"No," she protested, forcing her fingers to try to latch onto a button. "No, I'll do it."

But her fingers slid purposelessly across the button.

Jake just pushed her hands away. "We're going to have to get those warmed up. And your feet. Are they numb, too?"

Amanda nodded, her gaze down to where his hands had begun to work her buttons. She was still so cold, so tired, so wretchedly miserable. And now, she was blushing crimson with distress.

"You should have had long johns on."

"Jake, you can't . . ."

He impaled her with his best glare. "Maria and Betty aren't here, Amanda. You don't have a whole lot of choice."

She ended up closing her eyes, too shaken by Jake's proximity, his purposeful intimacy, to face him. He stripped off her shirt and then slid the nightgown over her head, only unsnapping her bra when she was marginally covered. Then he slipped her arms into the sleeves of the gown and unsnapped and unzipped her pants. Amanda could still feel the quick brush of those fingers against her breasts, and it unnerved her.

"Well, at least you got some real clothes," he informed her, his voice edged with impatience. "It probably saved your skinny hide."

That got her eyes open. "Skinny?" she demanded.

He grinned. A real grin, the kind two people trade who've shared something special or perilous. "Thought that'd bring you around," he taunted. "Now, sit down so I can get your boots off."

Amanda dropped onto the edge of the bed, warmed more by that smile than by any fireplace or dry flannel. Feeding on that smile, savoring it like first sunlight. Then she saw the quick betrayal on Jake's face when he bent to pull off her boot.

"Jake, no!" she protested. "Your ribs."

"Don't start again," he grated, unzipping the high-quality leather and sliding it off her foot. "My ribs are fine."

"Oh, yeah," she challenged, suddenly afraid again. "They look great."

Jake lifted his head and met her glare with a heat that silenced her. "Now, let's get those hands in some warm water."

Amanda didn't know what misery was until the feeling came back in her fingers. Jake had to physically hold her hands in place to keep her from pulling them out. First they tingled. Then they burned. And then they shrieked.

She sobbed then.

"I told you to wear my gloves," Jake told her, rubbing her hands between his own as they sat on the big couch in front of the fireplace.

Amanda couldn't even answer. She tried to pull her hands back. She tried to bend those throbbing red fingers and couldn't.

"Shh," Jake soothed, pulling her closer, chafing her hands, his arm circling her. "It'll be all right. It'll only be a few more minutes."

Amanda buried her head in his chest and bit back every swear word she'd ever heard. "I'm . . . sorry," she gulped, desperate for composure, knowing she wasn't going to find any soon as she soaked the shirt Jake had changed into. "I'm a . . . dumb greenhorn."

Jake chuckled, stroking her hair with his free hand, his other capturing Amanda's awakening digits. "No, you're not," he argued gently. "You're just not a Wyoming rancher. Next time it snows we'll make sure you're at the ranch already."

"Next time I'll visit in July."

His hands were so rough, so callused from hard work. How could they be so very gentle? How could his voice, so hard and commanding, be so tender? Amanda ached with the comfort of his hand in her hair, with the warmth of his breath on her cheek, with the steady strength of his heartbeat so close to her ear. She closed her eyes and gave herself up to his care, gradually losing the pain in her fingers, gradually losing the tears of frustration and fear.

Jake's hands slowed. His breath quickened. Amanda heard the silence grow in the room, felt the stumble of his heart. She heard her own heart follow, and realized suddenly just where she was.

The fire crackled and popped. Outside, the wind whined, and somewhere a clock ticked. There on the couch, the silence stretched and tautened and gelled into something completely different. Something sensate. It smelled of leather and wood smoke and hard work. It sounded like the rasp of labored breathing. It felt like the frayed bonds of control.

Jake lifted her hand to his mouth. Amanda's gaze followed. His eyes were closed as he kissed those swollen, aching fingers. His jaw was tighter than tensile steel. The sudden thunder of his heart betrayed him.

Amanda lifted her sore fingers and rubbed them against the rasp of his jaw, and something deep inside her melted. Something well built and jealously guarded crumbled. Jake opened his eyes and Amanda was lost.

He wrapped her into his arms just as he had on horseback, but tighter, closer, more completely, so that nothing could come between them. He bent to whisper her name, the sound of it ragged as the wind. He kissed her, and Amanda knew the feeling of freedom.

She'd never known that hunger could be so delicious. That command could taste so sweet. He brushed her lips and then returned, his mouth as soft as morning air. He lifted a hand and wrapped his fingers into her hair. And then he took the kiss that he wanted. He sipped, he plundered, he bruised with an intensity that stunned Amanda to her very core, that kindled a dark fire Amanda had never suspected. She met him, opened to him, parried with him in a honeyed waltz of desire and need.

Amanda sank into him, into his touch, into his smell and sound. She drank his harsh moan and offered her own sigh of surprise. Lightning leaped from his fingertips and curled from his mouth. Celebration exploded into yearning and swept away objection. Amanda arched against him, her breasts aching for the brush of him. She tortured her own fingers with the silky mantle of his hair and partnered her tongue with his. And when she felt his hand drop to cup her breast, she knew that this was what she'd been searching for all this time.

"Boss!"

The back door slammed, and boots clattered on the mud-room floor. Amanda almost came right up off the couch. She was sure her heart stopped completely. The only way she knew Jake was as shaken as she was that he had to lower his head and collect himself before answering Clovis's anxious page.

"What, Clovis?"

By the time the little man burst into the living room, Amanda and Jake were a respectable distance apart on the couch. Amanda clutched her hands in her lap and Jake raked his through his hair.

"Willy just got back. We got three more pregnant mares we can't get rounded up."

Jake didn't even turn to acknowledge his foreman. He nodded, his eyes flinty. "Saddle Bill for me. I'll be right there."

Amanda didn't get the chance to object.

"Don't say a word," he said as he climbed stiffly to his feet. "This isn't going to get done without me, and without foals, I have no ranch."

Amanda fought the urge to reach out to him. His forehead was taut again. His skin wasn't blue anymore. It was paper white. He was too tired and sore to go out again, and they both knew it. And Amanda knew that there wasn't anything she could do about it.

"I'll have something to eat when you guys get back in."

Jake swung around on her. "You get some rest. You've had a rough day."

Amanda shot him a sardonic grin. "And you haven't. Go on. It's about time you learned what this greenhorn can do."

"I already told you," he said, brushing a finger across her cheek. "I don't think you're a greenhorn."

"I'm still waiting to find out what you think I am," she said.

But Jake did no more than shake his head and walk away. Amanda couldn't move from the couch for a long time after she heard the back door slam again. She hadn't realized she had tears left.

Jake wasn't entirely sure he could put one foot in front of the other. His head was reeling, and his chest felt like it was going to cave right in. He ached everywhere he wasn't numb, and he still had to get back in for something to eat.

The wind was easing up a little. The snow had finally stopped after depositing about two feet, but it was drifting dangerously, so that they'd almost lost one of the mares. As it was, he was afraid some of the stock they'd left out in the pastures would be forfeit. But it looked like he was going to save the foals.

"Come on, boss," Clovis encouraged him as he pushed open the barn door. "Maybe we can get something hot in us. Make us feel better."

Jake didn't even notice that Clovis was looking worried, and that the worry was aimed right at him. He was too tired. He hurt too much, and the day wasn't over yet. They still had to get the horses fed for the evening and check on the foals they already had. But for now, Clovis was right. Maybe they could find something in the main kitchen. He hadn't realized until Clovis said how hungry he was, that he was, too.

The smells met them the minute they stepped into the mudroom. Simmering meat and spices, hot coffee, apples.

"Hey, howdy!" Clovis crowed, shucking his coat and shaking the snow off him. "There's real food in this house."

Jake peeled off his gloves and shoved them into his pocket. He picked at his buttons and did his best to slip out of his coat without lifting his arms. When he couldn't quite complete the task, he bit back a groan. The pain shot right up his neck this time, taking his breath away.

"How many people for dinner?" he heard and lifted his head to see Amanda standing before them clad in Lee's flannel nightgown, robe and a flour-dusted apron. Another image of her briefly flashed, tear-streaked and soft, her breasts so heavy and full in his hands, her moans the music that drove a man mad. How could she possibly believe that he didn't think much of her? He thought too much of her.

Her face crumpled briefly into distress and then settled itself back into greeting. Jake fought the sudden urge to pull her back into his arms.

"Four of us," Clovis told her. "Did you really cook dinner?"

She chuckled as she led them both into the kitchen, where the fireplace there crackled and a Coleman lantern hissed on the table, providing the only light. "Didn't have anything else to do. Since the electricity's out, there wasn't any television, and somebody threw my computer away."

"They—"

No more was said. Jake took his first good whiff of what smelled suspiciously like stew and almost fainted from relief. He wasn't going to have to scare up cold cuts and beer. There was real food, hot food, and light and warmth from the kerosene heaters. He might just make it, after all.

"Jake."

He almost didn't hear her. "What?" he asked.

She was smiling, a bright, false smile that belied what he was sure he looked like. "Get washed up. Dinner will be on in five minutes. Okay?"

Rubbing at his raw face with a cold hand, he nodded and turned to his room. Aspirin wasn't going to do it this time. He wasn't going to make it through the night this way. He wasn't going to make it through dinner, not with Amanda sitting so close to him, smelling like smoke and spices, not with his body caving in under him even as it ached for her. Jake felt as if he were breaking apart into a million pieces, torn by what he wanted and what he knew he could have. Battered by experience even more than work, drained by the effort of control.

There was only so much he could do; didn't anybody realize that? There was only so much any man could do who'd been dealt his cards. But day after day, year after year, Jake fought the elements and the ranch and the odds, and then walked back in to face that house alone. And he knew now that that wouldn't change. Because the kind of person he wanted to share his house with was Amanda. The kind of woman who built something for herself from nothing, who had the courage to calmly face trouble and realistically face danger, and then could pull herself back together to take care of somebody else. The kind of woman who challenged him toe to toe and then made him laugh.

But Amanda Marlow was someone he could never expect in his house. Not now, not ever. And aching for her wasn't going to change that. It wasn't going to change him, and that was what made that kind of dream impossible. The woman he could have he didn't want, and the one he needed, wanted, desired, he could never have.

Jake trudged over to the the bedside table where the two medicine bottles still waited unopened alongside a full glass of water. He picked them both up and looked at them, desperate for the relief they could offer. Weighing them, studying them, balancing them so that the pills inside clicked against the plastic.

Frustration welled in him like acid. Futility beat him down. The pain that blossomed had nothing to do with his injured ribs. Jake Kendall hadn't wept since his mother had died. But he fought tears in that empty, silent room with the sounds and smells of life not more than thirty feet away. And that hurt worst of all. Giving in to the fury of it, he hurled the bottles as hard as he could, shattering one against the far wall. Pills skittered across his hardwood floor like beads from a broken necklace. The little plastic bottle rolled unseen beneath his chest of drawers. And Jake Kendall turned away and slowly trudged into the bathroom to wash his hands for dinner.

She hadn't meant to see it. She'd only come back to help. Jake had looked so haggard standing in the kitchen, the pain and fatigue etched on his face, the hours dragging him down, and she knew he was still showing a facade. Clovis, José and the other men would never know just what that day had cost Jake. Amanda only meant to slip back into his room and help him change into a dry shirt without anyone realizing he needed the help.

She'd reached the door to his room to find him standing with his back to her, the bottles of medicine in his hand. She sensed a torment in his rigid posture, felt in him a pain so ferocious that no physical injury could have accounted for it. And then she saw him throw the pills, a harsh groan betraying him, like the moan of a wounded animal as he'd turned toward the bathroom.

Amanda fled for Lee's room before he caught her. Shaking. Suddenly seeing images she hadn't even thought about for twenty years. Hurting so deeply inside that nothing would salve her anguish. Suddenly plagued by a suspicion that had its roots in habits she'd observed half a continent away. A suspicion that resurrected the old frustration into new pain.

She'd compared Jake to Uncle Mick. Could he have been more like Uncle Mick than she'd realized? Could that be the burden he carried around in silence, trapped deep where no one would think to look, contained in a carefully controlled world where everyone knew him, where he knew everyone?

Dear God, she thought, squeezing her eyes shut against sudden tears. Could something like that have happened to Jake? Could a man like him have settled for it? All these years, alone in the midst of everyone, shutting himself away where no one would see him. Could *that* be the secret to Jake Kendall?

She had to be sure. She couldn't simply walk in on him making rash accusations. She had to spend her time in his house wisely, so that she could know for sure. So that she could help him if he'd let her.

In the meantime, she knew just what to do now. After all, it was what she'd done so long ago for Uncle Mick.

The kitchen echoed with male high glee. Clovis and José introduced Amanda to Willy—a nineteen-year-old, with glossy blue-black hair and the best posture she'd ever seen—who usually drove in from the reservation. She also met James, a grizzled man of indeterminate age who cursed as much as Willy blushed. Amanda ladled stew onto their plates and shared their stories of the blizzard, all the while keeping an ear to the back of the house. She poured generous helpings of steaming coffee, set out the bread, and then filled a glass of water at the sink, which she carried out of the kitchen with her.

She found him buttoning a dry shirt. His fingers shook and his jaw was clenched. Amanda faltered at the door, hurting more for him than he did himself.

"Here," she said without preamble. "You take this from me, and I'll do that for you."

Jake looked up at her, and she died a little. He was too exhausted to maintain that precious control of his, and she saw the frustration and pain he'd carried into that room with him. She saw wariness and fear. And she breezed right by them all.

"You got my hands to work," she said, handing him the glass, "now it's my turn to return the favor. It looks like it's still a real bitch of a night out there."

Amanda almost thought she caught a hint of a grin from him.

"It is."

She nodded and buttoned. "In that case, the stew should help. You're lucky Maria had the stew meat out thawing already. Without a microwave, I never would have managed otherwise."

Jake looked down at her progress. "Smells good."

Amanda kept buttoning, her fingers fumbling almost as badly as his, but for different reasons. Neither of them seemed to notice. "It should. I won awards for that stew. Of course, the apple pan dowdy is even better."

"You cook, too?"

She could have wept at the harsh edge to his voice, the splinters of frayed control. Instead, she lifted her gaze to his and laughed. "You'd be surprised what I can do, Jake. Of course, I guess since we're going to be stuck together for the next day or two, you're going to find out."

For a moment she was afraid he was going to break, that he was going to allow the truth to escape between them, the raw desire each of them fought, the growing attachment. The ambivalence. But he just gave her back half the smile she gave him.

"If you can cook," he said, "you don't have to do anything else."

Amanda finished buttoning his shirt and stuffed it down the back of his jeans, her hands as quick and competent as his had been. She left the front for him to finish. He handed the glass to her.

"Nope," she said with a definite shake of her head. His front shirttail was still hanging out, and his jeans were mostly unzipped. Amanda refused to pay any more attention to them. Instead, she reached into her own robe pocket and pulled out what she'd brought in with her. "Here. Take these."

Jake stared at the two pills in her hand with something like astonishment. It quickly faded into distrust.

"Where did you get those?"

She grabbed his free hand and set the pills firmly in his palm. "I decided," she told him brightly, "that I'd had just about enough of this macho... stuff. Nothing short of the codeine in these pills is going to suffice tonight, and we both know it."

"But how...?"

She shrugged. "I came in to tell you dinner was ready and damn near killed myself on all the pills on the floor. Lucky for us it was just the antibiotic. That was only about fifty bucks a bottle, so it's no great loss. These little babies, on the other hand, can still come in handy." She looked straight into his eyes, challenging him. "Especially for somebody with broken ribs who's ridden through a blizzard to save a stupid writer, and then spent the rest of the afternoon saving his herd of horses. I'd think he'd be a little sore."

He tried to hand them back. "I still have work to do tonight. The horses have to be fed."

Amanda promptly set her fists on her hips again. "If you can't trust that bunch of freeloaders in the kitchen, then I wish you'd just stop feeding them and be done with it."

"They're not freeloaders!"

Her smile was sly and triumphant. "Then I imagine they could manage feeding a bunch of horses all by themselves. Couldn't they?"

He couldn't think of an answer. Amanda motioned to the pills with her hand.

"I'm not feeding you till you take them."

Jake had a pretty impressive scowl, even for the condition he was in. "One."

Amanda glared right back. "You know the difference between a terrorist and me?" she demanded. "You can negotiate with a terrorist. Now, take the damn things so I can get some dinner myself. I'm starved."

His expression crumbled into surprised humor. Amanda held her breath. She saw him jiggling the pills in his palm, as if weighing options. She saw something like relief skitter across his eyes, and her suspicions grew apace with the pain. In the end, he popped the pills into his mouth and took a sizable gulp of water to wash them down, and the relief was Amanda's. At least she'd found a way to get him to take the medicine.

"Two every four hours isn't going to kill you," she taunted. "Just make sure if you ride, it's on Buck. That way if you fall asleep, he can always find the way home."

"Don't push it, Amanda."

She grinned and shoved her hands into the deep pockets of her robe so Jake couldn't see that they were shaking. "Come on out to eat. After the rest of the hands head out, I'll show you the folk remedy I just remembered."

Jake's eyebrow lifted. "A folk remedy?"

She nodded. "I should have thought of it before. It's a miracle-worker."

"There's no wildlife involved, is there?"

She smiled. "No wildlife. Now, get your pants zipped and get in to dinner, young man."

Amanda saw Clovis look up when Jake followed her into the kitchen, and knew how very worried he'd been for his boss. When the older man saw that Jake was actually smiling—well, as much of a smile as Jake ever afforded Clovis—his relief was almost palpable. The conversation picked up, and Amanda joined the men at the big table for stew, bread and coffee.

"You're hired, Miss Marlow," Willy praised her, his voice low and his plate empty. "This is the best stew I've ever had."

"I do rabbit and squirrel, too," she assured him.

"A real Renaissance woman," Jake growled into his own quickly vanishing dinner.

"That's right, Mr. Kendall," she retorted happily. "I've been known to shoot my dinner, as well."

Jake's grin was sly. "Remind me to keep her away from the barn cats."

The chuckles were easy and comfortable. Amanda dished out the apple pan dowdy and poured more coffee to groans of appreciation.

"How'd you manage this, girl?" Clovis demanded, his gesture taking in the food and warmth and light Amanda had managed to provide. "You a city girl and all."

Amanda sneered. "City girl. Watch your language, Clovis. Besides, it's amazing what you can do in an electrical outage with a gas stove and a closet full of backup supplies."

"Did you refill the kerosene heaters?" Jake asked.

Amanda's nod rode on an impressive scowl of her own. "A real handy thing to have," she said. "You might think of keeping one in the cabin."

He lifted an unconcerned eyebrow. "I do. But I pull it out to help keep the foaling barn warm in the winter. Since nobody stays in the cabin then, anyway."

"This isn't winter," she reminded him.

"It's winter here until the last snow. And that's sometimes May. I guess the Appalachians don't do it that way."

"No," she answered. "They have a strange phenomenon there they like to call spring."

The food disappeared, the coffee was enjoyed with the discussion of how they'd managed to handle the surprise blizzard, and then Clovis led the men back out into the night. He didn't say a word when Jake announced that he wasn't going to help, but Amanda saw the quick glance of gratitude the little man flashed her. Hats were slapped on, coats donned, and the wind snaked in the back door as the voices drifted back to the barn.

"Need some help?" Jake asked as Amanda cleared the dishes. His voice was already more relaxed. So, come to think of it, were his features. The flickering yellow light from the lantern washed over his face in gentle waves now.

Amanda smiled to herself as she carried the plates and cups to the sink. "Not now," she assured him. "You head on into the living room. I'll meet you on the couch."

Jake cocked an eyebrow. "The couch?"

"That folk remedy," she retorted. "Remember?"

His nod was slow. "Oh, yeah. Hope it's as good as codeine."

"Nothing's as good as codeine," she assured him. "That's what I've been trying to tell you."

Jake heaved himself to his feet and headed into the living room. "I'm stubborn," he said as he went. "At least, that's what Betty says."

"Betty's right," Amanda assured him.

By the time Amanda made it into the living room, Jake was stretched out on the couch, his boots up on the arm, his hands across his stomach. The firelight warmed him, and the shadows protected him. His face was relaxed now, his eyes shut. It made such a difference. Suddenly he wasn't the hard man who had sought so hard to intimidate her. He was the gentleman who had offered his horse, the big brother who had fought so hard to see that his brother and sisters had a better life. He was the neighbor who could be depended on and trusted.

Amanda was tempted to let him be. But she knew just where that would get them both. Leaning way over the back of the couch, she ran a hand along his cheek.

"Hey, big boy," she greeted him in a sultry voice, "I want your shirt off."

The more
you love romance . . .
the more
you'll love this offer

FREE!

Mail this heart today!
(See inside)

Join us on a Silhouette® Honeymoon
and we'll give you
4 Free Books
A Free Victorian Picture Frame
And a Free Mystery Gift

IT'S A
SILHOUETTE HONEYMOON—
A SWEETHEART OF A FREE OFFER!
HERE'S WHAT YOU GET:

1. Four New Silhouette Intimate Moments® Novels—FREE!

Take a Silhouette Honeymoon with your four exciting romances—yours
FREE from the Silhouette Reader Service™. Each of these hot-off-the-press
novels brings you the passion and tenderness of today's greatest love stories…your free passports to bright new worlds of love and foreign adventure.

2. Lovely Victorian Picture Frame—FREE!

This lovely Victorian pewter-finish miniature is perfect
for displaying a treasured photograph. And it's yours
FREE as added thanks for giving our Reader Service a
try!

3. An Exciting Mystery Bonus—FREE!

You'll be thrilled with this surprise gift. It is useful as well as practical.

4. Free Home Delivery!

Join the Silhouette Reader Service™ and enjoy the convenience of preview-
ing 4 new books every month delivered right to your home. Each book is
yours for only $2.96* each, a saving of 33¢ each off the cover price per book—
and there is no extra charge for postage and handling. It's a sweetheart of
a deal for you! If you're not completely satisfied, you may cancel at any time,
for any reason, simply by sending us a note or shipping statement marked
"cancel" or by returning any shipment to us at our cost.

5. Free Newsletter!

You'll get our monthly newsletter, packed with news about your favorite
writers, upcoming books, even recipes from your favorite authors.

6. More Surprise Gifts!

Because our home subscribers are our most valued readers, when you join
the Silhouette Reader Service™, we'll be sending you additional free gifts from
time to time—as a token of our appreciation.

START YOUR SILHOUETTE HONEYMOON TODAY—
JUST COMPLETE, DETACH AND MAIL YOUR FREE-OFFER CARD

*Terms and prices subject to change without notice. Sales tax applicable in NY. Offer limited
to one per household and not valid to current Silhouette Intimate Moments® subscribers.
All orders subject to approval.

© 1991 HARLEQUIN ENTERPRISES LIMITED

START YOUR
SILHOUETTE HONEYMOON TODAY.
JUST COMPLETE, DETACH AND MAIL YOUR
FREE-OFFER CARD.

If offer card below is missing write to:
Silhouette Reader Service, 3010 Walden Ave.,
P.O. Box 1867, Buffalo, NY 14269-1867.

DETACH AND MAIL TODAY!

NO POSTAGE
NECESSARY
IF MAILED
IN THE
UNITED STATES

BUSINESS REPLY MAIL
FIRST CLASS MAIL   PERMIT NO. 717   BUFFALO, NY

POSTAGE WILL BE PAID BY ADDRESSEE

SILHOUETTE READER SERVICE
3010 WALDEN AVE
PO BOX 1867
BUFFALO NY 14240-9952

Chapter 9

Jake's eyes popped open as if they'd been spring-loaded. "What?"

Amanda just smiled and lifted the bottle of liniment she'd carried in. "The remedy."

Jake looked over and scowled. "A back rub?"

"The best," she assured him, moving around to the front of the couch. "Sure to cure all ills."

"But I just got this shirt on," he protested, still not moving.

"You do the buttons and I'll do the rest."

Jake groaned and closed his eyes again. "I don't suppose I could talk you out of this."

"Do you know how sore you're going to be tomorrow if you don't get those muscles relaxed a little?" she demanded. She almost lost her train of thought when she looked down on him to see the firelight wash his forehead. Shadows collected in the hollows of his cheeks and flickered through the fan of dark lashes against his cheek. They pooled into the hollow of his throat like dark water, and Amanda couldn't think past wanting to dip her tongue in it and drink.

"I am relaxing them," Jake protested, still not moving. "I'm laying them down on this couch."

"Not good enough. Come on, be a big boy and get it over with so I can get some sleep."

"I don't suppose there are any alternatives that let me stay right here," he countered, his voice gravelly with weariness.

Amanda couldn't help the smile. The only alternative she could think of wouldn't have been found in any book of medicine, folklore or otherwise. But, oh, as she looked down at the whipcord body stretched out on that couch, at the soft, beaten denim jeans that fit so snugly, she wouldn't have minded trying.

Jake caught her in that smile. When she let her gaze stray back up to his face, it was to find those icy blue eyes focused on her. Those icy eyes that suddenly looked so curiously like flame. They stole Amanda's breath and shattered her sense. She could feel the scarlet flush of exposure creep up her cheeks.

"Amanda," Jake grated, his jaw tight again.

She came very close to giving in to the instincts that chorused in her, instincts older than time, instincts that fed on the sight of fire-warmed skin, the sound of a rasping breath, the smell of leather and hard work and fresh wind.

At the last minute she reeled back in her control and turned her attention to uncapping the liniment. "No negotiations," she insisted, nudging his leg with her own. "Get the damn back rub or I just pour the liniment over your head and leave you here to freeze."

In the end, she sat behind him on the couch pouring liniment into her hands. Jake waited, his head down, his elbows on his thighs, the firelight flickering in his hair and along the sleek lines of his bare arms. Amanda set the bottle back down and turned to her work.

She did her best to remain objective. Jake was as tight as a guidewire, his muscles knotted beneath her fingers. She kneaded and rubbed, working from his neck down, over his shoulders, his back, each vertebrae of his spine, her fingers digging into sore spots and unraveling tension.

He groaned once, and the sound thrummed right through her. Amanda hadn't meant for this to be anything but therapeutic, but it was hard to keep it that way. Jake's back was so solid, so sinuous against her hands. His skin was warm, his body every fantasy she'd ever entertained about the male species. She could smell the twin tangs of soap and liniment on him, could hear the soft fall of his breathing, could feel the sleek muscles and tendons beneath her hands. She imagined what he'd feel like against her, around her, in her, and it threatened to overwhelm her.

"Boy, that fire's hot," she murmured, wiping a slippery hand along her forehead.

Jake didn't answer. He didn't move.

"Jake?" she whispered, leaning a little to the left to see the angles of his face limned in fire. "You okay? Are you too hot?"

Amanda almost groaned at the question. She was the one who was too hot. Her hands ached to wander farther afield. Her breasts burned for another taste of Jake's hands.

But Jake still didn't answer.

"Jake?"

That was when she realized that her treatment had worked. He wasn't relaxed. He was asleep. Between the hot food, pain medicine and massage, he'd finally given in to the battering abuse his body had suffered over the last few days. His eyes were closed and his head down, that tumble of dark golden hair falling forward over his forehead.

Amanda wasn't sure what to do. She was afraid that if she tried to get him into his own room, he'd wake up enough to demand a walk out to the barn. There was an afghan on Lee's bed. After carefully easing Jake back, she ran in to get it. Then, covering him, she slid down on the floor next to the couch to make sure Jake would be all right there with that medicine on board.

Amanda reached up to brush the hair back that fell in his eyes and ran an exploratory finger along the line of stitches that had crusted over. She could see the bruises Sidewinder had left behind, both on Jake's face and his chest. She could tell how much Jake had been hurting. Well, she'd just stay here to make sure he didn't hurt himself any more.

Amanda didn't realize that she'd laid her head down on the couch alongside his, or that the fire had almost burned out after she'd closed her eyes. She didn't know she fell asleep until Clovis found them there three hours later.

* * *

"Boss! Hey, boss, you awake?"

Amanda's eyes flew open and her head shot up. For a minute she couldn't quite decide where she was. The room was cool and dim, and it hissed.

The hissing was what brought her back—hissing from the kerosene heaters and what was left of the fire. Amanda looked down to find that Jake was still asleep, his features more relaxed than she'd ever seen them, his limbs sprawled over the just-too-small couch. At the last minute she overcame the urge to caress that weather-roughened cheek just once before getting up.

"Boss?"

Amanda climbed to her feet before Clovis could make it into the living room.

"Clovis, what do you want?" she whispered, tiptoeing out to the kitchen.

Clovis was just entering from the mudroom, another layer of snow decorating his coat. His hat was in his hands, and he looked like a man entering his first church.

He nodded shyly in greeting. "Amanda."

It must have been the low light, Amanda decided, and the hour. He was acting as if he was in her bedroom instead of the kitchen.

She tried to smile away his discomfort. "Is it snowing again?"

He took a quick look at the dusting of white on the front of his coat. "Sure is. Not near as bad as before, though. Is Jake awake?"

She took a second to pull a hand through her hair as she shook her head. "He's asleep. You're not going to wake him, are you?"

"I'm afraid I have to. Bitsy's foaling."

Amanda looked back toward the dark living room and stepped closer to Clovis. "He can't, Clovis. He's just done too much today. He needs to get some sleep. You're not having any problems with her, are you? You don't need me to call the vet?"

"Oh, no. Nothin' like that. It's just that Jake likes to be there when a foal's born. It's his way. And I'm not one to presume otherwise."

Amanda nodded, understanding perfectly. "Well, I am. He doesn't need to hold her hand or anything, does he?"

Clovis flashed a startled grin. "She does most of the work. A real trooper when it comes to this kind o' thing. We never had to use the chains on her once."

Amanda didn't even want to ask. "In that case, give Bitsy my regrets. Jake'll be in to see her in the morning."

Clovis started wringing his hat. "Oh, I don't know, Amanda. He's gonna be real mad."

Amanda grinned. "I know. It's his way. Well, I don't mind him being mad at me."

Clovis actually tried to sidle by her. "Maybe if I just let him know..."

Amanda wasted no more time on tact. Grabbing a handful of Clovis's coat, she ushered him straight back into the mud-room. "No. Now, unless the barn's burning down and the horses have all escaped and there's a hurricane, you let that man sleep. He'll be out first thing in the morning."

"But—"

Amanda smiled as she pulled the door open. "Good night, Clovis. If you guys want some coffee or anything, I'd be happy to bring it down. But don't come back unless it's a national emergency."

For a minute Clovis stood out in the snow, a dumbfounded expression on his face, his hat in his hand. Amanda reached out, grabbed it from him and slapped it on his head for him. Suddenly, like a light coming on, he smiled. A big, bright toothy smile.

"Yes, ma'am," he conceded with a huff that passed for a chuckle. Then, shaking his head, he walked off.

Amanda shook hers a little too as she shut the door behind him. It was almost one in the morning. Amanda could see the snow dancing gently in the breeze. She could hear the crunch of Clovis's progress over the snow. Other than that, the world was silent and cold. Isolated. The snow paled the reflected clouds and sapped the darkness from the night. It was magical, mysterious and hushed. Amanda looked out into it and smiled with a satisfaction she hadn't known in a long while.

She was resetting the fire when Jake woke. He didn't just wake. He bolted upright. Amanda almost fell face first into the fireplace.

"Clovis," he snapped.

"Nope," she answered, finishing the task so that the fire snapped and popped at her, shooting sparks straight up the chimney and warming her nose. "He's a little older. And much more bowlegged."

Jake swayed a little on the couch, his hand instinctively on the ribs that must have reminded him not to move so quickly.

"Where is he?" he grated, rubbing the confusion from his face with his other hand.

Amanda wished she could simply enjoy the sight of that firelight on his chest and shoulders, still bare above the afghan where it had slid in his sudden movement.

"I imagine he's at his place, where he belongs," she mused instead, turning deliberately back to the fire so Jake didn't catch her lie. "Probably asleep or something."

Jake shook his head. "Bitsy looked like she was going to go tonight. I should check."

That brought her right around and to her feet. "No," she said. "You shouldn't. You should get the rest of the first good night's sleep you've had in a while. You should let that codeine make you feel better and then have a decent breakfast before going back out to that barn tomorrow."

Jake looked up at her with the kind of expression he probably reserved for uninformed customers who made unreasonable demands. "Horses usually foal at night, Amanda," he informed her. "And, like I said, foals are an important part of my business."

Amanda set her hands on her hips, hoping Jake didn't catch her deception. "And would Clovis come right up here the minute there was any kind of trouble?"

Jake actually retreated to a rueful grin. "Yeah. He would."

"Do you feel better?"

He pushed his hair back off his forehead. "Did I fall asleep on you?"

Amanda's answering smile was brash. "I promise not to tell anybody."

Jake's gaze dropped a bit, his expression a little bashful. "I'm just so... tired." He was rubbing at his face again.

Amanda once again took matters into her own hands. Stepping up to him, she reached down for that hand and tugged. "Come on, Jake. It's time you went to bed."

Jake looked up at her, his eyes glittering in the firelight. "It's cold in there," he protested in a husky voice.

Amanda did her best to ignore the sparks that seemed to explode from the rasp of a callused hand. "You have a big down comforter," she said. "Besides, I can't go to bed with you on the couch, because I keep worrying that you're going to fall off."

His face folded fractionally into amusement. "You wouldn't fit with me on the couch, anyway," he retorted. "Unless we really worked hard at it."

Amanda immediately blushed, millimeters away from yanking her hand back and escaping. "You know what I mean."

Jake squeezed Amanda's hand, and the sparks multiplied, skittering up her arm. "Lee's bed doesn't have a comforter. You'll freeze in there."

She shrugged, her eyes down. "I'll sleep here."

Jake slowly climbed to his feet alongside her so that his chest was inches from her nose. His bare chest. His glistening, hair-roughened chest that she'd been fantasizing about ever since she'd first seen it.

"Then I couldn't get any sleep worrying that you'd fall off," he protested.

Amanda looked up, expecting to see taunting, maybe invitation. What she saw was darker, harder. What she saw in those shimmering blue eyes was the same throb of desire she felt in her own chest. The struggle to keep distance, to prevent mistakes. The slow topple of barriers that were far more formibdable than hers.

"Amanda..."

It was a sigh, a groan. It was promise and plea. Amanda trembled, now in his grasp, her body suddenly raw and anxious, her heart racing, her chest on fire. She looked at him, di-

sheveled from sleep, haggard from pain and struggle, flayed
raw with loneliness. She heard the harsh cant of his breath, the
echo of his heart, so close to her lips. She felt the fine tremor
of his control, suddenly as tenuous as hers.

She'd meant to find this moment since she'd first seen him,
she knew that. She'd peeled away his defenses and crept close
for a peek inside him, knowing that whatever it was that made
up Jake Kendall sang to her the age-old song of attraction, of
commitment, of affection. She'd steeled herself for that first
contact, that kiss that had sparked such a terrible yearning in
her. She'd harried him, instinctively seeking more. Seeking this.
And still, still she wasn't sure if it was right.

It might not be right. But it was what she wanted. And she'd
known it deep inside for a long time.

Amanda hadn't anticipated what kind of lover Jake would
be. She'd just trusted that hint of vulnerability in his eyes. Now,
hands entwined, gazes locked, she was afraid. There was in-
credible gentility in this man. But there was fierce need, a need
so great it could consume her.

It consumed her. It swept over her with the speed of his first
kiss, his mouth slanting across hers in a harsh, groaning union
that left them wrapped in each other's arms. It ignited her,
whipping up flames that seared at her, that propelled her to
answer Jake's intensity with her own.

He crushed her to him. He lifted a hand and cupped her face
to him, tilted her head back so that he could slake his thirst with
her. His fingers were rough, but the whisper of his breath on
her was as sweet as morning. The thunder of his heart shuddered through her. The solid wall of his chest comforted her
and tormented her. Amanda lifted her own hands, sought the
ridge of muscle, the tickle of hair, the security of warmth. She
reeled with the heat of him, trembled with the force of him,
melted with the tenderness of him.

His hands were restless, his mouth insatiable, his body impatient. Amanda felt it all, drank it like potent wine and stumbled with the drunkenness of it. His arms, his shoulders, his
chest. So solid, so sleek with firelight and shadow, so fluid in
her hands. His hips raked against hers; his legs insinuated between hers.

He bent a little, his one arm sweeping down her back, and Amanda stiffened.

"Oh, no, you don't," she protested on a small rasp, all the breath she had left.

Jake's eyes glittered like dark diamonds, hard and mesmerizing.

But Amanda had anticipated him. Bestowing a shy smile, she lifted her hand to his cheek. "You're not hurting those ribs just to show me what a male you are. I can still walk."

She turned to take a step toward his room and wobbled a bit. It made her giggle for the first time in five years. "Well, kind of," she admitted.

Jake wrapped her in his arms and buried his face in her hair as they stumbled together to find that big, soft down comforter.

Amanda's fantasies had entertained gentleness and patience, languid words of love rained down with the torment of sensitive fingers. She'd never anticipated the desperate feel of Jake's hunger. She'd never imagined the fire he'd set or the grace of the ballet danced by two sweat-drenched bodies.

She knew that night. She tumbled to the bed, entwined in Jake, her body a riot of sensation, her voice mingling with his in ancient music. He tasted her breasts again. He filled his hands with them, teasing them through the soft flannel until the nipples tautened into pebbles. He filled his mouth with them, laving them with his tongue, suckling, caressing, nipping, until Amanda raked his back with impatience. She arched against him, rubbed against him, delighting in the rasp of hair against the sleek skin of her belly. Hushed by the throb of him against her. She let him sweep her gown off and demanded the privilege of torturing him with the calculated descent of his zipper. And as much as she loved the sight and feel of soft denim on his legs, hugging his taut, square bottom, she loved even better the hug of her own hands there, her fingers measuring steely thighs and tickling the tender skin behind his knees.

He never took his mouth from her. From her breasts, her throat, her belly. He tasted the inside of her elbow and licked her fingers. He nibbled her earlobe and then tickled the shell of her ear with his tongue. And always he returned to her mouth, his kisses bruising her, battering her, bringing her to life. She tasted cloves and coffee on his tongue and smelled the snow on his hair. She mingled sighs with him and sobbed when he cupped her face between his work-roughened hands and kissed her eyes closed. He drank from her, danced with her, worshiped her. No man had ever brought her to such life, had ever driven her to such torment. No man had ever whispered her name as if he were praying.

The comforter was forgotten, unnecessary. Amanda was wrapped in Jake, arm and leg and mouth. She was drowning in him, sailing with him. The fire he'd stoked in her belly licked upward, outward, sparked, flared and melted. Wherever his fingers played, the embers burst to life. Where his tongue followed, they crested.

She felt his hand on her thigh and welcomed him, furious to have him in her. She heard his moan when his fingers first dipped into her, and touch and revelation jolted her. She cried out, the pain of his touch exquisite, the feathering of his caresses agonizing. She clutched at him, raked her own hands through his hair and demanded her own kisses. She pulled him against her, hard and urgent, and instinctively lured him on.

She shuddered, shuddered again. The crest was building in her, lapping against her belly, washing deep and hot in her. Riding, whirling, balanced on a knife's edge, so close to climax she wept with it. She threw her head back. She opened her eyes. She saw the fire in Jake's eyes, the harsh edge of control, the sheen of sweat on his forehead and the beautiful smile that was hers. And then she reached to him, taking him in her hand. She saw the shock of it register along his jaw, heard the harsh rasp of surprise in his voice. She saw his eyes widen, darken. She smiled to him, then, and guided him to her.

"Wait—" Jake rasped, teetering at the edge of control. "I'm not—"

"I am," was all she said.

Patience was swept away. Jake tangled his hands in her hair and lifted her face to be kissed. He plunged into her, slick and hot and sweet, deeper than the fire, deeper than the need, deeper than loneliness or desire could go, and Amanda wrapped herself around him and pulled him deeper. She arched and rocked, her hands holding him tight, his hands and his mouth devouring her. She whimpered, whispered, moaned. She felt his body tremble for release and knew the cost of his patience. And then, suddenly, like a white-hot storm, the fire swept her away, too. Shuddering, shimmering, singing, balance and thought shattered into sensation. She cried out to him, laughing, weeping with the enormity of it, when with a rasping cry, he followed. She held him tighter, tighter, whispering to him as he buried himself in her, as he, too, shuddered to release.

The moan of the wind reached them first, where they lay tangled and spent, Jake's face still nestled against Amanda's shoulder. She stroked his hair, savoring the weight of him, the warmth of him, the quiet strength of him. She fought the need to pull away, afraid that once separated they wouldn't be able to find their way back.

Even so, Jake finally had to roll away. Gathering her into his arms, he cushioned her against him, rubbing his cheek against her hair.

"I think," he said lazily, "that we should finally think about using that down comforter."

Amanda knew she wouldn't feel the cold for a while yet. Even so, the cover might shield them somehow from the world, from the morning that was sure to come and the problems they were going to have to address. "A good idea," she agreed, still not moving.

He chuckled. "I'll move if you do."

She yawned. "You move first."

They did get the comforter eventually, and snuggled beneath its feather-light warmth, still wrapped in each other's arms, still silent with satisfaction, still smiling with discovery. Still refraining from what would await them when they woke.

But that would be later, Amanda knew, her eyes closed against Jake's chest, her fingers entwined in his, her leg thrown over his. For now, she couldn't ask more than to savor these few moments when they could both afford the illusion of perfection.

Chapter 10

Amanda really wasn't surprised that Jake was gone when she woke. Even so, she felt the sting of emptiness, the first flush of fear. How would Jake view what had happened last night? Would he hold the memory as precious as Amanda did? Would he realize that what they had shared had been much more than just chemistry and hormones?

Jake had betrayed himself. He'd shown Amanda how much he needed her, how much he cared for her. Jake, a man of few words, had shown by his actions what Amanda had come to mean to him.

And Amanda, who lived with words every day of her life, had been shaken to silence by what had lain unidentified inside her. Amanda, who had spent years trying to organize her existence into some kind of meaning, hadn't had a clue as to what she'd been about. She'd always known she'd had commitment, perseverance, inquisitiveness. She hadn't known, though, that bubbling at the core of her had been such a trenchant passion. Such life that it could burst over her like fireworks. Like dawn on a cold winter's morning, crystalline and pure with the colors of heaven.

She hadn't known that she hadn't understood before quite what it was to fall in love. Because although she'd once been engaged, it hadn't been until last night that she'd really understood. Falling in love wasn't reason and sense, it was splintering need, it was aching uncertainty and gnawing ambivalence. It was knowing that the problems you faced might be more than you could solve, no matter how much you loved someone. It was facing those problems, anyway, and hurting all the more for it.

Amanda showered and dressed alone. She brewed up a pot of coffee in a cold kitchen, knowing that Jake hadn't eaten after all before going down to the horses, and stared out the window into the shimmer of yet more blowing snowfall, wishing with all her heart that she knew what to do next.

The phone rang while she was looking through the office.

"Oh, good, the lines aren't down, after all."

Amanda sank into a chair by Betty's desk. "Just the electricity. How are things in Boston, Lee?"

"Boston's Boston," the girl retorted. "How's the ranch? Why didn't you tell me that Jake had broken his ribs? Is he all right? How did you get back from the cabin? I'm so glad you're okay. Is Jake?"

Amanda didn't know whether to laugh or sigh. "He's fine," she assured the girl. "Just a little cranky and sore. How'd you find out?"

"When I couldn't get anybody at the house yesterday, I called Maria. Was Doc McPherson by?"

"He stitched up a cut on his head and prescribed some medicine."

"Which Jake didn't take."

"You've been through this before."

Lee's giggle was bright and rueful. "Poor Betty. Did she have to stay with him?"

"No, she didn't. I did. Your brother almost landed out in the snow."

There was a telling pause. "*You* stayed with him? All night?"

Amanda scowled, still scouting the room. "It wasn't as interesting as it sounds. I yelled and he snarled. Betty showed up just in time to keep one of us from getting shot."

There were piles of forms on the neat desk, bills of sale, horse breed registry applications, stud books with notes scribbled in margins and checkbooks for utilities, taxes and other outsiders who didn't trust a man's word or his cash. All in the same handwriting.

"No, you don't understand," Lee protested. "I mean that Jake . . . well, I mean, I really love my brother and all, but . . ."

"It would have been easier if somebody had warned me," Amanda agreed.

She was rewarded with another giggle.

Signatures. There they were, on the bills of sale. Just what she'd suspected. It gathered in her chest like weights, the collecting of inevitability. The approach of decision and action.

"Amanda?"

Amanda set the stacks down and gave her attention to Jake's sister. "I'm sorry. I'm a little tired. Your brother came out on horseback to the cabin to get me yesterday. It was a long day."

"On horseback?" Lee demanded. "How romantic. How scary."

"How cold."

"Sorry about that. I tried to call, but nobody was home. I forgot about the heater."

"Uh-huh. Then Jake threw my computer in the snow because he decided it was unwieldy on horseback, so I'm stuck here without any company—except for the OK Corral—and nothing newer to read than your old schoolbooks."

"Threw it away? Why'd you let him do that?"

"He was driving."

"Oh, Amanda, I'm sorry. Did you lose anything?"

"No. I'd backed it all up on disks, which I managed to save. But I can't use them without a computer, which leaves me with little to do except practice scales on my dulcimer."

"Well, you could teach yourself the piano. Or maybe go through the *National Geographic*s in Zeke's room. I'm afraid Jake let all the subscriptions lapse when we left."

"I noticed."

"If it doesn't have to do with the breed of a horse, he doesn't care."

"What does he do in this house for relaxation?"

"The only time he's in that house anymore, he's asleep."

Amanda fought the urge to smile. Well, not quite, she couldn't help but think, her body remembering without her permission and tingling in the oddest places. But that wasn't something she needed to share with Lee right now.

"I guess I'll just have to find paper and pencil and do things the old-fashioned way. Then I'll figure out a way to keep Jake from driving me nuts."

Amanda almost groaned out loud at that one. Lee didn't even seem to notice. "Don't be silly," she admonished. "Jake's as happy as a pig in a peanut patch. Now he's got an excuse not to leave the ranch at all."

Amanda lifted an eyebrow. It was his way, she could almost hear his sister say. Just like everyone else did.

"A pig in a peanut patch?"

Lee giggled. "I stole that one from you."

"Well, you can have this one, too. Your brother's so contrary, if you threw him in a river, he'd float upstream."

"That's him, all right. Isn't he cute?"

Amanda was glad Lee couldn't see her grimace. "Darling," she retorted, and hoped she sounded disparaging enough.

Amanda had just said goodbye to Lee when Betty called to say that the roads were going to be impassable for another day at least. She rattled off a list of things Jake needed to do, and concluded by admonishing Amanda not to wander out in the snow, since Wyoming blizzards were no place to be traveling, no matter what the need. Amanda hung up shaking her head, and went right back out on her hunt.

The *National Geographic*s took up four entire shelves in Zeke's room, a male haven with a decorating maturity arrested somewhere around the freshman year of college. The magazines were arranged in order and meticulously shelved. They were also thumbed like rosary beads. Amanda held them in her hands like a penance and stared sightlessly toward Jake's room. She decided that it was about time to say good morning to him.

She found him over in the mares' barn. Shaking the snow from the collar of the sheepskin coat she'd stolen from Gen and Lee's room, Amanda started down the stalls, petting a proffered nose here, sneaking a peek over a half door there. She found Jake about five stalls down on the left. Seated cross-legged on the straw, his head bare and his voice gentle, he was busy singing to a brand-new foal. If Amanda hadn't already lost her heart, that would have done it.

The mare looked up at Amanda as she leaned over the door. A pretty little chestnut with a blaze, she was slowly swishing her tail and watching Jake get to know her baby with placid acceptance.

The foal was four legs and a head, a wobbly, ungainly little thing with a high, reedy whinny. It stood right alongside its mother as Jake stroked its coat.

"You're a sham," Amanda accused gently, smiling at the sight of Jake singing and caressing the day-old animal. "Here I thought you were rough and gruff, a real Marlborough man. You're nothing but a teddy bear."

"Keep your voice down," he retorted, still in that same singsong voice, his attention on the little animal who was nose-to-nose with him. "I have a reputation to uphold."

"I think an ad in the paper should do it," Amanda quipped, resting her forearms over the door and leaning in for a better view. "Maybe an announcement over at Stilwell's."

"See what I have to put up with with?" he asked the foal. The animal sidestepped a little, butting into Jake with its too large head. Jake just kept stroking and singing, his broad, callused hands as gentle as birds in flight. "Smart-assed authors who think they know everything."

"They do," Amanda assured him, filled with the sweet beauty of the scene. "And they all say that you're just a pussy cat in a Stetson."

"I'm really mad at you," he said, although the timbre of his voice didn't change. The little horse lifted its head and nibbled at Jake's hair, and Jake crooned a little more, rubbing his hands over the dark gray coat. "Clovis tried to wake me."

Amanda couldn't take her eyes from the gentle communion before her. "Women have babies all the time without men helping them," she assured him, leaning her forearms on the door. "I was told Bitsy was no different."

"I should have been here."

"You should have been asleep. Is it a boy or a girl?"

He rubbed his hands up and down the little horse's neck, and then dropped a hand to bend the left foreleg. "A filly. She's a beauty, isn't she?"

Amanda tilted her head a little. It was difficult to call brand-new foals cute. They were so disproportionate, so wobbly. But there was that same wonderful openness that all babies possess. "Gorgeous. She's gray. Does that mean we have another Grayghost foal?"

"Grayboy. This is Grayghost's first grandbaby. Amanda, meet Graylady."

"My pleasure," she said, grinning. "What are you doing?"

His answering smile was crooked. "Bonding. The best way for this little lady and me to work together is for us to start now, while she still weighs less than I do. Isn't that right, old girl? Right now, before she figures out she's supposed to be scared of me. So we come in and introduce ourselves and scratch her favorite places and get her used to having me touch her."

"What are you doing to her feet?"

"The sooner you get her used to having her hooves lifted, the easier it is to care for them later, and to have her shod. Tomorrow we'll get a halter on her for the first time."

Amanda was enchanted. The little animal tottered around Jake like a trusting child. The mother butted Jake every so often, demanding her own attention. Jake gave it with generous lashings of praise and profuse apologies that he hadn't been able to attend the big event itself.

"That's what they all say," Amanda offered dryly.

Jake did his best to ease back to his feet, but he was still a little sore for that. When he lurched, the foal was startled and whinnied. Jake crouched back down and blew into her nose, very gently. Amanda was amazed. The little animal settled right down, nuzzling Jake with that velvety dark nose of hers.

"Secret code?" she asked.

Jake smiled as he unlatched the door to step out. "It's the way horses greet each other. The great secret to training horses. Best way to control a horse is to think like a horse."

"Can I do it, too?" she asked, still watching the foal as she redirected her attention to her mother. It was evidently breakfast time, and like all children, she was impatient.

"Maybe in a couple of days," Jake offered, stepping out and bolting the door behind him. "Too many people at once is too much for her and her dam. Get to know her mama, though, and it'll be easier to be friends with her."

Amanda looked up at the soft light that lingered in Jake's eyes. "You do this for every foal born here?"

He watched the baby he'd just left and shrugged. "A guy's gotta like something about his job."

Amanda huffed, much as Clovis did. "Like I said. A rank fake."

Jake returned his attention to her, and the light in his eyes melted a little, shifted into something more uncertain. Amanda wished they could have talked before he'd left the bed that morning. She was so afraid suddenly that he wouldn't be able to now.

"You didn't eat breakfast," she accused gently. "Did you?"

He picked his hat off a nail in the wall and plopped it back on his head. "I was late for work."

"How are your ribs feeling?"

He at least had the grace to shrug a concession. "Better. I guess I might have needed a little food and sleep."

"And codeine."

Another shrug. "Aspirin probably would have worked just as well."

Amanda knew better than to push.

"It's boring up there without my computer. Is there anything down here I can do?"

Amanda was hoping for levity, for companionship. When Jake turned his gaze on her, she knew both would come with a price.

"Amanda," he said, lifting a hand to touch her, but never quite doing it. "I'm sorry. I shouldn't have—"

Amanda couldn't bear the pain that flared in those beautiful blue eyes. "I don't want to hear 'I shouldn't have,'" she interrupted, grabbing hold of his restive hand before he could pull away. "I want to hear, 'Wow, Amanda, was that a surprise. Later we might talk about it in light of what's happening between us.' ''

She almost begged out loud for a smile. Even an argument. Something that told her he'd fight for them.

But he shook his head. "I wasn't fair to you."

Amanda did laugh, then, a sharp report of surprise. "You were a gift to me last night. Don't ever think different." She squeezed his hands between hers, intent. "Please, Jake."

She saw the torment he was trying to hide, saw the impulse rise to cut her off. Saw it die. "This isn't the place to talk about it," he finally decided.

Amanda nodded. "I'll sure agree to that. How 'bout later over wine? By the fireplace?" She leaned very close, so close that she could almost smell his discomfort. "Naked?"

The barrier shut with an almost audible clang. Jake pulled away and straightened. "You want to help, see Clovis about feed. I have to check on the stock we left out in the pasture."

"It's still horrible outside," Amanda protested.

Jake didn't even smile. "Not much choice, is there? We're not in Boston now, Amanda."

She watched him go and fought new tears. Bitter tears born of hard experience and the flush of newness. Angry tears at having to be falling in love with the last man who'd let her.

Well, at least she knew one thing. He was acting like that new foal in there, skittish and shy. Amanda had a lot more bonding to do before she dropped any kind of rope over that neck. Because the rope she suspected she'd have to drop would hurt, and it would hurt bad. She just had to show him how much she could help ease the pain before she did it.

Jake worked himself back into a state of exhaustion and still it didn't help to get Amanda off his mind. She'd been a revelation last night, a miracle. She'd been light and fire in his hands, her skin so soft he'd wanted to lay his head against it and dream, her eyes so deep and sweet that he'd drunk from them like a well. As he pitched bales of hay to the pastured horses, he thought of the dance of her body in the shadows. As he broke through the ice to get the horses water, he remembered the song of passion on her lips. As he trudged through snow and ice and wind, the temperature cold enough to take off the tips of his ears, he was warmed by the memories of her candor, her spirit, her hunger. Nobody had ever argued Clovis down over a foaling mare. No one had ever brought Jake Kendall to his knees with just her memory.

He plodded back up to the house, wishing she'd be gone, terrified she would go, wondering what he was going to do about it. When he threw open the back door, the wind swirling in behind him, it was to smell the bouquet of cooking food and hear the narcotic of laughter. Her laughter. For a minute he could do no more than stand there, his eyes closed, his hands clenched against the pain. He'd have to get her to leave before she found out. Before she shamed him with her pity.

"There you are," she greeted him brightly from the kitchen door. "We were just about to send out the Saint Bernards."

Jake opened his eyes and damn near walked back out the door. She was in Lee's jeans, and they were too tight. Too delectably tight. She wore a soft cream angora sweater, and had her hair piled up on her head, so that damp curls clung to her neck, just where the most tender skin was. His body reacted so swiftly, so fiercely, that he almost had to turn away again.

"Had a lot of work to do," was all he could say, pulling off his hat and knocking the snow off against his leg. "Clovis in here?"

She nodded, her eyes a little darker, her hands on her hips as if she was going to challenge him again. "And José. And Willy and James. We've been waiting dinner on you."

He shrugged out of his coat and hung it up, his ribs grating and his arms sore. "You didn't have to."

"I knew that," she said with a saucy grin. "But it's always so much nicer at dinner when you're there scowling at me."

Jake looked up at her, surprised. She just flashed him some teeth and spun on her heel.

"Ten minutes," she announced. "The you-know-what is still on your nightstand."

"I don't—"

But she was already gone.

Jake heard the men greet her, heard Clovis's awed respect, Willy's shy attraction, José's amusement. She'd won them over with nothing more than a ladle and a sense of humor. She'd won him over with less. With more. With everything and nothing, no more than the way she stood when he challenged her, the way she lit up when she was able to learn something new. The way she made no excuses for her passion.

God, he was falling in love with her. He rubbed at his face, tired of the aching, of the loneliness, and walked on into the bedroom to get ready for dinner, wishing he knew what he was going to do about her.

Dinner lasted forever. Jake imagined that the food was good, but he had no taste for it. Amanda had cooked up ham casserole and corn bread tonight. She'd evidently spent the majority of time he hadn't been with her helping Clovis and José in the barn and then cleaning up and cooking in the house. And she looked like she'd just stepped off the pages of a magazine as she sat at the other end of the table, flickering candles the only light on her hair and in her eyes, her laughter cascading around the room like bright water.

"By the way," she said over the coffee and cookies that José was putting away like hardtack in the desert, "your sisters called. Both of them. And Zeke. And Betty and Maria and Doc McPherson. I told them all that you were just fine, that the horses were fine, and that we had a beautiful new baby on the ranch."

"We have five so far," Clovis argued instinctively.

Jake drank his coffee in silence.

"Your sister the doctor says that you should take the antibiotic," Amanda continued, "just like your doctor the doctor said. Your brother the anthropologist and your other sister the student took bets that you'd die of lockjaw first."

Jake glared at her, even more angry because he wanted to laugh with her. He wanted to smile and joke and tease, just like Clovis and José were doing. But that would be letting down his guard, and except for last night, Jake had never let down his guard before. So he sipped his coffee and did his best to let the conversation flow over him.

"Another fine meal, Miss Marlow," Willy crowed, tipping his chair back. "I don't half mind gettin' snowed in with you as the cook."

"Somebody like you," José added with a nod, "I expect fancy things. Not good food."

Amanda grinned at them both. "I'm saving the escargot for Sunday dinner," she assured them.

She didn't belong here, Jake thought again. Not really. She'd get tired of the empty miles and the harsh weather quickly enough, no television, no conveniences, no nightlife. As soon as the novelty of playing homesteader in a storm wore off, she'd be back on a plane so fast her ears would pop.

He tried, really tried, to picture the room without her. To picture the ranch without her. To picture his bed without her.

He couldn't do it.

Amanda looked up when he stood. "Heading in for bed?"

"I'm going on down to the barn to check on Filbert. He has an abscess we're treating."

Clovis scrambled to his feet. "I can do that, boss."

Jake glared at him. "I'm not so sure you'd tell me if he had problems," he snapped and turned away, feeling even worse. It wasn't Clovis he was angry at. It wasn't anybody. But he was angry.

Amanda had never in her life been a calculating female. She wasn't sure she could get away with acting like one now. But, looking at her reflection in the mirror, she knew she had to try. Jake had been crusty as hell tonight, but that crust had been pretty damn thin. It wouldn't take much to break through and let loose all that confusion seething beneath.

She didn't go in for fancy underwear. A single woman trying to keep warm in a New England winter didn't really have much use for satin and lace. As a teacher living alone she preferred athletic bras for jogging and undershirts for sleep. So that was what she'd managed to stuff in her bag before Jake had yanked her out of the cabin.

She tried her best to assess the look. It might work. Her panties were good old cotton, but they were very French cut. Her undershirt was sleeveless with a scoop neck that gave away just enough to send an imagination into gear and nicely cupped the rest.

Not that she had any misconceptions about the package she was trying to wrap. It was plain, just like her mama had said. Plain and a little skinny, so that the only attraction for single men had seemed to be her fame. But it was all she had. And Jake hadn't seemed to mind it covered in flannel last night. Maybe if she added a long, loose flannel robe, it might just distract him enough to get a reaction. Amanda took a few more minutes brushing out her hair so that it looked just a little sleep-tousled, and then headed in to fall asleep in front of the fire.

Jake wasn't sure what to expect when he walked back into the house. He could see from the barn that most of the lanterns were out. Smoke still curled from the chimney, so the fire was still going. Maybe Amanda was asleep. It would be better if she were. But he was honest enough to admit that he hoped she was waiting for him.

"Amanda?"

His only answer was the hissing from the lanterns and heaters, the crackle from the fireplace. The house was cool and dim. Battling the hollow ache of disappointment, Jake shook off his hat and coat and hung them up. He raked his hands through his hair and rubbed at the weariness on his face as he walked on through the kitchen.

There was still a pot of coffee on the stove. He stopped to pour himself a cup before heading into the living room. There was stuff Betty had left him to sign from two days ago he should probably do, and all the heaters needed to be checked for fuel. And he should stoke the fireplace for the night.

Jake came to a shuddering halt in front of the couch.

"Amanda?"

She was asleep, curled on the couch, her hair tumbled over the fabric like a fall of silk, the dark green robe she'd borrowed gaping to reveal the sleek line of her leg, the creamy skin of her throat. Jake couldn't move. He couldn't approach or leave. She was beautiful, soft and mysterious and sweet, and he knew every curve and hollow of her body now. He ached for her so hard he thought he'd shatter.

"Amanda? Wake up."

She murmured something in her sleep and turned a bit. The robe gaped even more, revealing the undershirt and panties she was wearing. White, cotton, so simple and practical it should never have looked sexy. It sent his pulse rate rocketing. The material draped down her chest, baring her throat and shoulders, with only thin straps contrasting to her skin. It molded to her breasts, the breasts that Jake had held in his hands, had tasted and teased until her nipples were as taut as they were now from the cold. Even those plain white panties, cut high so that a man could sate himself on the sight of her legs, shouldn't have been sinful. But they were. Jake heard a soft sloshing sound and realized that he'd clenched the mug so tightly that he was close to crushing it between his hands.

He reached over to close her robe and brushed her thigh with his hand by accident. Amanda smiled. Jake straightened as if he'd been electrocuted.

"Wake up," he begged, reaching down to nudge her shoulder. Instead, he found himself fingering her hair, gently brushing it back from where it had tumbled into her face.

Her lashes were so long, so dark against those pale cheeks. Her mouth was so full, so ripe. It tasted like dark honey and left a man wild with hunger.

"Oh, you're back," she murmured, and Jake realized that her eyes were open. Sleepy, sensuous, their smile dark like a moonlit glade.

He did his best to reel in his control. "You're gonna freeze in that."

She looked down at her attire. "The fire must have burned down. I was really too hot before."

Jake motioned with a jerky movement of the mug. "You wear that all the time?"

She grinned ruefully. "Not as much romance in writing as people think. This is as exotic as it gets."

Pulling herself up, she raked her fingers through her hair and curled her feet underneath her. "Come and sit down," she offered.

Jake couldn't quite move. He was afraid that if he did, he wouldn't stop at sitting down. His hands itched for the feel of her again. His mouth was dry and his palms wet.

Amanda looked up at him, her eyes guileless and smiling. "Nobody's here," she admonished. "Your reputation's still safe. I promise not to tell anybody that you were a nice person to me, if you just sit down and relax a minute."

All Jake could do was shake his head.

Amanda tilted hers, so that her hair slid down the side of her throat, so that it curled over the tops of her breasts, burnished mahogany silk against pale cream satin. Textures and memories.

"Jake," she whispered, sounding almost disappointed. "I don't bite."

His smile was dark. His hands trembled. "Oh, yes you do. And it hurts like hell."

Did he see tears? Had that been what he'd wanted? If it was, it wasn't now. He couldn't bear the idea of hurting her.

"Amanda, I—"

But it seemed to be her turn to shake her head. "No," she said, her voice deliberate. "I'm not listening to excuses or apologies. I'm not listening to anything unless you sit down first. Please, Jake."

He did. He sat down and prepared to apologize, to excuse his behavior the night before. But this close he could smell the soap on her, the wild tumble of wind and sunlight in her hair. A woman like her should have smelled exotic and expensive. Amanda smelled like a high meadow in the spring, and it was destroying him.

"Good," she allowed, "you can compromise. I'd wondered."

"Amanda—"

She didn't seem to hear him. Reaching over, she stole the mug from his clenched fingers and took a long sip of coffee.

"Ah," she sighed, eyes briefly closed. "Good and strong. Just the way I like it." Opening her eyes, she impaled him with an impish grin. "Another myth shot to hell. Everybody thinks an author drinks Scotch or champagne for breakfast. I drink my coffee black and my Scotch on chicken. I do admit to a weakness for red wine. I was going to try and ply you with some, but I noticed you don't stock any. Not even for cooking."

Jake did his best to maintain some control. "I don't drink wine."

Her face folded into a dry grin. "I think I just said that."

"Amanda."

"Yes?"

"Close that damn robe."

She took a look down at the same view Jake had. "But Jake," she protested, "it's just my old cotton underwear. It's hardly sexy."

"Don't," he grated out, yanking the edges of the robe closed himself. "Don't play games with me, Amanda."

Could she really have been that innocent? She looked up at him in surprise, but Jake could have sworn he caught a shadow of relief in her eyes. Gratitude.

Gratitude? How the hell could that be?

But she didn't even give him the chance to consider it. "I think it's time to talk about last night, Jake."

Jake looked hard at her, tried his best to find a schemer there, a shallow opportunist. He desperately wanted her not to be what he wanted, because otherwise he couldn't bear to give her away.

But there was no guile in those eyes, just concern. Just soul-deep beauty and life. Just the deadly narcotic of simple desire.

"You obviously think that last night was a mistake," Amanda said without preamble, her voice soft, her eyes dark. "Did you want to tell me why?"

Jake couldn't stay there. He couldn't look at her and lie. He sure as hell couldn't tell the truth. Lurching up from the couch, he strode over to face the fireplace.

"Don't you think it was a mistake?" he demanded.

"No." It was almost the voice of a child, soft with injury, hesitant with uncertainty. "Why should I?"

He turned on her. "Because you don't belong here. You don't belong with me. You never did, no matter what happened last night."

Jake saw the pain he was inflicting. He saw a vulnerability he'd never thought to find in Amanda's eyes. Not this woman who spent time in New York and Hollywood, who was quoted in gossip columns and anthologies. She had no business looking suddenly so frail.

"Look around you, Amanda," he insisted. "This is what I am. It's what I have. A ranch, some horses, and a family I've raised since I was twelve. I've never been to a restaurant fancier than Stilwell's. I left Wyoming once, and damn near walked home to get back. I wear old jeans and older boots, and it's been since Lee graduated high school in June that I've had a suit coat on. Is that the kind of life you're looking for? Tied to one place? Working twelve to fourteen hours a day just to see that your animals get the basic care, having to schedule your whole life around the needs of the ranch, working yourself to death just so your children can do the same?"

Jake was shaking. His chest was on fire, and his gut was churning. He impaled Amanda on the truth, the truth he'd let her see. He battered her with reality and saw her features soften with consideration.

"Well?" he demanded yet again, pushing, driving her away while he still could. "Are you ready to give up those fancy clothes and your passport for all this?"

She met his gaze then, and her eyes were thoughtful instead of outraged. Quiet rather than angry. But her answer, when it came, was devastating, anyway. And just what he thought he'd wanted.

"No," she admitted simply. "I'm not."

Chapter 11

Amanda balanced on a knife's edge. She trembled with the terrible chances she took. Her heart thundered in her ears, and her throat burned with the deception she practiced. Even so, she kept her voice calm and quiet. She faced the raw torment in Jake's eyes and smiled. She sat still before him when what she wanted to do was curl into herself, protect herself from the disillusionment that bubbled free in Jake.

"That's what I thought," was all he said before he turned away again.

Hold me, she wanted to beg. Come to me, wrap me in your arms and let me take away that pain, that loneliness, that terrible distrust. Let it be like it was last night, before you thought to question what your instincts were telling you.

"You sure like to draw your own conclusions," she mused, gaze on his taut, straight back. Knowing just how heavy the burden was that he carried. "What I was thinking was that I'd like to combine the two." Turn around, Jake. Face me and let me close. Don't make me taunt and torment this out of you. "I've been on the road too long, Jake. I want to go home."

He turned then, but his judgment was still in his eyes, and it was harsh. "Then go home."

She did her best to smile, but knew she faltered. "Not West Virginia," she amended. "West Virginia really isn't home, anymore. People treat me like a specimen there." She laughed, a short, bitter sound. "Heck, they treat me like a specimen everywhere. I've been bouncing from city to city, trying to find one place to belong, and I think I've found it."

He clenched that mug before him as if he were thinking of throwing it. His jaw was like steel, his eyes dark. "You belong here?"

She shrugged, and her shoulders shrieked with the strain. "I came here to write, Jake, that was all. And then, day after day up in that cabin, I realized that I'd rediscovered something precious. Something I hadn't even known I'd lost. The silence, the harsh majesty of the mountains. The simplicity of life. Now, I don't think I can leave again."

"Then what was that about combining lives?"

Smiling, she uncurled her legs and climbed to her feet, her hands holding the edges of her robe together, her fingers taut against the soft fabric. Still she didn't back down. "I like to travel, Jake. There's so much out there beyond the Rockies. So many people to meet, so many beautiful cities and countries. I'd like to spend some time in Scotland, wander around the fjords of Norway, take a sailing ship through the Caribbean. I'd like to study new folklores in countries I haven't visited before." She let her smile grow wistful with the yearning she knew had crept into her voice. "And then I'd like to come home," she said. "Here."

He reacted as if she'd flayed him, his face frozen and taut with the pictures she'd painted. With the temptations she'd scattered before him. She knew now that those magazines hadn't been an aberration. Closed away, year after year, all alone, Jake had held those pictures in his hands and yearned for something he'd thought he couldn't have.

"Here where?" he retorted. "Wyoming? The Rockies? Lost Ridge?"

Amanda gathered her courage. "The Diamond K."

Their war was fought for a minute in silence, her intent green eyes battling his tormented blue. The fire crackled and hissed. The wind moaned low outside. Shadows collected and shuddered along Jake's features, deepening his distress. Punctuating his pain. Amanda didn't think she could stand any more.

"You decided that, did you?" he challenged, dead still, his voice as raw as a winter wind.

Slowly Amanda shook her head, her gaze never leaving his, her hands trembling. "I hoped it."

"And I was just supposed to wait here while you wandered around?"

"No." She took a breath, knowing how close she was, how perilously she balanced on the brink of disaster. "I wanted you to come with me."

His laughter was short and sharp, a bark of disbelief. "Just when am I supposed to do that?" he demanded. "Haven't you been around to see the work that goes into this place?"

"Yes. But I know, too, that you've spent every waking minute since your twelfth birthday providing for everybody else in your family. Now they're all out in the world, successful and independent because of what you gave them. And you're still here working every waking minute. I think it's time you did something for Jake Kendall."

That was what broke him. So quickly that Amanda couldn't even brace herself, Jake hurled the mug against the wall. The ceramic exploded, painting the wall in a ragged coffee stain. He stood rigid and unyielding before her, the frustration on his features turning them to stone.

"Well, I guess you haven't heard, lady," he snarled, trying to frighten her. Failing. "That's just not the way it's done here. It wasn't when my grandfather lived, or my father, or me. We're stuck here, tied to this place and this land and everything that it involves. I don't travel, and I don't learn about somebody else's culture, because it's all I can do sometimes to keep my head above water here. And this is the real world, not some fairy tale spun by a bored teacher who wants to reinvent the world just for her benefit. Live a real life, Amanda, and then come tell me how to run mine."

Amanda battled tears. She dipped her head a little, trying so hard to know how to handle this. "You think I invented all that about having an outhouse and going barefoot just to sound romantic or something?" she asked. She faced him then, her hands clenched tight against his distrust, against memories she'd only danced around for so long, against the pain of loss and the dread of separation. "Jake, I can't think of a thing that's romantic about an outhouse. Or being so poor that we didn't have the money for shoes or electricity or a phone of our own. There were days when the only meal I got was the school lunch. There were nights when we all slept in the same bed just to keep warm because we'd run out of fuel.

"You want to know why I don't go back to West Virginia? It's because it took my family. All of it. My father and my brother and my uncles were all killed in a mining accident the day after my seventeenth birthday. I stood by a mine site for four days waiting for them to bring their bodies up. And I stood there with nobody because my mama and my Uncle Mick were already dead. I was already leaving when it happened. After that, I just didn't turn back. So, yes, Jake, I think my life was just about as real as it gets."

"It was different for you," he rasped, the anguish palpable.

She nodded. "Yes," she admitted. "It was. I was able to make my own choices then. I didn't have the weight of three siblings depending on me. But you have the opportunity now, Jake. Don't you think it's worth taking? Don't you even want to give us a chance?"

He started a little, as if struggling with warring instincts. Amanda held her breath, so close to him and yet held impossibly far away. "No," he insisted, sounding even worse. "No. I don't."

"Why?"

"For reasons you'll never understand," he snapped and whirled from her.

"Why," she demanded. "Because I was able to get away and you weren't? Because I'll never know what it was like to have been trapped back there with no way out?"

He whirled on her, rigid with torment. "Yes! Yes, damn it."

"And you've already decided that I'm not worth sharing that with? Make me understand, Jake. Help me see this from your point of view."

He tried to turn away again.

"Jake," she protested, reaching out to him. "I love you."

He stopped. His head came up and his chest heaved convulsively. "No."

She tried her very best to smile. "You keep disagreeing with me. I find that so irritating."

He didn't move. So she did. She walked right up to him and rested a hand on his arm. It was rock solid with tension.

"Jake, last night—"

He jerked upright, glaring at her. "Last night I took advantage of you."

She looked up at him. "No," she said gently, "you didn't. Last night I walked in with you. And Jake—I want to walk in with you again."

"Amanda, don't—"

"Damn it, don't you understand yet?" she demanded, tears burning her throat. "I'm past arguments and rationalizations. No matter what you say or do, I'm going to love you. I'm not just lonely or infatuated or—"

Suddenly she was in his arms. "Oh, Amanda," he groaned, surrounding her, stopping her open mouth with his own. "Shut up. Just—" And then before Amanda could protest or even think, he'd swept her up in his arms. "Just shut up...."

She'd stolen his control. She'd sabotaged his strength. Before Jake knew what was happening, he had her in his arms and was stalking toward his room.

"You talk too much," he growled against her mouth, that whisper-soft mouth that infected his thoughts, that hungry, hot mouth that tormented him and mesmerized him. He took that mouth, wrapped his fingers into her hair so that she couldn't escape, even if she'd wanted, and plundered the soft, secret recesses, mating his tongue with hers, sipping the tang of coffee and capturing that full, petal-soft lower lip between his teeth to tease it. To tease her into groaning, deep in her throat, so that he could bend farther and taste it against his tongue. She let her head fall back in his arms, her hair cascading over his hands, his forearms, her moonlight-pale throat offered to his lips.

"You drive me crazy," he muttered against the flutter of her pulse. "Never give a man a chance to think..." The bed. He reached it and eased into its nest with her still in his arms, her skin hot and flushed already, the cotton not enough barrier to his anxious hands. "Never give him a chance to say no..."

She smiled. Stretched out beneath him on the bed, her hair a dark aura against the soft cream-and-green comforter, her eyes deep emeralds in the night, she smiled, and Jake felt himself stumbling right into her winsome challenge. "Do you want to say no?" she demanded, her voice husky, her hands hesitating at the brink of his shirt.

Jake buried his hands in her hair, in her silky, sweet hair that smelled like sunshine, and caught her like a butterfly. "It's too late," he managed just shy of a growl, and then eased his burning, aching body down to hers. "It's way too late to say no."

He wanted to frighten her, to intimidate her with his desperation. She needed to know that he was past patience, he was past sanity and reason. The hot fire in her eyes was singeing him. The sweet flush of her skin was drowning him. The secret pleasures of her body were tormenting him.

But she wasn't afraid. She wasn't hesitant. Jake had almost wanted to see caution in those dark, deep eyes. He'd wanted to see retreat. Instead, he saw delight. Instead of dying, the fires flared, the flush deepened and pulled him right under. Amanda yanked open buttons and pulled at his shirt with trembling hands. Jake helped her, they helped each other, until she could reach his skin as he could reach hers.

He felt her delicate fingers skim his chest like whispers and groaned with his body's harsh answer. The need he'd shoved down too long. The hunger he'd buried beneath work and discipline and denial. Amanda was setting it loose like a wild animal, and it sprang. It took her, hands and mouth and tongue, devouring, quenching, sating itself on her.

Jake shook with the fury of passion. He gasped with the wild music of her response. She arched beneath his touch. She whimpered with his kiss. She urged in murmurs and praised in throaty moans, her hands even more bold than his.

Jake filled his mouth with her. He filled his hands with her. He sank into the languorous forest of her eyes and captured her body like a fall of sunlight between his hands. Between his desperate hands, his hungry hands. His hands that swept throat and cheek and ear, that plundered belly and hip and thigh. He explored her breasts through cotton, the skimpy shirt doing no more than complementing the soft fullness of her, the sigh of material caught between his thumbs and her taut, attentive nipples tormenting him.

He gathered those breasts in his hands, the shirt bunching up in his palm, the barrier just enough to tease them both. He dipped his head to taste that cotton with his mouth, with his tongue, with his teeth, and then he nudged at the top of the shirt with his mouth until he could slip his kisses in beneath. He slipped his hand along the edge of her panties the same way, torturing them both with the cool, plain material that kept him away from the hot silk beneath.

He skimmed her with his fingers and felt her leap beneath him. He raked her thighs with callused fingertips and felt her ease open in invitation. He pushed that cotton shirt up with both hands and feasted on her breasts. Amanda sang to him, her hands in his hair, scoring his back, snaking beneath the waist of his jeans.

"Off," she gasped, yanking, "I want them off—"

Together again, they worked them off, and his boots. Together they turned back to sweep the final barriers away. Cotton whispered in the night. Amanda's skin gleamed like moonlight beneath Jake's hands. Her eyes glowed. Her fingers tempted and teased. Jake wanted to just look. He wanted to fill his eyes just as he had his hands. But it was too late for that. It was way too late.

He brushed her tangled hair back from her forehead, drank from the dark well of her mouth. He plunged his tongue deep inside her, tasting, tempting, pulling panting little whimpers from her as she danced in his hands. He slid his hand down her sleek belly to dip beneath the nest of curls there. She lifted her hips to him, pulled at him, her breasts thick and delicious against his chest, her hands insatiable. He slipped his fingers in between the hot petals of her and shuddered with her cry of discovery. She was so slick, so swollen. Her body was a gift for him, her gathering pleasure so entangled in his own that he couldn't tell them apart anymore. He felt her wrap her own fingers around him and almost let the world splinter away.

But he didn't. He stroked and he kissed and he touched. He held off as long as he could, the ache so hard he could barely stand it, the agony the sweetest he'd ever known. And then, when he felt the shudders build, deep inside her where he knew he wanted to be, when her eyes flew open in surprise and her whimpers grew to cries, he accepted her welcome and slipped home.

She was crying. She was crying his name. She was scrabbling at him, her body easing into the ancient rhythms, her skin sheened with perspiration, her eyes wide and wet. Jake closed himself in her, wrapped her around him, so tight and warm it was agony. It was life. It was home. He answered once, crying her name as the world finally gave way, as he spilled deep inside her, as he spent himself in her arms, shuddering and gasping with the release of control.

"We forgot the comforter again," she murmured some minutes later, still wrapped in him, her heart not yet slowed or her respirations eased.

Jake could barely pull a coherent thought together. All he knew was that he was warm in a way he'd never been in his life. Warm and content and, just for a moment, happy.

"What?"

"The comforter," she repeated with a disinterested yawn. "We're going to have to cover up soon. It's gonna get cold."

Jake didn't care. He couldn't quite pull himself past the moment, past the easing thunder of his heart or the lingering taste of coffee and tears on his tongue, or the alien warmth of a woman in his arms. A woman he suddenly couldn't get enough of.

His hands were still restless with her, smoothing her hair, outlining her shoulder and hip, dipping into the hollow at her waist and tucking themselves up beneath the warm weight of her breasts. His body couldn't get its fill of her, at once sated and empty again, filled with memories and yet demanding more.

Jake nuzzled his cheek against her hair and wished with all his heart that he never had to worry about lasting past this moment when everything was so right. When Amanda still didn't realize what a coward he was.

God, how he wanted to go with her. He'd wanted it before he'd ever met her, to wander along the banks of the Seine and fly over the top of the world, to swim the moonlit waters of the Aegean and sit down to a meal with a person who didn't know how to speak his language. It had been a cancer that had gnawed at him since the day he'd picked up his first *National Geographic,* that had grown in silence and festered in isolation. It was a dream he'd never see, and he knew it.

But to go with Amanda. To see her eyes light up with discovery, to hear that unquenchable hunger in her voice, to have the world opened up to him with her words and reflections. To know...to know...

"Jake?" Her voice was sleepy and satisfied, the kind of music a man only dreams of.

He stroked her hair and fought the bitter taste of loneliness. "Yes?"

She snuggled closer, her small hands wrapping tight around his waist, her head tucked beneath his. "Couldn't we try?" she asked. "Couldn't we just take it one step at a time?"

Jake couldn't help a bark of surprised laughter. "Amanda," he admonished, "I think we've jumped a couple of steps in the last few days."

She stilled in his embrace. "Do you want to go back?"

And in the end, all he could give her was the truth. "No. Never. But that still doesn't mean that there's anywhere to go from here."

"Do you believe me?" she asked. "That I'll love you no matter what?"

It was an effort to breathe. To work past the truth. "I think you believe it."

She lifted herself up on an elbow so that she could face him. She was moonlight in the darkness, mystery, compulsion. Her hair brushed her shoulders with dark fire, and her areolas were dusky roses. Jake ached hard for the taste of them again. For the taste of her. He wanted to bury himself so deeply in her that nothing else would matter. That nothing else would exist. He wanted peace, and Amanda was the only place he found it, even for a little while.

He saw some kind of battle being waged in those deceptively serene eyes. He saw it tighten and shift in her, and then ease away into a soft smile of determination. "Well, then," was all she said, "I'm just going to have to get you to believe it, too."

Jake wanted to protest. He wanted to warn her about the dreams of nighttime that dissipated in the sun. He wanted to prevent her from making it more difficult for him when she finally left, because he still knew she would. A woman like Amanda. A woman who'd gone the places she'd gone and done the things she'd done. She just wouldn't settle for returning to the old life, no matter what she thought.

A woman like Amanda. She deliberately leaned over him, turning him onto his back, her hair and her breasts skimming his chest, her eyes melting from determination into seduction.

"I'll have to show you," she insisted, her voice like honey as she bent down to kiss him.

And she did. She showed him. She turned her own passion loose on him and made him forget the morning.

Amanda was a rank coward. She should have confronted Jake last night, should have shared her suspicion as she'd intended and eased his burden of deception. He'd been alone for so long, even amid a family that loved him, a town that respected him, that she couldn't bear his being alone any longer.

But she still wasn't absolutely sure she was right. She had suspicions, saw a pattern. She had the nag of familiarity. But any number of things could account for Jake's actions. Amanda might lay her theory at his feet to have herself proved wrong, to learn that it was her he disdained and not himself.

And even if she was right, she wasn't absolved. If she was right... Oh, God, the weight of that collected in her with the memories she hadn't resurrected in so long—the frustration, the anger, the accusations.

Jake Kendall was a proud man, a man who had constructed an entire world around him without anyone being the wiser. A man who called his own shots and made his own rules. A man who would not admit any weakness easily, even if that weakness were only in his own mind. Amanda knew. Her Uncle

Mick had been a proud man. He'd lived until his fortieth birthday practicing one of the most clever deceptions a man could, getting Amanda to do his work for him, to intercede with the outside world for him. Uncle Mick had hoarded *National Geographic*s, too. He'd dreamed of going to faraway places and doing exotic things. But without money, he'd always said, he'd just be happy to look at the pictures.

To look at the pictures.

Amanda looked at her own reflection in the mirror and realized that she'd passed up her chance to force the issue last night. She couldn't pass up that chance again. She couldn't let Jake go on torturing himself with the thought that she didn't know. That no one knew. That once they did, he would somehow be less of a man.

If she was right.

But even if she was, the battle had just begun.

Fate conspired against her—the weather and Betty's legendary dedication to the Diamond K and the erratic foaling habits of mares in the spring.

For the next four days, the temperature rose back into springtime, melting the ravaging snow and uncovering the bodies of three of Jake's yearlings out in a far pasture the hands hadn't been able to reach. Three more horses gave birth in quick succession, one of them in a labor so protracted that the vet had been called out and the chains put into use. Amanda had watched, thinking that she'd certainly seen such devices in woodcuts of medieval tortures, and then thankful for them when the foal arrived healthy and both baby and dam were back on their feet.

Betty coerced her son into breaking out the four-wheel-drive truck and made it back over the roads before they were passable, bringing Maria and an end to the cozy kitchen meals.

Neither Betty nor Maria said a word about the coffee stain on the wall. Within half an hour of showing back up at the ranch, Betty had walked into where Amanda was picking at her dulcimer and handed her a cup of coffee, her only comment, "You realize, don't you, that nobody on this good, green earth has ever succeeded in keeping Jake Kendall from one of his mares before." And then she'd simply walked away, smiling and shaking her head with what Amanda thought was great satisfaction.

As the snow melted, the world cranked back into gear and Amanda felt herself being left behind. Electricity flickered on, life returned to order, and Amanda had no excuse left to remain behind at the ranch house. Finally she saddled up Sweet William, hooking her bag and dulcimer over the saddle horn just as she had coming this way, and headed back to the cabin.

"I can't guarantee the electricity's back on up there," Jake protested, his hand on Bill's withers, his eyes brimming with unspoken emotion.

Amanda thought she saw distress, hoped she saw disappointment. She smiled for him, anyway, resurrecting every moment they'd spent in proximity with that big down comforter. "If it isn't, I'll come back for my heater," she assured him. "Besides, the electricity won't do me much good without a computer."

"About that, Amanda, I'll—"

"About that, Jake," she interrupted, knowing exactly where he was going with it. "I'll probably have to go into a city a little bigger than Lost Ridge to replace it." She shrugged. "Probably needed a new one, anyway. Do you want me to look into something for the ranch?"

His scowl was magnificent. "I'd rather ride buck naked through a sandstorm."

"That's quite an image." Amanda proffered a grin. "With or without your hat?"

"I'll repay you for the computer."

"You did," she assured him. "You got me here before my toes fell off. I'll see you in a couple of days, Jake."

For just the briefest of moments he let his eyes communicate for him. She saw the surge of yearning, the uncertainty, the fierce need. She saw him shutter it all away again.

"Don't forget that Lee's coming in."

Amanda nodded. "Don't forget where I'm staying," she suggested, her own expression not shuttered at all.

Jake tensed alongside her. He dipped his head a little so that she couldn't see past the brim of his hat. Amanda ached for him, ached for herself that she had to leave him, burned with the world that had flooded back in just when she'd thought they might escape it. Even so, she patted his gloved hand once where it rested near her leg, and turned Sweet William off toward the high meadow. And she fought tears all the way along that chattering, crackling mountain stream to where the rustic little cabin waited in cold silence.

Jake lasted two long days. He put up with Clovis's fussing and Betty's bossing and the demands of the ranch that had once kept him too busy to think. He stalked his silent house late at night when Amanda should have been there, and fought the urge to ride through the dark to that little cabin. Each time he set his hat up on the rack in the mudroom, he expected to find Amanda there on the couch, just as he had that last night they'd made love. He swore he still smelled her on his sheets, heard her laughter in the fire, caught her shadow next to his own when he woke.

But she wasn't there. He was alone, just as he'd always been. No, he realized, not as he'd always been. Before he hadn't known what he'd forfeited. He'd shut it out as deliberately as the regret of lost parents. He'd constructed his life so that it would be superfluous.

He'd been deceiving himself. All along, every cold winter night and soft spring morning. He'd been waiting for Amanda to arrive and bring the world to life. For Amanda to leave again, taking the warmth and grace and beauty away with her again.

The sun was riding high in a cold blue sky when he set off for the meadow on Alabaster. A little barn-sour after all the bad weather, the white Arabian quarter mix danced beneath him. Usually Jake let Alabaster have his head, but his ribs still weren't quite up to it yet, leaving the horse as impatient as the rider.

The snow was almost gone, the spring wildflowers beginning to peek through. The stream tumbled and sang to his right and the mountains brooded beyond. It was a glorious spring day. The world was coming back to life, there were new foals in his yard, new business waiting to be transacted. Jake's favorite time of the year, his mind full of plans and action, his body ready to gear up after a hard winter.

Today, he left the ranch behind. His mind was ahead, on that cabin. On the cabin's occupant. He hadn't slept, he'd lost his taste for whatever food Maria had fixed, and he'd been chewing Clovis out for imagined mistakes. If he didn't resolve his own problem soon, he wasn't going to have anything to go back to.

If he didn't resolve his problem soon, he wouldn't care.

It was exactly as it had been that first afternoon. Alabaster flicked his ears and whuffled. Jake saw the red four-wheel vehicle parked alongside the cabin. And then, like a gift being opened, he turned his horse toward the cabin to find Amanda standing in the doorway.

She wore a dark gray cable sweater and cream slacks, and her hair was gleaming with its midnight sun. Jake felt the desire slam through him. He clenched the reins in his hand, afraid of losing control, of completely coming apart out there in the middle of the field.

"This is private property," he taunted, knowing damn well that his voice was too harsh. He couldn't help it. His hands shook. His belly was on fire. He wanted her so badly that if he weren't careful, he'd take her right there in the doorway.

She smiled and he was lost. "I know," she answered his greeting, leaning against the doorway, coffee cup in her hand. "I figured I'd negotiate with the owner to stay just a little while longer."

"Negotiate?"

He brought Alabaster to a halt at the porch, but couldn't dismount. He couldn't move or he'd give himself away.

Amanda stepped forward and rubbed a gentle hand over the horse's nose, her gaze never straying from Jake's. "Yeah," she answered, her voice slowing, thickening like warm honey. "I thought I'd invite him in where we could get comfortable. And we could talk a little, and maybe share something to drink...."

Jake managed to raise an eyebrow. "Are you talking bribes here, young woman?"

Her smile widened and her eyes darkened. "If that's what you want to call it. Did you know that there's a big, soft down comforter on this bed, too?"

Jake never remembered swinging from the saddle. He didn't remember whether he tied up Alabaster or how he got inside the door without spilling the coffee in Amanda's cup. All he remembered was walking into her arms, and then the world was lost.

She was right. There was a down comforter on the bed, but they didn't use that one, either. They didn't even make it as far as the bed before Amanda lost her sweater and Jake his hat, jacket and shirt. They stood, entangled in each other, starving for union, desperate for the life they'd only found in each other's arms. Gasps gathered into moans and crescendoed into words, repeated words, names, each other's names, endearments, silly and sweet and harsh, cries of surprise and sighs of satisfaction.

She was life in his hands, writhing, dancing, singing. She was the deepest of nights, with her dark whispers of passion, and the hottest of suns, scattered over him by her clever hands. Jake ravaged her mouth. He praised her skin and revealed her mysteries. Her body, so familiar to him, so completely new, urged him on. When he didn't disrobe her quickly enough, she pulled her undershirt up over her own head with shaking hands. Jake caught her there, trapping her hands over her head, bending to capture her mouth, her throat, her taut, high breasts in his hungry mouth. He undid her slacks one-handed and slid them from her hips, still not letting her help, demanding her satisfaction before she took his.

Lifting her against a chest that forgot to protest, he carried her to the bed and fell into it with her, the springs creaking welcome, the sunlight showering them in their private world. He kissed her, plundered her. He teased her into agony with his hands, never letting her go, consumed her with his mouth, the taste of her salty, soft skin driving him wild. The nub of her nipples between his teeth, against his tongue, torturing him.

She bucked against him, arched against him, rubbing against his chest and belly like a cat, moaning incoherently, her eyes wide, her lips parted. She begged him home with her whimpers and her body, but Jake still wanted more. He swept away her panties, those useful cotton slips of nothing, and tasted her excitement. He dipped, plunged, sipped, until she cried out, again and again, her helpless hands freed against him, her hair spilling over the bed, her back arched. She tugged at him, pleaded, wept. And Jake, knowing he couldn't wait any longer, finally let her have her way.

Amanda was splintering, her body a shower of light and sound, shuddering, spinning, shivering with urgency. She felt Jake slide up alongside her and took her own kisses. She claimed her own territory with hands that curled into hair and traced muscle and tendon, that tormented, slipping in beneath the taut material of his jeans and hinting at the pleasure she could give. His groan was harsh against her, his hands abrupt. Amanda smiled, captured that groan with her mouth and then began her real torment.

Rubbing, rubbing, a cat in the sun, her body desperate for the hair-roughened contact of his, she fumbled with his belt. Fumbled more with the zipper, until his throat rumbled with protest. And then she tasted that, bent to take his nipple in her mouth and tease it to the same attention as hers. She pushed his jeans down and away, his shorts, and had him to herself. And just when he was beginning to take her shoulders in hand, she pulled away and took her own taste.

His cry was guttural. Her hands refused to still. He writhed just the way she had, and it made her smile. Boots cracked against the wall and denim shuddered to the floor. And Amanda, suddenly powerful in a way she'd never known, eased herself down onto Jake. He took her breasts in his callused, rough hands. He panted, his eyes dilated and deep. Amanda rocked. She filled herself full with him, deep and hard and hot, and she tormented him yet more. And, suddenly, she was the one tormented. She was rocking faster, and the shudders of pleasure, of unbearable fire, caught up with her. She opened her mouth, startled that it could happen again so quickly, so intensely, and then cried out, overtaken, overwhelmed. Jake clutched at her shoulders, pulled her down to him, and rasped out her name, again and again, shuddering to silence.

Finally, when the sweet inertia ebbed a little, Amanda was caught by a bubbling delight. Still in Jake's arms, both of them slick and spent, she found herself giggling.

Jake moved his head around a little. "Something wrong?"

She tried to shake hers, only to bump into his chin. "It just seems like we never say hello anymore."

She could feel his answering chuckle rumble in his chest. "Hello, Amanda."

"Hello, Jake."

They managed finally to find their way beneath the comforter. "You're an addiction," he protested, stroking her hair.

She squeezed her eyes shut. "I missed you."

"Me, too."

"Does this mean we do it my way?"

Another stifled chuckle. "I think we just did."

She gave him a cuff on the chest. "I'm serious, Jake. I've been miserable ever since Betty walked back in that house and we didn't have any time together."

"I'll fire her."

"You can't."

"You can work for me, instead."

"No, thanks," she demurred. "I'd make you go to computers, and then you'd have to just fire me, too."

"Did you get your new one?"

She nodded, soaking in the steady cadence of his heart against her cheek. Burrowing more deeply into the soft comfort of his shoulder. "The other one was a computerpop. So I got a fancier one, and it does everything but cook my breakfast."

He stretched a little. "Not a bad idea."

"Breakfast? It's almost noon. Haven't you eaten yet?"

"Probably before you were awake. But it's time for lunch now. What do you have stashed away for a hungry rancher?"

She couldn't help another giggle. Jake tousled her hair. "Besides that."

Amanda managed to crawl out of bed and even locate her old robe while Jake pulled on his jeans. The two of them padded together over to the kitchen, sated and lazy and smiling.

"I'm really glad you thought to keep this cabin here," she admitted with a shy smile, the surprise of their passion still hot in her chest.

Jake's grin was much more rakish. "It does come in handy sometimes."

Amanda abruptly straightened from where she'd been bent over the refrigerator checking contents. "Have you used this place before? To, uh . . ."

"Tryst?" he teased, sidling up beside her and slipping his hands around her waist. "What do you think?"

Amanda bent back to her perusal in just such a way that her backside came in correct contact to elicit a delighted moan from Jake. "I think that you were probably the kind of teenager who never made it further than the seat of your daddy's pickup truck. And that as a man you were too all-fired responsible to ever bring a woman around with young kids in the house."

Sneaking a quick glance around behind her, she was delighted to see Jake's chagrin.

"Bingo," she crowed.

"You think you're so smart," he taunted, running his hands down the robe where it draped over her thighs.

She immediately hit her head on the refrigerator. "Stop that. I'm cooking."

"I'll say."

Straightening, she shoved eggs, butter, cream and ham into Jake's hands. "I've had a craving for eggs Benedict," she announced, walking on by.

Jake stared at her. "Here?"

Amanda made it a point to look around. "Well, I prefer them over the open fire, but I guess this'll have to do."

They bantered like an old couple, teasing and laughing, the ranch and the world a great high meadow away. For at least now, the two of them were caught in a bubble of contentment, pretending that they were the only two who existed, for just this moment in time when nothing could touch them.

Amanda left Jake baby-sitting the poaching eggs as she cleaned off her mess from the little kitchen table. She was gathering together the ranch material when she noticed a square of paper she'd been using as a bookmark. It made her laugh.

Jake looked up. "What's so funny?"

Amanda picked up the little paper, bright with scrawled flowers and letters, a crudely made card Lee had drawn for Jake on his birthday years ago. "To the best, best, best, best big brother in the world," it read. Then, after some consideration, evidently, she'd scratched out one of the bests. Amanda handed it over without thinking.

"I found this in with the papers Betty gave me," she said, already piling more books together. "You really must have done something to make her mad."

She hadn't thought. She'd been so lulled by the surprise of Jake's arrival, the whirlwind of their lovemaking, the soft laughter of companionship. She'd given him the card instinctively. When she lifted her attention back to him for an answer, she saw him consider it.

"I don't remember what," was all he said, his voice suddenly lifeless. But Amanda saw the way he looked at the card. Flat, unseeing. And when she turned away to carry the books to the couch, to give him room for the privacy suddenly she knew he needed, she saw the way he rubbed that card, like a talisman in his hands. She saw the bittersweet longing in his eyes which she could never salve for him, and her heart stumbled with terrible comprehension.

Because at that moment Amanda knew. She had her answer. Jake didn't know how to respond to her. He didn't know, because he didn't know what the card said. Jake couldn't read it.

Chapter 12

Amanda didn't know what to do. She should have walked back into the kitchen and asked him for the truth. She should confront him with it so that they could get it out in the open and get past it.

But suddenly, facing it, naming it, she was afraid of it. Jake had spent his entire life maintaining a lie, a crippling, debilitating lie that kept him at arm's length even from the people he loved the most in the world. She'd just seen the pain in his eyes. She knew how much he loved Lee. She could only imagine what it would have meant to him to read her sentiments to him, to carry them away with him somewhere and not have to share them with anyone. She knew what he'd lost, what he'd forfeited.

But she knew that right now she couldn't face him with her knowledge. Not when the anger and sympathy battled in her for him. Not when it would show so plainly in her expression that it would drive him away. It had happened once before. She couldn't let it again. She couldn't.

"Hey, what about these eggs?" he demanded from the kitchen, only the slightest edge to his voice giving him away.

Amanda fought the rush of frustration, the urge to salve that pain that had been accumulating for all these years. She had to step carefully now, and this would be the first one.

Until she knew what to do.

Until she had the courage to do it.

"Just what I like to see," she retorted with a too-bright grin as she turned back for the kitchen, "a seminaked man in my kitchen."

Jake turned on her, outraged. "You don't mean that *you* use this cabin as a place for a . . ."

"Tryst?" she countered, sidling up to slip her arms around his bare chest, seeing the dark residue in his eyes and hurting for him. "You betcha, buddy. And I plan on continuing that, too...if I can find a rancher who will take time out of his busy day, that is."

"Only if you keep feeding me lunch."

"Watch it, big boy. I know where those broken ribs are, and I know how to hurt them."

"So do I," he said. "You made me get on a horse and ride you through the snow."

Amanda gave him a quick punch to prove her point. He grunted agreeably and then dropped a kiss on her forehead. "Explain this to me," he begged, wrapping his arms around her in return. "I haven't taken time off from the ranch since I was in the hospital the time Alabaster broke my leg. And yet, here I am, in the middle of a work day, with my shoes off, making eggs Benedict, and I can't seem to want to go back to fixing fences."

"Sounds to me," she offered lazily, hoping the staccato of her heart didn't give her away, "like you're falling in love."

"I'll let you know," Jake informed her with another, longer kiss that involved some sighs, "after I've eaten the eggs Benedict."

She really gave him a smack for that one. They ended up having to poach more eggs.

Amanda had no one to go to. No friend who would keep her confidence, no mentor to share sage counsel. She was two thousand miles from her resources, and caught in a town that would broadcast any and all attempts she made for help.

So the next day, instead of bringing her books back to the table, she climbed into the car and visited Pinedale, a town a good distance away. It took her most of the day just to track down the literacy resource group there. She returned the following day to update her information so that when she finally faced Jake with his secret, she could do it armed with the most current literature, the best outlook.

Amanda knew better, though. Reading was tough enough when you were seven, and everybody was learning at the same time. It was quite another when you were a grown man, struggling to comprehend something most people by then take for granted. It was the solution as much as the problem that battered at a man's pride, and that was the only answer she had to give Jake. Even knowing that learning to read would be the logical answer, Amanda knew she had an uphill battle to get Jake to do it.

At first she was angry. At Jake, at his parents, at his family. How could a man so intelligent, so driven and quick, not demand the right to read? How could he just accept his handicap as a failing and leave it at that? Amanda had been brought up in a worse environment than Jake had, but she'd made it. She'd attacked school like a holy mission, had seen books as the magic carpet out of a house where chickens scratched at the door and old cars lay in pieces out in the yard.

But Amanda had been given the chance to go to school. Her parents had struggled hard to give her that, if they couldn't give anything else to her and her brother. It had gotten her away. For William Paul, the mines had gotten him first.

It was the gift Jake had given his family. A gift he'd given at his own expense, pushing them through their schooling by sheer willpower, sometimes. Nagging, demanding, encouraging. And all the while left behind by the very gift he was giving. Because to give them the chance to stay together, to stay in school and escape the grinding poverty that was all his father had been able to leave him, he'd forfeited his own chance at freedom.

Not freedom from the ranch. Amanda truly believed that Jake Kendall would wither up and die any place other than the

Wyoming mountains where his horses grazed the meadows and the mountains crowded the sky. But the freedom to dream, to ever step beyond the tiny, controlled world he'd created and then finally become imprisoned in.

Jake's way. Everybody said it, but nobody really understood it. And that made Amanda angriest of all.

She had to get him away from the ranch to talk to him. And she had to do it before Lee came home. She wasn't looking forward to it.

The card. That stupid, silly little card he hadn't seen in years. Jake shook just thinking about it, the crinkle of that paper in his hands, the bright smudges of colors Lee had collected into flowers. The silly sentiment he'd made her read to him, because she knew he liked her to read as much as possible. Just to learn. To learn to read well so that she could do whatever she'd wanted in the world.

He could still hear her reedy little voice, caught between defiance, assurance and fear. Reading her own words, and then carefully explaining to him that she'd had to scratch out one of the bests because he hadn't allowed her to have her very own cat in the house. Not a barn cat, she'd explained, that ate mice and moved too fast to catch. A nice, fat tabby that would give her hugs when Jake wouldn't.

He heard the words again, heard his own gruff laughter at his sister's logic. But he'd never been able to have those words to himself. Never once, in all the years the kids had written, Gen from med school, Zeke from the sites, and now, Lee, his baby sister, so far away he couldn't ever think of visiting her, and it had been Betty who'd heard about her loneliness first, her sense of disorientation in the big city, her homesickness. It had been Betty who had smiled first, like a caregiver seeing a child's first steps.

Jake was jealous. He was sick at heart. He was so tired of it all, so much more alone. Because now Amanda was here, and he was kept from her, too.

He'd seen her handwriting on the yellow tablet on the table, quick, strong strokes with an ink pen. He'd seen the way she'd dealt with the computer, an old friend, an easy tool, and felt foolish that he couldn't even get one to start up.

He wanted his situation to change. He ached to see those places Amanda had talked about. He wanted to share the world with Amanda and then be able to come home and take charge of his own business. He wanted the chance to ride his own horses in competition.

But he knew better. And that was what followed him through the day and slept with him in the night. That was the only companionship he'd be allowed, and the pain of it was fresh and sour all over again.

He didn't hear from Amanda for three more days. He'd been up to the meadow again to find Sweet William grazing and the red car gone, and returned to work even harder, sensing already somehow that she was moving away. Afraid she was. He knew it was coming. He just couldn't stand the thought that it was coming so soon.

Not till Lee leaves, anyway, he rationalized. She'd at least stay to visit Lee.

Jake spent his days as he always did in the spring, working with the new foals, easing them into their working relationship with humans, sharpening the older horses after the lethargy of winter, opening the training back out into the fresh air where it belonged after those months in the indoor ring. He spent too much time on horseback for his ribs to heal quickly, but it didn't matter. He spent too many hours outside to do anything but drop into a dead sleep when he got home, but that was the only way he'd rest. Clovis and José trained more horses than usual, and this year he let Willy begin. But this year his heart wasn't into it.

"Boss," Clovis announced, leaning over the fence to the corral where Jake was working Sidewinder on a lungeing line. "Why don't you go ahead and knock off early? We're all goin' into town tonight. Horses is all fed and bedded down."

Jake barely looked away from his work. "Yeah, Clovis. Okay."

"No, boss," his hand insisted. "I mean it. You're gettin' that raggedy look about you again, and you've been a mite... peevish lately. What with Lee comin' in a couple o' days, you might think to ease up a little so's you don't snap the little thing's head off.''

Jake actually worked up a grin for his foreman. "Peevish, is it?" he retorted.

"If you'da'yelled at anybody but Betty this afternoon, she might have taken real offense."

Clovis was right. Jake had no business taking this out on the people who worked for him. He had a lot of failings, but being hard on the help wasn't one of them.

"Okay, Clovis," he conceded, actually slumping with the weariness of it. "Let me put Sidewinder up and I'll close shop for the day."

"Good." The little man stepped down. "By the way, I'll betchya if you ask Sweetpea real nice tomorrow she might let Grayboy come callin'."

Jake really did grin at that. The thought of that majestic act reduced to candy and flowers was enough to brighten anybody's day. "I'll give her the good news," he assured the man.

Jake hoped Maria had left something for him to eat. With everybody else in town for the evening, she wouldn't have to worry about feeding them. He probably should apologize to Betty, too, while he was at it. He shouldn't have ridden her case for short-ordering the feed. It was the feed store's fault, not hers. Besides, he knew better than to think he could run the ranch without her after all this time. If it weren't for Betty, nothing would get done. For yet the hundredth time, Jake wondered if she knew. If she guessed. He'd never had the courage to find out. He didn't now.

Betty was gone. Maria was gone. Jake took a bemused look around as he stepped back out of the stallion barn to find that the only cars remaining were his pickup and the four-wheel drive he used when he didn't feel like climbing a horse.

He looked up to the house and got more confused. Had the electricity failed again? There were a few dim lights up there, but they flickered, just like lanterns or candles. Jake took a quick look over his shoulder, but the yard lights were still on. For just a second, his heart lurched. Anticipation sweated his palms. Could there be somebody in the house, after all?

Somebody who'd lit candles deliberately? He loped up to the back door without another thought.

Again he was greeted by a banquet of aromas—wood smoke and food. These food smells were different, though, alien and piquant. Not stew, not steak, not any of the food groups he recognized. Hanging up his jacket, Jake peeked around into the kitchen.

"Ever had Chinese food?" she greeted him with a broad smile.

Jake stepped in, his pulse racing at the sight of her, his gut suddenly on fire, with dread, with hope, with all the warring emotions a man battles when he knows he's falling in love. More when the man knows that it won't do him any good.

"Chinese?" he echoed a bit stupidly.

Amanda was standing over by the stove where she had piles of chopped-up food waiting to go into the skillet. Garlic. That was what Jake smelled. Garlic, spices, exotic, enticing aromas. And soft, dancing amid them, the smell of spring.

Amanda nodded, and her hair drifted like smoke. "Chinese. I thought I'd start with something simple. Beef with broccoli, cashew chicken, maybe some fried rice. What do you think?"

He thought he'd rather forget the food and concentrate on her. She was in a dress tonight. Suddenly he realized that it was the first time he'd seen her in a dress, a soft, simple dress the color of an autumn evening sky, that clung to her just the way that damn cotton T-shirt had, and revealed almost as much leg as those panties. He was already beginning to ache, and he hadn't even got his hat off yet.

"Hello, Amanda," he managed.

Her sudden smile was like a starburst. "Hello, Jake. Take off your hat and stick around a while." Then she quirked an eyebrow at him. "Unless you're looking for a sandstorm."

Slowly he palmed his hat and lifted it off. "Chinese," he murmured yet again, dragging a hand through his hair to force it back. "I've never had Chinese food before."

Amanda just nodded and went back to the food. "That's what I figured. I think you'll like it. I'm still chopping here, so I think you'll have time for a shower if you want before we eat."

Jake felt awkward and foolish. Blind-sided. He stood stock-still in the kitchen doorway, his hat in his hand, only knowing that Amanda was quickly driving him to distraction, and that he couldn't keep up with her.

"How'd you do it?" he demanded.

Amanda looked over her shoulder. "You mean how did I manage to clear the entire ranch of people so we could be alone tonight? Not an easy thing to do by any means. But it seems as if you've been a mite testy the last few days. Everybody thought it would be a great idea if I could somehow see my way to...getting you into a better mood."

Jake's eyes flew open. "They said that?"

Amanda chuckled. "Betty? Be serious. She didn't say anything more than 'tell him he doesn't deserve you.' Have you been cranky with her?"

Jake nodded his head before he realized it. "I was coming up to apologize when I saw the lights...by the way, where are they?"

He got another smile for that, a smile full of memory and promise. "I kind of liked the atmosphere better before. More intimate, don't you think?"

There was one Coleman kerosene lantern on the counter. Everywhere else the light was provided by firelight and candlelight. The house shuddered with it, undulated with it, a sensuous, soft light that seemed to melt reality. It made Jake's mouth water and his belly ache.

"I'll take that shower now," he suggested, realizing that he was starting to wring the brim of his hat the way Clovis did. Turning on his heel, he hung it up out of the way before he started chewing on it, too. "Unless you'd like to join me."

The thud-thud of the cleaver slowed noticeably, but refused to stop. "This is all timed," she demurred. "But don't use up all the hot water. We might see our way back in later."

Jake choked down images and fantasies and took himself off before he lifted her right onto the counter and ruined that pretty dress of hers.

Amanda listened to Jake's boots echo on the hardwood floor. She waited for them to diminish toward his bedroom, waited for the door to close. Then, shuddering, she dropped the cleaver and shut her eyes.

She wasn't going to be able to do it. She was going to approach him wrong, state her case badly, break his heart.

She *was* going to break his heart. There was no other way to let him know he wasn't alone. She just prayed that she wouldn't shove him so far away that he wouldn't let her share.

"You shouldn't teach him," the counselor in Pinedale had told her. "The stress is too great for people in a relationship. The frustration levels are particularly high. You don't need him blaming you if he can't manage as quickly as he'd like."

But they hadn't found an alternative. The towns within a negotiable distance that had programs also had close business ties with the Diamond K, and so far the counselor hadn't found any viable alternatives. Jake's best chance to learn would be with a one-on-one tutor, someone to badger and bully and encourage him the way he had his siblings. And all the best information prevented Amanda from being that tutor, which meant that more people would have to know. And how many, to Jake Kendall, would be too many people?

Maybe just one. Maybe just her.

Amanda timed it to the minute. She was pulling the cashew chicken off the stove when she heard Jake return. The other food waited out on the table, and she'd opened the bottle of plum wine she'd bought. Maybe he didn't like red wine, but there were few things more delectable to her than a good plum wine with Chinese food.

"It smells . . . interesting," he allowed.

Amanda set out the dish and turned to greet him. Her words died in her throat. He stood in the door like a young man on his first date, uncomfortable and stiff. He had jeans on, and they looked brand-new enough to cause a rash. Over those he'd worn a sweater that one of the kids must have bought him and he'd left in his room rather than insult them by giving it away. He obviously thought it looked ridiculous because it had been knitted in shades of teal blues and cream. Not a man's sweater at all, she could almost hear him say. What he hadn't realized was that he could wear a ruffled nightgown and bunny slippers and still look like a man.

The thick, soft sweater was devastating on him, V-necked enough that Amanda got a hint of the delicious dark gold hair that she loved to finger on his chest, and just the colors to bring out the startling blue of his eyes. He'd shaved, and his hair was still wet, clinging in soft waves to the back of his neck. It was all Amanda could do to keep her hands off him.

"My God," she gasped with coy surprise. "You own something that doesn't have flannel or goose feathers?"

Jake's scowl was impressive. "You got dressed up. It was the least I could do."

Amanda smiled for him. "I got dressed up to seduce you, Jake. You did that in a down vest and boots." She held up a hand. "But don't change again on my account. I think I could really get used to you in sweaters."

That didn't seem to ease his discomfort any. Amanda went right to plan two and walked up to him. Lifting her face to his, her body insinuating itself against the cloud-soft sweater and the rasp of jeans, she gave him a welcome kiss that noticeably changed the configuration of those jeans. And then, before either of them could do anything about it, she stepped out of Jake's reach.

"Let's eat," she suggested.

Jake's eyes were as dark as night. "My idea exactly..."

She spun out of his way and headed back to the table. "Come on, Jake. I want to see what you think of my cooking."

She heard his impatient growl and ignored it, wishing her hands weren't clammy, that she had a better plan than show him what he was missing and then wing it. Praying that love would be enough to help them beyond the revelation and all the pain it would unleash.

"I told you I didn't drink wine," he protested when she poured him a glass a few minutes later to go with his food.

"Just try it," she insisted. "It's the perfect thing to drink with this."

"Amanda—"

"How are you ever going to know if you like something if you don't try it?" she insisted, just a little too sharply.

Jake lifted an eyebrow at her. "This stuff must be real important to you."

Amanda did her best to offset her tension with a playful scowl. "Chinese food is my life. Now, come on and try it."

"You're sure you're not trying to poison me?" he demanded, picking through the vegetables on his plate.

"I'm trying to teach you that there's more to life than steak at Stilwell's and stew in the kitchen."

Jake shot her a glare. "And just what good is that going to do me?" he demanded. "Last I saw there weren't any Chinese restaurants in Lost Ridge."

She held her breath, praying for patience, for insight. "But there are in San Francisco. You can smell them when you ride the cable car. Chinese food, fresh air, salt water and flowers. I'll tell you something. San Francisco is the best-smelling city in the world."

"And you want me to go there."

She smiled, her hands clenched in her lap. "I just don't want you to count it completely out. Try the Chinese food, Jake. Maybe next week I'll make you veal scaloppine or coq au vin."

"Next week? How long were you planning on staying?"

The room crackled with unspoken questions, with demands and pleas and questions. Amanda answered them. "I don't know," she admitted, casting a quick glance down at her plate. "I have quite a lot of dishes I'd like to try out on you. And I'm going to be taking a class in Thai cooking this summer. I could be here for quite a while."

"Thai cooking? What the hell's that?"

She looked up at him, grinned. "Do you like peanut butter?"

She could see the bemusement, saw the humor struggle to break through, saw the crust of discipline that covered desperation.

"Yeah," he finally admitted. "Why?"

She nodded. "Then you'll love Thai food. And Indonesian, come to think of it. Now, try this before it gets cold."

He did. Amanda held her breath, held her place, not sure what she wanted, knowing that if Jake did like it, if he had been dreaming of trying it just once in his life, she was torturing him. Hating it, knowing she'd do it again if it didn't work this time.

His eyes lit, a dark, private fire smoldering way inside him. He didn't say a word for ten minutes, tasting one dish, then another, then the wine, his concentration centered on his meal as if he were the first man to test uncharted waters, as if his perceptions of it would have to be carried back to an unknowing world.

He never noticed that Amanda barely touched her food.

Finally he lifted his gaze back to hers, and Amanda saw the full weight of what she'd done to him.

"New York has great Chinese restaurants, too," she told him, her voice small, her fingers clenched around the stem of her nearly empty wineglass. "And Italian and French and Spanish."

"Does New York smell great, too?" he challenged wryly.

Amanda couldn't help but grin. "No. But it's . . . there's an energy there, a rocketing, pulse-pounding life that you won't find anywhere else on earth."

"You really like it."

She shrugged. "I'd like to go there sometime when I'm not alone. There's so much to share. . . ."

Jake's eyes betrayed him, just briefly, when the pain seared them, tightened them. When, for just a heartbeat, he let her know how much he wanted that, too. But he retreated too quickly to catch.

"It's not going to work," he told her, setting his utensils down.

Amanda tried not to stumble over the sick dread in her stomach. "What?" she asked. "You don't like it?"

But Jake was already shaking his head. "There's more to it than Chinese food and New York, Amanda, and you damn well know it. Don't you understand yet? I can't give you the life you want."

Amanda's heart threatened to stop. "Who says?"

He glared at her, his armor thick, his anger old. "Are you prepared to spend your life with a man who can't talk about any more than a horse's bloodline? Who hasn't been out of town in five years, even to see his own sisters and brother? Who wouldn't be able to go with you to your award ceremonies or sit in your classes or even stand up with you at a party of people who are important to you? You might fit into my life, Amanda, but I don't fit into yours."

"I want you there, Jake."

The chair scraped in protest as Jake lurched to his feet. "But I don't belong there," he insisted, tall, rigid, threatening. "I'm a rancher, damn it, not some literary critic. Just what do you think would happen when you try and tell me all about the plays you saw, or the books you read or the research you were doing? Do you think I could really talk to you about those? Do you think I'd even know what the hell you were talking about?"

"A step at a time," she begged, hands on the table, desperate to stand, knowing her legs wouldn't hold her. Terrified of the next few minutes. "Please, Jake. Just don't say no."

"What do you want me to say?" he demanded, and she heard the raw ache in his voice. "That I'd be happy embarrassing you for the rest of your life?"

That *did* bring her to her feet. "Embarrassing me?" she retorted, sincerely outraged. "Jake Kendall, I never want to hear that from you as long as you live."

"Look at me," he challenged, the bowls on the table clinking at his sudden movement. "I don't own a suit, Amanda. I've never owned a pair of shoes that didn't have pointed toes and heels for riding. I drive around in a fifteen-year-old pickup truck with a gun rack in the back."

"I don't care."

"Well, I do!"

That was when Amanda knew there was no turning back. Jake pulled away from the table and stalked off, and she knew he was hiding from her. Hiding the shame he'd hidden for so long. Hiding the truth that he thought she couldn't bear. She followed right after him, her heels clicking on the hardwood floor, her heart slamming into her ribs.

"Answer me one question," she said, both of them faltering to a stop by the fireplace, where the molten light softened
the stark emptiness of a room decorated in denial.

He refused to turn to her. She kept her distance, the sight of
his taut, dark features tearing at her.

"What?"

And so she asked, "Do you love me?"

For a moment, silence held suspended between them. The
world slowed to an uneasy pause, the air in the house heavy and
still, the fire the only punctuation. Amanda could barely hear
it for the blood rushing in her ears.

And then, Jake answered. "Yes," he said, the raw torment
in his voice more answer than his words. "I love you,
Amanda."

She should have wilted with relief. The tension still mounted,
inexorably, stifling her, stealing her air. "Then sit down with me
for a minute. I have a confession to make."

Jake turned on her, his hard eyes gleaming oddly in the half
light, his jaw hard enough to shatter a glass. Amanda reached
out a hand to that jaw, tested its strength, its defiance. To for-
tify herself on the hard, proud life it protected.

"Please," she asked again, gently, simply.

He surrendered to her plea and lifted a hand to hers. His
hand trembled, too. His heart thundered just as hard. Amanda
thought her heart would break now, even before she did what
she'd come to do. She didn't have the strength for this, not
again, not with this man who was the sum and total of a well-
deserved pride.

They sat together on the couch, Jake still silent and formal,
Amanda folded into herself, trying to gather her courage.

"I found your magazines," she said, not quite brave enough
to face him. "The ones you hide in your room."

The silence shifted, chilled. Amanda wanted to shut her eyes
from it. From him.

"So?"

She took a breath. "You remember my telling you about how
much you remind me of my Uncle Mick?" she asked. "Well,
Uncle Mick used to keep magazines. *National Geographic*s. He

loved to look at the pictures of the world, places he knew he'd never see. He said that it was going to be the best he could manage. He kept those magazines like a prized collection in a gallery, and knew just what pictures were in each one. I'd walk into his house and find him fingering those pictures like he could transport himself there just by touching them.''

Amanda fought the words, the poignancy of old memories, the fear of a tenuous future. She curled her hands in her lap, holding on to her purpose like a gift clasped in sweaty palms for a very special guest. And then, because she knew she had to, she turned to face Jake with the rest.

"Uncle Mick used to have me do his writing for him. Applications, letters, things like that. He said he had terrible handwriting, and if you ever saw his signature, you'd believe it. He couldn't read from a book to me because his eyes were bad and he just kept forgetting to get in to town to get glasses. Uncle Mick never went anywhere," she said, seeing the dawning apprehension in Jake's eyes and dying even before, "not even into Wheeling, because he said that crowds bothered him." Jake knew what she was going to say before she said it. Amanda said it, anyway. "I was fifteen before I realized that the reason he'd never gone anywhere was because he couldn't read the street signs. He was trapped in a little town of a hundred people, on a farm where he couldn't raise anything, by a problem he was too ashamed to admit."

Jake's facade was crumbling, and beneath it Amanda saw the most terrible grief, a raw, frightened kind of shame she'd never known, even walking into class that first day at university with her secondhand dress and West Virginia accent. Desperate to reach out to him, to let him know how she felt, still Amanda held herself apart, knowing that that more than anything else in the world would shove him away.

"Nobody knows," she said, her voice soft. "Do they?"

She held her breath for reprieve, and in the end, got none. Jake's eyes iced over and his voice carried her sentence. "That I'm illiterate? No, Amanda. Nobody knows. Now, if you're quite finished, I think it's time to go."

Chapter 13

Jake had nowhere to run. Still, he ran. He climbed off the couch, leaving Amanda silent and alone, and walked to the kitchen and began flipping on the lights and cleaning up the dishes.

It was a funny thing. A long time ago, back when he'd still dreamed about things like that, he'd dreamed that someone would come along and discover what he'd been hiding, would magically know somehow that he couldn't read. They would come to him and tell him, and suddenly it would be all better. He wouldn't be alone anymore. He wouldn't be the only one who knew that he couldn't read a dinner menu or a street sign or even the silly notes his little sisters wrote to him on the bathroom mirror in soap. And it wouldn't hurt so much anymore.

How wrong he'd been. It didn't hurt as much. It hurt more. It hurt so much he didn't think he could breathe past it. He didn't think he'd be able to get to sleep tonight or wake up in the morning or face any of the people he'd see.

He'd been wrong. He was more alone now than he'd ever been in his life.

"Jake, don't do this," Amanda whispered behind him. "Please."

Jake didn't answer. He collected the used dishes from the table, the delicious aromas taunting him, and carried them to the sink to get rid of them. To purge himself of them, of her, of the soft pain in her voice when she'd faced him.

Squeezing his eyes shut, Jake dropped the dishes in the sink. He couldn't face her again, couldn't seek those gentle green eyes for his peace. Because, now, all he'd find there was pity.

He supposed he heard the clicking of her heels behind him. He didn't pay attention. Gathering up another load with hands that shook like he had the ague, he toppled them into the sink and began to run the water.

But suddenly she was standing before him, glowing like a Madonna in the harsh kitchen light, tears coursing down her face. And that was what shattered his pride.

"Go on back," he rasped at her, the shame dragging him down, breaking him. Of all the people in the world he hadn't wanted to be exposed to before, it had been Amanda. And now, in her eloquent eyes, he saw why. "Go back to your ivory towers and your theories and fairy tales, little girl. I have a ranch to run."

"Why?" she demanded, standing up to him, standing right in front of him so he couldn't escape. "Why are you running away?"

Jake's smile was hardly congenial. "I'm not," he assured her. "I'm going back to where I belong. I suggest you do the same."

He managed to turn away from her, so he could scrape the rest of the food down the sink. Pungent and delicate and delicious, tastes he'd never experienced, forbidden fruit. Just like Amanda. Exactly like Amanda.

"Just like that?" she demanded, pulling on his arm, trying to make him face her. "'Oh, well, Amanda, there's nothing we can do now, I can't read and you can, and so there's nothing more for us here?'"

He spun on her, making her flinch. "What would you like me to do, Amanda? Would you like me to ask Lee, or Gen or Zeke? My family who all have college degrees? Would you like me to tell them that I can't even read their damn letters? Would you like me to head on in to Lost Ridge and ask around about where I can learn to read? There are two hundred and twenty-seven people living there, and I do business with the majority of them. I've built a reputation on trust and honor and the strength of my word, just like you said. I've managed to earn a certain amount of respect in the area, because I know what I'm doing and I've never, ever lied to anyone. So, how do you think those people would react if they knew I'd been lying to them all along? What do you think they'd think if they found out I couldn't even read the bill of sale I was handing them with their horse?''

"They're your neighbors, Jake," she protested. "Not your enemies. Besides, who needs to know?"

"It's a small town, Amanda. You tell me."

He turned again, desperate to be free of her, to be alone again with the cancer that ate at him, wishing she'd never seen it and reacted.

"I can find out for you," she offered. "Go someplace you don't live, someplace they don't know you—"

"No!" he roared, his fury pushing her back. "I'll be damned if I'm going to let you do something like that."

"You didn't believe me, then," she said behind him. "You didn't think I meant it when I said I'd love you no matter what."

His hand was on the door. He was only a few steps from escaping, from running out and getting in the car and flying over the dark roads until he couldn't see those eyes again. But her words gnawed at him. He had to know. Like picking at a sore, he wanted the worst of it.

"Just when did you find out?" he asked, and then turned again. She'd never moved, never thought to shy away from him. It shuddered through him. He didn't know what to do anymore. He didn't know where to go from here. "How did you know?" he demanded. "Nobody's ever known. Nobody's even suspected."

Her smile was so sad that Jake damn near reached out to her. "Little things. Familiar things. I wouldn't have guessed, either, if it hadn't been for Uncle Mick. You remind me so much of him."

"And I suppose you taught him to read and he lived happily ever after."

Her eyes were huge and dark and hollow. "No," she admitted. "He wouldn't let me. He said it shamed him too much. He never left that little world. Never stopped looking at the pictures in *National Geographic*. He died not knowing how to read the stories he'd been telling all those years."

The truth of it speared through Jake like lightning. Sharp and devastating, impaling him on the future, on the years alone, piling up like so much dead wood until it all toppled from the weight. Closing himself further and further away, from his friends, from his family. Closing himself off forever from Amanda.

"You did this on purpose tonight, then," he accused, gesturing to the debris in the sink. "You decided to whet my appetite a little and see if it would pay off."

Amanda straightened before him, her slim, small body as taut as a violin string. "Yes," she admitted. "I wanted you to know that it's out there for you. It's all possible, everything you've ever dreamed, wanted, hoped for. And I wanted you to know that I won't give up. I'm not letting you loose until you know that."

"No," he retorted, walking right up to her, towering over her, doing his best to intimidate her. "No, Amanda, no. It's too late. It has been for years. I'm not telling my family and I'm not telling my friends just so you'll feel better. I'm doing fine the way I am, and that's the way it's going to stay."

"Are you?"

"Am I what?"

"Doing fine. You work yourself into exhaustion with your horses because it's the only thing you think you can do. You can't go visit your family and you can't date anybody for fear that they'll find out. You can't read a paper or a book, and I have the feeling that you've never even seen Grayboy compete because you're afraid of being lost in a strange town. Are you fine, Jake?"

"Don't, Amanda," he commanded, knowing he was teetering on the edge and hating her for it. Hating himself more than he ever had, even with all the practice he'd had. "Don't push."

"What else am I supposed to do?" she asked, hands clenched and white, her face so drawn Jake wanted to help her somehow. "I love you. I know what you're going through, and I want to help you do something about it."

He took her by the shoulders, fought the urge to shake her, to drag her to him and kiss her senseless, to take her back to that bed one last time and pretend she'd never found out and it could still be the way it was the last time.

"It had to be you," he said, dying in pieces with the feel of her in his hands, with the sight of those liquid green eyes. "It had to be you who found out the truth about me. About what I am."

Sudden outrage flashed in her eyes. "And just what are you, Jake? Are you human? Are you a man who's done his best?"

"I'm illiterate, Amanda," he snapped, his voice as hard as his words. "I'm a failure. You, of all people, should know. You got out. You fought your way past a childhood that makes mine seem like *Leave it to Beaver* in comparison. You're an author, for God's sake. A teacher with degrees from some of the most important universities in the country. What do you think that makes me?"

Jake wasn't sure what to expect. He didn't expect Amanda to start cursing at him. Cursing at him in language he'd rarely even heard out in the corral. Her eyes snapped fire, and her hands hit her hips, and she pulled herself right out of his grasp.

"A failure?" she spat, now truly worked up. "How dare you, Jake Kendall? How dare you call yourself a failure for sacrificing everything you wanted in your life just so your family could survive? My God, do you think you had a choice? You were only seven when your father started pulling you out of school to try and help around the ranch. Seven! It was all you could do to help your family keep the title to the land, much less see your little sisters and brother to school. But damn it, you did it. You worked so hard that you're a legend in the entire state, turning a failing, nearly bankrupt cattle ranch into the most respected horse ranch in the West. And you did it alone, even with the handicap of not being able to read. You did it so well that you put your sisters and brother through some of those same universities all by yourself so they could be what they wanted. And along the way you gave ex-convicts a second chance, and old drunks who didn't have anyplace else to go. You saved them, you made them productive, and you call yourself a failure?"

She cursed again, sharp and succinct. "Sure as hell redefines the term failure in my book."

"How did you know about that?" Jake demanded.

"About José and Clovis?" she retorted. "Don't be silly. People have been dying to talk about you from the minute I set foot on this ranch. Whether you want to believe it or not, you great big stupid oaf, there are a lot of people around here who care for you."

God, if only it were that easy. If only Jake could simply announce, By the way, I haven't been able to read all these years. Everybody be patient with me while I catch up.

But he knew better.

He knew better.

"Amanda," he said, "I've worked my whole life to gain the reputation I have in this town. To finally amount to something—"

"*Amount* to—"

"Shut up, Amanda. You grew up on a poor farm. You know what that's like. What it was like for me was that it wasn't until I snagged Grayghost that people finally stopped calling me 'that poor Kendall boy.' I grew up with the pity of this town, because of the ranch, because of my father, because that's the way they'd always thought of the Kendalls. Just a little touched because they wouldn't give in to the inevitable and either sell the ranch or turn it into a tourist concern." He held her hard in his gaze, not letting her shirk his intent. "That look is burned in my memory worse than the sight of my daddy dead out in the barn, or the first time I tried to do business and couldn't read a contract. That look is what propelled me all these years. Now that I've finally broken free of it, I'm not going back."

"But Jake—"

"It's not something you can do in the privacy of your own home, Amanda," he challenged. "And I can't afford to do it any other way." God knew, he'd tried. He'd tried to understand the kids' books, to pick apart letter sounds that made no sense, to understand how to put them together. He'd fought, late at night, with those books, while everyone else had been asleep. But in the end, he'd had nothing to build on. Not even the memories of a schoolteacher's interest, because all the teachers had known he was that poor Kendall boy and just figured he was a lost cause.

Well, he was.

"I'm not doing it," he told her. "Not now, not ever."

"Because you're the only grown man in the world who can't read?" she challenged yet again. "Well, let me tell you, pal. One out of every five adults in this country can't read. And it's not their fault, it's the system's fault. One out of five. Heck, you probably know somebody else in Lost Ridge who can't read."

He went rigid, pushed to the limit, the hurts too old and too deep to reason with. "Don't preach to me, Amanda," he demanded. "It's not going to change things. I'm not doing it."

"Even for me?" she asked. "Even if I helped?"

Jake sighed. He ached to take her back in his arms, to wallow in the silky sea of her hair. To make everything, everybody, just disappear. "Not even for you, Amanda."

"I won't give up."

"Then you should probably just leave."

But she shook her head. "I won't do that, either. One step at a time, remember?"

"Amanda, I told you—"

She stepped back up to him then. Settled her arms around him and lifted that sweet, infuriating face to him. Jake thought he could easily drown in that tide of bittersweet green. "I love you," she said. "No matter what. I told you that. You won't get any pity out of me, Jake Kendall, because you don't need it. You won't get any concessions, either, because I've been here before. I know what you're doing and why. And just think of this when you're thinking about what you want to do. Illiteracy is like alcoholism. Like an addiction. The longer you go, the more time and energy you spend on it, just to keep it a secret, until you don't have the time or energy left for anything anymore. Until your whole life is wrapped up in trying to keep your secret. Well, somehow I'm going to change your mind. And when that happens, we're going to work it through. To-gether."

"Amanda, you don't—"

She stopped him again. This time she kissed him. Reaching way up, on her toes, her hands curling into his hair, her lips hungry and sweet, that dress no more than a suspicion between them.

"Do you love me?" she asked.

"Amanda—"

She stopped him again. Again Jake lost control of his thoughts. He felt his own hands circle her, lift her so she could be closer, so he could taste her better.

"Do you love me?" she repeated on a whisper.

He had no answer but the truth. "Yes," he grated against her soft, soft throat. "Yes, damn it, I love you."

"Then don't keep any more secrets from me," she begged, eye to eye, heart to heart. "And I won't keep any from you."

"It's not that easy, Amanda," he insisted, his voice ragged with desperation, his hands clutching her to him while he could. "This isn't a damn book where everything gets better just because you want it to."

Her eyes softened into seduction and set him to trembling. "Nobody's here," she said rather than answer him. "Just us. That means that we could make love anywhere, and nobody'd know."

"Amanda—"

"We could even make love down in the barn, on the hay. I've always wanted to do that, haven't you?"

Jake finally set her back on her feet. "Stop it, Amanda. Stop it or I will."

She lifted her face back to his again, rubbed up against him in that age-old invitation that no man properly knew how to refuse. "How, Jake? How do you intend to stop a woman who loves you so much she paid off all his hands to go in to see a movie so she could have you all to herself?"

His control shattered. His resolve vanished. Lost somewhere beyond her eyes, beyond the breath of her scent and the sweet weight of her body, was the knowledge that this couldn't cure anything. This couldn't keep her happy when she lost the ability to communicate to a man who couldn't read the words she worked so hard to write. It couldn't prevent the love from withering in her delectable, deadly eyes, couldn't keep her tied to this ranch with him when she had the whole world to conquer.

It didn't solve anything. But the minute Jake tasted the plum and ginger on Amanda's mouth, it didn't matter.

"You need a bigger couch," Amanda murmured into Jake's throat.

He didn't move from where they'd ended up on the rug in front of the fireplace. "I need a less athletic woman," he argued.

"Don't be silly," she disagreed, caressing the ribs she was sure were still sore from the move that had taken care of the size of the couch. "You just need more practice."

She felt his groan all the way to her still-tingling toes. "If I practice anymore, I won't have the energy left to get up on a horse."

"A horse," she mused, knowing what kind of reaction she'd get. "Now, there's an idea."

"Amanda," he objected, right on cue, "I am not trying any calisthenics on a horse with you."

She giggled. "Spoilsport."

He ran slow fingers through her hair. Amanda closed her eyes, the sensation delicious and sad. She'd wanted so much from the conversation tonight, even knowing ahead of time how likely she was to get it. She'd wanted revelation, relief, action. Even wrapped in Jake's arms, their bodies and minds as intimate as couples get, she'd known that there had been no relief. There had only been more pressure, and she didn't know what to do about it. Except keep right on loving him. Without reservation, without condition. She'd lost Uncle Mick. She wasn't going to give up on Jake. And in the meantime, she could do worse things than reinforce the fact that he was, no matter what, still the sexiest, strongest, most compelling man she'd ever met.

"I love you," she whispered, letting her own fingers dance through the hair that crinkled across his chest. The view was wonderful, all the way down to his toes, the firelight bathing him in warmth, gilding muscle and tendon, washing over the planes of his sleek, hard body the way a new sun does the high meadow.

"I love you, too." But he sounded as if he were apologizing, and Amanda couldn't stand that.

She lifted her head, resting an elbow on his chest, and glared at him. "You'd rather you didn't?"

She'd surprised him. The corner of his mouth quirked as he lifted a finger to run it down her cheek. "I'd sure get more sleep."

She huffed in indignation. "We're just making up for lost time."

Jake chuckled now, and the sound of it lodged in Amanda's chest like spring wind. "Face it, Amanda," he challenged, cupping her bottom. "I can't keep my hands off you."

Amanda liked the sound of that even better. "I don't remember asking you to."

His palms were rough, too, and they felt delicious against her sensitive skin. She began to move against him, just a little.

"A woman like you doesn't wait her whole life for the feel of callused hands," he argued, even as his pupils dilated and his hands quickened.

Amanda couldn't help laughing. "A woman like me? May I tell you something about a woman like me, Jake? I spent the last six weeks before showing up here out in Los Angeles. Holl-ee-wood. I actually sat down to meals with people like Brett Clark. You know the guy, six feet four of muscle, savoir faire and brains? Every woman's dream in a tux? He asked me out a couple of times. He and three or four other people, because they knew who I was. They knew I'd written books that were going to be movies, so it was okay, I guess. And they did their best to charm me. And guess how many of them I ended up on the floor with?"

"Amanda—"

She scowled at him, loving the stern lines his face gathered into when he was admonishing her. "Don't 'Amanda' me. This is important. I went home alone every night for six weeks, and you know why? Because they bored me. Because not one of those guys was real. Not one of them had calluses on their hands, and I'll tell you something, Jake. Calluses say a lot about a man. I *like* calluses."

"You do?"

She shared a smile that promised dreams he hadn't even thought of. "I knew you had calluses the minute you first rode up to that cabin," she admitted. "I said to myself, 'Lordy, Amanda, there's a man who doesn't have to ask his astrologer if the signs are right to get a massage. There's a man who doesn't live just to hear the sound of his own voice. There's a man I'd like to get to know.'"

"Well, you did that."

Her smile broadened. She let her hand drift. "Intimately. And I plan on getting to know you even better."

His belly. Amanda loved his belly. It was so flat and hard, not from weight machines or personal trainers, but from hard, honest work. She loved to run her hands over the hair that trailed down from his chest, and then dip her fingers into his navel. She loved to see his reaction.

"Amanda, stop it," he protested, without pulling her hand away. "We can't figure that this is just going to solve everything."

"It's not," she assured him, turning her gaze to his mouth, on those lips that could torture her so easily. On the hard line of his jaw that brooked no argument. Except hers. "But I love you," she repeated, lifting her gaze to his eyes, which she loved the best. "And since we only manage to get together about once every four or five days, it seems that this is the best way to cut through all the small talk and let you know."

Jake obviously didn't seem to know whether to be surprised, outraged or amused. "You do have a way with endearments," he admitted, reaching up to tangle a hand in the hair that fell along the side of her face. Amanda smiled at the shower of sparks his fingers ignited, at the intoxicating play of his hand in her hair. She whimpered when he pulled her down to him.

"And where did you get that lingerie?" he demanded against her mouth, his hand holding her, his lips teasing her. "I thought you were an all-cotton woman."

She giggled, breathless and suddenly shy. "I was," she admitted, her hands splayed out against his chest, her hips seeking his. "Those were a free . . . aaah, gift with the computer."

His chuckle incited her. "Just for you, huh?"

"No," she answered on a whisper, on a promise. "Just for you."

He groaned, deep and primal. He pulled her to him, so close even the firelight couldn't come between, and rolled with her. Amanda felt the cushion of the thick rug against her back, felt the hair-roughened weight of Jake against her belly. She looked up into eyes made molten by desire, and knew what it was like to become irrevocably lost, because she became lost in those eyes. She became lost in the feel of those hands that praised her in ways no person had ever thought to praise her before. She became lost in the growl of his hunger and the delicate dance of his tongue against hers.

There was no rush this time, no all-consuming fire. This time there was discovery, exploration. This time Jake held Amanda's hands in his, keeping her still, while he watched her body in the firelight. She blushed with his frank appraisal, sank into his delighted smile.

"You're so beautiful," he whispered, dipping his head to kiss her throat, her ear. "So very beautiful."

She arched to his touch, hungry, cold without him, aching suddenly for the torment of his hands. For the touch of him against her hands.

"No," he denied her, catching her hands again. "It's my turn to show you just how much I love you."

Amanda lost her breath. She knew Jake could hear her heart, it tripped so loudly in the silent room. She knew he could see the flush of pleasure bloom on her skin. She'd never had a man look at her the way Jake did, or touch her with such reverence. She'd never wanted one to.

His hands skimmed and searched. They paused, tormented, teased. Skirting the line of her ribs, under her arm, around to her waist, he let his fingers hesitate just shy of her breasts, knowing already that they waited for him, seeing the hard peaks of her nipples just at his approach. He swept the lines of her legs, caressed the backs of her knees, her calves, her thighs. He cupped her bottom in his hands and then tested the sensitive skin at the small of her back.

And all the while, he watched. He watched her body respond, her belly tighten and her breasts tauten. He watched her eyes widen and her lips part and her head fall back. He watched as she began to writhe beneath him and smiled when she whimpered his name.

And Amanda, caught in his hands, by his mouth, saw the heat rise in his eyes, saw the wonder, the yearning, the love he couldn't express any other way, and knew what it felt like to soar.

Finally when he took her breasts in his hands, he couldn't keep her still anymore,. She wove her fingers into his hair and held him to her. She balanced herself against his chest, against the solid swell of his shoulder. She measured his arms, sleek and strong enough to control half a ton of animal, and claimed his torso. She watched, too, seeing the dark gold hair against her breast, the sun-darkened hand on her belly. She relished the contrasts, sleek against rough, hard against soft, light against dark. She savored the sensations, the curling, writhing fire that licked through her, the chill of kissed skin in the air, the delicious agony of tongue and lips and teeth tormenting breasts. She couldn't hold still, couldn't stay quiet. She couldn't imagine any sweeter torment. And then Jake edged his hand up along her thigh, and she arched to meet it, to meet him, and knew she'd been wrong.

"Please, Jake," she gasped, clutching him, the gathering fire demanding union, the dark lightning his fingers ignited splintering through her. "I can't . . . wait . . ."

He silenced her with his mouth, his quirky, insatiable mouth. Amanda begged, but he didn't hear her; she cried, and he drank her tears. She lost thought, lost time, lost place. There was only Jake, only his hands, his mouth, his tongue. Only his body, so warm and slick and sweetly familiar against hers. And finally, when she thought she couldn't stand it anymore, when she scored his back with her nails just to keep from falling apart, he slipped inside her.

"I love you, Amanda," he whispered to her, his hands in her hair, his sweat-sheened body filling her arms. "I love you."

But Amanda couldn't answer. She could only hold him, pull him into her, again and again, dancing on a tide that consumed light, sound, time. Lifting, singing, sailing into the sun where the words became meaningless and the act itself was all that was needed.

"It still doesn't solve anything," Jake murmured in her ear much later.

Amanda smiled. "Yes, it does," she disagreed. "Now I'll know where to get all my computers."

He didn't answer. He just stroked her hair where it lay tumbled across his chest. And slowly, quietly, they fell asleep before the fire, there with just an old afghan over them.

It didn't occur to them what a bad idea it was until the next morning.

"Hey, Jake!" Lee yelled from the back porch as she slid her key into the lock. "I'm home!"

Both Jake and Amanda bolted upright and stared at the door not more than fifteen feet away.

"Uh-oh," Amanda moaned, and then found herself being yanked into the bedroom, leaving all her clothes behind on the floor.

Chapter 14

"Chinese food?" Lee demanded from the kitchen. "Somebody cooked Chinese food in this house? Jake, where are you?"

"I'm right here," he growled, emerging from his bedroom, belting his robe over the pajama pants he'd just thought to put on. Lee didn't notice him kick the scrap of blue material under the couch as he walked past. She didn't immediately notice Amanda following from her room, belting a robe over a flannel nightgown. Nor did she see her kick two very small scraps of silk and lace after the dress.

"Hi, squirt," Jake greeted her as she turned the corner into the living room.

Amanda waited behind, doing her best to look innocent. Content just to watch.

Lee rushed into her big brother's arms and got her hair tousled with her hug.

"You weren't supposed to be here for two more days," he accused. "What's going on?"

She backed up a little, flashing him a sly grin. "Trying to keep something from me? Hi, Amanda. I thought you were at the cabin."

"I was," Amanda greeted her, knowing how good the girl's intuition was. Her brand-new underwear was probably gathering dust bunnies for nothing. "I rode over yesterday on horseback to visit. By the time we finished eating dinner, it was too late to ride home. Thanks for the nightgown, by the way."

The girl's trademark blue Kendall eyes sparkled with mischief. "My pleasure," she assured her. "By the way, the candles were a nice touch."

Lee was only Amanda's height, but she was a Kendall in every other way, with honey-blond hair, ramrod posture from all the years spent sitting a horse, a sleek figure and those water-blue eyes. If Jake had had any sense he'd be worried as hell about the boys circling her on campus. Luckily she also had most of the Kendall common sense.

"Chinese?" she demanded yet again. "You really got Jake to eat Chinese?"

"Oh, shut up," Jake snarled.

Lee's laughter was delighted. "And to think. You're still alive, Jake. You lied to us all these years."

"Have you had breakfast yet?" Amanda asked, noting that the sky was lightening in the east through early morning fog. It wouldn't be long before everybody else started showing up. In fact, she was amazed that Clovis hadn't already been up to check on why Jake hadn't been down for morning stables. Of course, the fact that Sweet William was still in his stall might have told him something.

"No," Lee admitted. "I've been on the road most of the night."

Jake started to attention. "All night? What the hell do you mean?"

She just patted him on the arm. "I mean that I was able to catch an early flight. Only it went to Denver, so I had to hitch a ride."

"Who with?"

Lee leaned over to give Amanda a grin. "Isn't he cute? He still doesn't let me cross the street in Lost Ridge."

"Lee—" It was not an amused sound.

Lee seemed to respect her brother's temper. "Two of the other kids from school," she assured him. "Both of whom strictly adhere to the tenets of a religion that forbids the driving of a car over fifty-five miles an hour or playing loud rock and roll while doing so."

Amanda saw Jake struggle against his little sister's sharp whimsy. "Both of them girls."

Lee nodded, her eyes big and serious. "Planning to be nuns. In fact, I think they were headed from here to the convent."

He tousled her hair again. "Somebody spoiled you rotten, kid."

Her smile was brilliant. "Can't imagine who. Now, how 'bout breakfast? Is it going to be moo shoo pork or lo mein?"

"Eggs," Jake barked. "And bacon. As soon as I get dressed."

Lee swung her carryall around and followed toward her room. "Getting good information, Amanda?" she asked, her eyes on the rigid set of her brother's shoulder, her expression betraying her struggle to repress her delight.

"When I'm not stuck in blizzards or tending to the sick," Amanda acknowledged.

"Did he get you a new computer?" she asked loudly enough to get her brother's attention before he shut the door.

"He did not," Amanda informed her. "I got me a new computer. You'll have to come up and play with it."

"I'll—good God, what's this?"

Both Amanda and Jake spun around at the unholy glee in Lee's voice. Amanda was terrified that the girl had decided to search under the couch. Instead, she reached over to the coffee table and picked up the sweater Jake had worn last night. "The sweater," she breathed in awe, holding it out before her like the lost family jewels.

Amanda wasn't exactly sure what to say. Jake looked thunderous.

"Lee—" he threatened.

Amanda couldn't help but grin. "Now I know why you do that so well."

Lee was looking between the two of them as if she'd just been privileged to a vision. "Tell me it was you, Amanda. Tell me you got Jake to actually *wear* it."

Jake tried another verse of the same song. "Lee—"

"We bought it for him, you know," Lee told Amanda, her eyes still wide, the corner of her mouth crooking. "For his birthday two years ago. There's only so much you can get a man who spends his big evening out every week down at Stilwell's or the volunteer fire department playing poker. But we never really *expected* him to *wear* it."

"Why not?" Amanda demanded. "It's beautiful."

"Of course it is. Gen spent darn near a hundred dollars on the damn thing. But we knew better than to think that would make a difference. We had a bet going, you know. Gen swore we'd have to bury him in it just to see if it fit."

"That's enough," Jake snapped, not nearly as upset as he sounded. "You know, there are always flights back to that big city you like so much."

Lee turned astonished eyes on her brother. "Leave?" she demanded. "And possibly miss the chance to be here and actually witness you doing something really cataclysmic, like giving one of your horses away?"

It couldn't have been better timed. The back door slammed open and Clovis strode in. "Boss? That you? I see that Sweet William's back in his stall. Does that mean Amanda's down from the cabin?"

That did it. Lee dissolved into peals of laughter. Jake deserted them for his room, and Amanda stood there, trying to figure out how she was going to retrieve her dress without anybody knowing.

It didn't take long for the entire ranch to reverberate with the effects of Lee's return. Betty actually sniffled a few times. Maria sang while she cooked, and José invoked several saints while he saddled Lee's mare. And Willy, who was so sweet and quiet, blushed furiously when Lee gave him a big kiss hello.

Of course, Amanda felt the effect most of all. Lee chattered nonstop through breakfast, shared the latest news from school while Amanda got ready to leave, and then demanded to join her for the ride to the cabin.

The two of them headed off without so much as a farewell from Jake, who was already closeted back in the breeding shed with Clovis and Grayboy. Something, Lee assured her, that she had to see while she was here. Something, Amanda knew, that she wasn't quite ready for. Not with Jake standing alongside her.

The morning was soft and alive, birds skipping over the fields, insects returning to life, the colors of a thousand different new wildflowers littering the grass. The stream sang to them and the breeze warmed them. And at the periphery, always, the mountains guarded them.

"God, I missed it," Lee breathed, resettling herself in her saddle as the horses walked up the meadow.

"I can understand," Amanda allowed. She never had gotten to her dress. For the ride back, she wore the same jeans and blouse she'd worn down. The bag in which she'd kept her dress hung empty from her saddle.

Lee looked over at her. "You like it here?"

Amanda didn't bother to disguise her smile. "I love it here."

Lee allowed herself a very satisfied smile.

"Don't look so smug. You're the smart brat, I'm the teacher, remember?"

"How was Brett Clark? Was he really everything people say?"

Amanda laughed. "He was the first person I've ever seen actually look at his reflection in a plate."

Lee giggled. "I guess this means you won't be moving in with him any time soon."

"I doubt sincerely that he'd be interested in homey aphorisms and weather forecasting."

"I heard a new one, by the way," Lee announced. "How's this? 'There ain't enough room in here to cuss a cat without gettin' hair in your mouth.'"

Amanda laughed, delighted at the new proverb. She collected them the way some people collected license plates and bottle caps. "Where from, do you know?"

"The Ozarks."

She nodded. "Great stuff from that neck of the woods. That's where I got the saying about your brother and the river."

They rode on for a few minutes more in silence, the only sounds the creak and jingle of the tack, the plodding steps of the horses, the small intrusion of the wildlife.

"What do you think of him?" Lee asked, and Amanda knew that she wasn't nearly as offhand as she tried to sound.

"He hasn't looked in his plate once."

Lee actually shook her head. "Jake has no ego," she admitted. "He really doesn't know how terrific he is."

All Amanda could give her was the truth. "I know."

Lee looked over, those Kendall eyes sharp and waiting. Amanda could see the girl searching for tactful words, and knew how very important the discussion was to her. She knew what Jake meant to his little sister, what the constant banter camouflaged.

"He's a little rigid," Lee said. "Has his little . . . ways about him. And he doesn't see the world the way a lot of other people do. For him, the only thing worth knowing about is the ranch and his horses."

"And his family," Amanda added softly.

Lee's eyes widened a little.

"I imagine sometimes it's hard for a man like him to say what he feels," Amanda suggested.

Lee turned her attention back to the trail. "I'd give back every cent of my tuition," she said, "wash dishes at Stilwell's the rest of my life and never put pen to paper if I thought I could make him happy."

"He knows," Amanda said. "But nothing makes him happier than seeing you in college."

"But what about him?" Lee demanded, her young face so very serious, so intense. "When does he get what he wants?"

Amanda came very close to holding her breath. "What's that, Lee?"

The girl gave in to an impatient shrug. "I don't know," she admitted. "But I do know that he isn't happy. He hasn't been for a long time, and it's making us all crazy."

Amanda ached to tell her, to share the truth. She wanted so badly for Lee to know that Jake only needed permission for the way out. He only needed his family's approval, their support. It would mean so much. It might make all the difference in the world.

But she had no right to ask. Only Jake could do that, and right now it didn't look as if he would.

Patience. Didn't St. Paul have quite a bit to say on the subject of love and patience? He had no idea, she thought dejectedly. No idea at all.

"Do you like him?" Lee asked, and suddenly Amanda heard the little girl who still depended on her brother, who still worshiped him, who hurt for him in ways Amanda couldn't even imagine.

Amanda smiled. She knew what Lee was driving at. Little sisters were sometimes notorious matchmakers. "Yes," she admitted gently. "I like him. Although, I have to admit I was just a little bit surprised by him the first time I met him."

Lee looked over, uncertain.

Amanda flashed her a grin. "Fussy?" she demanded. "Old maid? He's about as fussy as a marine DI."

Lee's laughter echoed out across the meadow. "Perception is everything, Amanda. He obviously hasn't told you to stand up straight or made you clean your room before dinner...." She shook her head, once again amazed. "Chinese. I'm going to have to call Gen and tell her. She won't believe it, either."

"Trust me, neither did Jake. He almost had a heart attack when he walked in and saw all those vegetables on the counter. At least I stuck to the ones he could name."

"I heard you stared down Clovis the other night, too."

Amanda almost sighed. "It wasn't exactly the Cuban Missile Crisis."

"Are you kidding? Amanda, you've set this place on its ear. You're the best thing that's happened to it since Grayghost won his first title. Better. Grayghost never got Jake to wear the sweater...do you *really* like Jake?"

Amanda finally gave up and reined Sweet William to a halt. "Let me put it to you this way," she said, facing the girl. "If I get a choice in the matter, I won't be returning to school in the fall."

Lee's eyes grew impossibly wide. Her mouth rounded into a perfect O, and she went completely still. That was when it really occurred to Amanda that she wasn't just taking Jake on. She was taking on his family. His sisters, his brother, his secretary, his foreman and everybody in the whole damn town. It should have overwhelmed her. If she got what she wanted, she'd go from a solitary life to one so crowded she'd be spitting cat hair.

But she saw the light in Lee's eyes, and she thought of the easy comfort she'd felt in Lost Ridge. She thought of the noise she'd always missed around a dinner table, of the fact that she'd never had a chance to share her success with her family.

She remembered like an ache the first time she'd had a manuscript accepted. She'd worked so very hard on it, pouring into it all the secrets and traditions and memories of her mountain, sweating over words, agonizing over the special flavor she'd wanted to impart. But when the editor had called her, there had been no one to turn to. No one to share the dizzying victory. No one who cared enough about her to be happy for her.

She'd never have to worry about that again.

"Would you mind?" she asked, just to get things started again.

Lee's abrupt laugh flushed a couple of crows from the brush. "Would I mind? Would I *mind?* I've been trying to figure out a way to get you two together since the first time I met you. What does Jake say?"

It was Amanda's turn for a laugh, although hers was far more disconcerted. "He might take some convincing."

Lee's expression dissolved into disgust. "Doesn't that just figure? That lughead. Well, we're just going to have to do something about that—"

Amanda reached over and grabbed the reins to Lee's horse before she had a chance to make good her threat. "No," she demurred, images of the collected Kendalls making her very nervous. That would definitely be the last thing Jake needed right about now. "Leave it to me. Please."

"But Amanda, what if he's stubborn? Did I tell you that he can be stubborn sometimes?"

Amanda managed a grin. "I found out on my own, thanks. I think that if all of you gang up on him, he's going to buck like Sidewinder with a saddle on."

Lee giggled. "That's a good one. I bet you're an author...do you really think so?"

"I really do. Now, let's go on up to the cabin. I want to show you some diaries that Betty found for me to read. They're your great-grandmother's."

"You're kidding. I never knew we had anything like that. Have you shown them to Jake?"

"Uh-huh." Not much else to say. Amanda turned Sweet William back on his way, and Lee followed.

"Did he ever read your book, Amanda?"

"No."

Lee sighed. "He's so frustrating sometimes. I really wanted him to read *Simple Gifts*. It reminded me so much of the people we grew up around. The minute I read it I knew how well you'd fit in at the Diamond K."

Amanda wanted him to read it, too. But, she kept reminding herself, one step at a time. One slow, careful step at a time.

"Just think," Lee said with a giggle, "if you guys did get married, we'd actually have to get Jake a suit. The whole state might turn up for a sight like that."

Amanda chuckled. "Nah. We'll just get somebody to marry us right in the corral. That way he could wear his boots."

"Everybody could sit right up on the fence."

"Have Stilwell's cater."

"Steak and fries and apple pie."

"I *might* get him to wear the sweater again...."

Jake felt as if he were rushing headlong into disaster. In no more than a few weeks his carefully constructed world had been turned upside down. Now there was a real chance it could topple altogether.

He couldn't look at Amanda without seeing the knowledge in her eyes, the tears she'd spent for him, the quiet concern.

The truth.

He'd tried to see it her way, that he really hadn't had any other choice. He'd tried to think past the old humiliation the town had unknowingly inflicted. But he had more than twenty years' worth of experience to overcome. He had a guilt the size of those mountains out there to face. And he was just too tired of facing it anymore. He wanted to live his life the way it was, work his horses, ride his land, visit with the people who knew him and didn't expect anything from him that he couldn't give.

He was teaching one of the fillies about saddles. They'd progressed past the saddle blanket. Today, Jake would cinch up one of the lighter saddles and let the animal get used to it. By the looks of her laid-back ears, it would take a little sweet-talk.

Jake could afford sweet-talk for a horse. A horse didn't expect things from him he couldn't give. A horse worked you hard, demanded your attention and your best efforts. This yearling was a bay filly named Lazy Susan, a sharp, fiery little thing who would probably be perfect for speed events when she got a little more sense and a little less sass in her. It was Jake's job to take care of both without taking the spirit right out of her. It was what he liked to do best.

Today, though, his mind wasn't on her. As he eased the saddle down onto her back, his mind was on green eyes. His memory was plaguing him with promises and demands. With offers so seductive that a man couldn't be expected to ignore them just for work. Offers that had nothing to do with that lithe body that had danced with his the night before. That had everything to do with the delicious appetite of the mind inside. The experience, the knowledge.

Jake wanted what Amanda had. He wanted her intelligence, her hungry curiosity, her insight and humor. He wanted to see the world through her eyes and hold her hand while he was doing it.

He wanted desperately to read her words.

He'd stood all alone in his room this afternoon, the copy of *Simple Gifts* in his hands, Amanda's glossy picture looking back out at him from the back jacket. Amanda in her other persona, her professional self, where she wore classic, tailored clothes and where her hair looked like a corona around a bright sun. He'd stroked the pages as if they were the rarest of silks, running his blunt fingers over the print, the letters blurring before his eyes, the meaning forever locked away from him.

This was as much a part of her as her laughter, as the way she cocked those fists on her hips when she was determined about something. This was a window into that deep, sweet soul of hers, and he wasn't allowed to see in. It threatened to break him when nothing else in thirty years had.

"Call out the press. Jake Kendall spends time with a horse."

Jake didn't bother to look around from where he was stroking the filly and bribing her with a little grain as she skittered beneath the unfamiliar weight.

"Hello, Lee. Have a nice time up at the cabin?"

"I had a great time. Did you know that Great-Great-Grandma Barkins was a pow-wow woman?"

Jake remained eye to eye with his charge. "Is that right?"

"It's a fact. Back in Kentucky before they came out to the territory."

"I know you're dying to tell me what a pow-wow woman is."

"You'd probably already know yourself," his sister taunted, "if you'd ever thought to go through all that stuff locked away in the attic."

"I wasn't the only one who grew up in that house."

She laughed behind him, and the sound was delighted and light. Teasing, taunting. Usual stuff. Amanda hadn't given him away.

He was going to have to live the rest of his life waiting for it.

"When was the last time you let me in the attic?" Lee demanded playfully.

Jake couldn't help a smile. "The day I caught you and Tommy Helpern playing doctor."

"Tommy Helpern's in premed now," she teased. "I imagine we could really work up a good game if we tried."

"Not if you want him to make it to med school," Jake retorted easily, hiding the fear, just as he'd always done. Showing one thing, being another.

"Do you know what a pow-wow woman is?"

"The person with the concession for Indian war dances?"

"Very funny, Jake. This is your own family we're talking about. Your history. Don't you care?"

"Of course I care, honey. But unless pow-wow women knew how to exorcise psychotic palominos, it doesn't make much difference."

"You still haven't given Sidewinder back?"

"I'll be able to ride him again in a week or so."

"Poor Amanda."

Jake turned around. "Poor Amanda what?"

Lee shot him a saucy grin. "She's going to get to spend another fun-filled night taking care of your busted ribs. By the way, that's a dandy of a scar. Is that from that last dance you had with him?"

Jake overcame the urge to rub at the scar just over his right eye. He'd taken the stitches out himself, but it still itched.

"I should have asked those friends of yours to take you with them to the convent."

"We're not Catholic, Jake."

"I'd pay 'em for the privilege."

She snorted unkindly, which made Jake grin as he turned back to the filly.

"She's a pretty little thing," Lee admitted. "Isn't she Buttercup's baby?"

"Buttercup and Detonator from over at Jensons."

Lee whistled. "She's gonna have some speed, then."

Jake nodded. "And a temper. She reminds me of you when you don't get your way."

"Snot."

God, it was good to have her home. Just like he had at Thanksgiving and again at Christmas, Jake battled the desire to beg her not to go back. Not to leave him in that empty house all alone. She was the last to go, the hardest given away. She was all that was left of his resolve to keep going.

"Amanda said to thank you again for the loan of Sweet William. Those two really seem to get along."

"Clovis tried to teach her to ride on Pokey. Bill seemed more her size."

Lee laughed. "Isn't she wonderful, Jake? Isn't she everything I told you in my letters?"

Jake squeezed his eyes shut for a moment, his hand on the smooth, warm coat of the filly, his mind a meadow away. His heart crumbling. "She reminds me of you," he retorted.

"Then you do like her!"

He turned a hard-won wry smile on her. "I said she reminds me of you. Which means she's a smart aleck who thinks she knows everything and doesn't mind in the least telling everybody."

Lee's answering smile was smug. "No wonder you like her so much."

"I didn't say that."

"You didn't have to," she teased. "I found her clothes under the couch."

Jake whirled around on her, instinctively furious, exposed, unnerved by the suddenly adult young woman who sat atop the corral grinning down at him. "Listen, you snot—"

She waved him off. "Oh, for heaven's sake, lighten up. I said you're doing it, not me. Although, if Tommy still looks as good as he did, I might take the risk—"

"Lee!"

She giggled and jumped from the fence. The filly danced away, still not used to all the extra stimulus. Jake didn't even notice. His eyes were on his little sister and the real joy in her eyes.

"I promise I'll behave," she told him, stepping right up to him and challenging him just the way Amanda did. "Although it'll probably give me a rash. But there is just one thing I want to say."

Jake groaned dramatically, hoping it hid the dread, the sick sensation of inevitability.

Lee cuffed him on the arm and then betrayed her real concern. "It damn near killed me to leave you, Jake. I felt like we were all deserting you. I've spent the last fifteen years of my life trying to figure a way to get you someone else in your life. Somebody who'd be here for you when we all scatter to the four corners of the world." She shook her head a little, her eyes brimming with emotion. "If it has to be Amanda, I'll just have to live with it. Especially since she's just about my second favorite person in the world—and don't you dare tell Gen or Zeke, or I'll cut your cinches when you ride Sidewinder."

Even with all the ambivalence making mincemeat of his stomach, Jake managed a smile. "Wouldn't think of it."

"I won't bother you any more about it. It's your decision. Yours and Amanda's. I just thought it might help you to know that if you'd like to fulfill my dream of having my very own sister-in-law, you have your family's wholehearted approval...at least, you have mine. I may have to bribe Gen and Zeke."

Jake couldn't believe it. He was actually laughing. "What more can a brother ask for?" he demanded, pulling her into his arms and lifting her off the ground in a hug.

"So, that's all I have to say," she said somewhere within the folds of his flannel shirt.

"I'm glad," he acknowledged. "This is really something that only Amanda and I can work out."

Lee gave him one more squeeze and then trotted back on out of the corral.

"Just don't disappoint us," she commanded slyly before she slid between the rails.

Completely helpless in the face of his sister's enthusiasm, Jake could manage no more than a return to the filly. She was just as high-spirited, contrary and cantankerous. But at least she couldn't talk back.

"Gosh, this is just like a real family," Lee gushed as the three of them sat to dinner two nights later.

"Lee!" both Amanda and Jake chorused together.

Lee nodded. "Oh, yeah. Right. I'm mute. A mime. Wanna see me walk against the wind?"

"I want to see you in a box," Amanda snapped.

"I'll get the nails and two-by-fours," Jake offered.

Lee just laughed. "Gosh, this is more fun than pushin' little biddies in a crick."

Jake stared at her. "What the hell does that mean?"

Lee shrugged. "I don't know, but doesn't it have a great sound?"

"Where," he demanded, "do you keep coming up with those damn things? You're beginning to sound like an almanac."

"From Amanda," she assured him. "There are a bunch of them in her book...oh, but that's right. You haven't *read* her book yet, have you?"

"Why should I?" he demanded. "You're reciting it over the dinner table!"

"I swear," she goaded, leaning just a little closer over the cake she and Amanda had baked that afternoon, "you're so grumpy you don't do a thing but sit in a chimley corner, rock your big toe and whistle hard times."

Amanda fought a grin. "You *are* a brat," she informed the girl.

Lee shot her a grin. "This way he won't miss me so much when I'm gone."

"I'd be happy not to miss you real soon," Jake warned.

Lee arched an eyebrow at him. "Well, then you won't mind if I go meet Tommy Helpern at the movies."

Amanda saw Jake's glare, saw the dance of affectionate challenge between the two of them. But she saw something else, something Lee didn't seem to see. She saw the strain her return had put on Jake. He'd been so quiet the last few days, so intent on his work, to the point of almost taking away José's chores just to keep busy. Bad storms the last two days had kept him inside, which had the same effect as trying to bottle an explosion. The longer Jake went without being able to ride off his problems, the worse it got. And Lee's innocent goading was only making it worse.

Lee was a blessing to him, but she was a burden. Every time she talked to Amanda about Amanda's work, or her own, or the studies she was immersed in, Amanda could see Jake tense. Every time she turned to include Jake in the conversation, he all but ran. And Amanda knew why. She knew he was waiting for her to betray him. To let it slip to the person he could least afford, that he couldn't read. That everything he thought Lee based her affection on was foundationless.

Amanda knew she'd precipitated the worst crisis Jake would ever face, and there wasn't a damn thing she could do to help. Except wait. Except keep his faith and hold his silence and provide his support until he could deal with it. Until he made his decision.

But the longer he went, the greater the toll it took on the both of them.

Maybe if they could just last through Lee's visit. Maybe then Jake would feel free to once again discuss his problem, to look at it in a more objective light without his little sister constantly buffeting him with her hero worship.

The weather had broken just before dinner, letting the late sun wash across the meadow in thick, golden shafts. Maybe tomorrow Jake could get a little of this out of his system by taking Buck on a long run somewhere.

"So, can I, huh? Can I go to the movies, Jake?" Lee prodded.

Jake all but snarled, "Make it a double feature."

"With Tommy?" she teased, getting up to give her brother a kiss. "I'm sure something could be worked out."

He just sighed as she trotted out of the room.

Amanda refilled their coffee and sat back down. "I'm amazed you don't have more gray hair."

Jake scowled. "I don't have any gray hair."

"Of course you do," Lee assured him, sweeping back into the kitchen with jeans jacket and purse in hand. "You got it when you taught me to drive. Can I have the pickup?"

"Take the Jimmy," Jake told her. "I don't trust you in my good truck."

"His good truck," Lee gloated over to Amanda as she slipped into her jacket and bent to kiss her brother goodbye in one fluid movement. "That truck's damn near as old as I am."

"And where did you start using language like that?" he demanded. "You learn that from Amanda, too?"

"Heck, no," Lee assured him, already at the door for quick escape. "Hers is much more colorful. I learned mine from you."

He barely lasted long enough for Lee to get out the door before he began pacing. Amanda kept her seat in the kitchen, ostensibly concentrating on her coffee and the last few crumbs of the cake she kept picking at as she listened to the retreating growl of the Jimmy and the agitated echo of boots trailing up and down the floor.

She should go back up to the cabin. She should have never come down, wouldn't have if Lee hadn't been so adamant. The tension couldn't get worse in the house unless Gen and Zeke walked in. Amanda knew that just her presence was forcing

Jake to a decision. She knew what he had to overcome to get there. She knew the dread of humiliation he battled.

So she sipped her coffee and watched a flock of birds sail across the mottled, gilded sky and waited there if he needed her, aching for him with a fierce regret that could never show on her face.

"I can't live like this," he suddenly announced from the doorway.

Amanda looked up to see the naked pain in his eyes and got to her feet. "Wanna talk?"

He shook his head. He dragged his hands through his hair. "I think you need to leave."

She went very still. "Tonight?"

Jake faced her, and Amanda saw the weight of his decision, saw the urge to flee, the fear, the anger, the hurt. "For good. I can't keep this up, Amanda, with you here every day. I'm having trouble enough just knowing that you...that you know. But trying to go on pretending that nothing's changed—" He shook his head again, his movements jerky and desperate. "I can't even face Lee anymore."

Amanda walked up to him, needing to be close, wishing desperately for the right words to get him past this point—to get them both past it.

"She knows something's wrong," Amanda told him. "They all do."

"Well, hell, of course they do. I've been as surly as Sidewinder since she's been home."

Amanda shook her head. "Not just now," she retorted softly. "They've felt it for a long time now. Lee told me that they're all worried about you."

Jake spun on his heel and headed back into the living room. Amanda followed, keeping a careful distance. He didn't need to be crowded right now. He needed to be helped.

"It doesn't matter," he argued, stopping over by the dark fireplace, his head down, his hands clenched. "I can't do it."

"What can't you do?" Amanda asked gently, her own hands clasped together to keep them to herself. God, how she wanted to hold him, to stroke his hair and nestle his head against her where he'd be safe, where he'd be protected and comforted. But that was the last thing Jake Kendall would be able to stand right now. "Learn?"

"I can't face them," he admitted, his voice raw with anguish. "I can't—I look at Lee here now, and I see that the hard work I've done with her is paying off. She's smart and sassy and independent. But how can I send her back out into the world with the knowledge that I've been lying to her all these years?"

"Jake," Amanda protested. "She loves you. She'd do anything to see you happy, don't you understand?"

"No," he argued, swinging around on her. "You don't understand. I can't stand the idea of seeing the look on her face when she finds out that I haven't been able to read one of the letters she's sent me. Not one. Not even the cards she wrote me in school and those little notes she used to slip into my dresser when she thought I wasn't looking. I still don't know what those ever said!"

"Don't you want the chance to read her letters now?" Amanda challenged. "And Gen's and Zeke's?"

"I can't!" he shouted, devastated. "I'm illiterate, damn it! How do you expect me to admit that to them? How do you expect me to suffer their pity?"

Amanda had no answer. Locked into the pain in Jake's eyes, she stumbled over her good intentions and her determination. How could she hurt this man? How could she—?

"Jake?"

Both of them whirled at the sound. Fear slammed through Amanda, even knowing already what she'd find.

It was Lee, standing in the door to the kitchen, her eyes on her brother, wide, tear-swollen eyes. Stunned, desolate eyes.

"Jake?" she repeated in that little girl's voice that suddenly shattered the rest of Amanda's control.

Jake shuddered beside her. His body went rigid, his own eyes stark as death. "No," he protested bleakly. "No."

And Amanda saw exactly what he'd feared the most. She saw the impact the truth was having on his sister. Lee looked as if she'd just lost her moorings. Emotions as raw as an open wound warred in her: shock, grief, confusion. Amanda took a step toward the girl, trying to pull her away before she could hurt Jake with her dawning sense of betrayal, but it was too late. Before Amanda could move, Jake turned on his heel and ran out the door.

"Jake!" she yelled, running after him.

"He can't read?" Lee demanded, her voice dissolving with the sudden, flooding tears. "Dear God, Amanda. He's never been able to read?"

Chapter 15

Amanda turned on Lee, flailing in her own emotions, lost the minute she'd seen the light go out in Jake's eyes. Torn between following him and facing his sister. She knew what she wanted to do, but she knew what Jake would allow. She stayed.

Lee looked almost as bad as her brother had. "All this time?" she demanded, her voice impossibly young, her eyes a wasteland. "And he never told us?"

"How could he tell you?" Amanda challenged. "He couldn't take the time out to learn when he was young. It was all he could do to keep a roof over your heads. He was seven when your dad started pulling him out of school to help, Lee."

"But now—"

"Now he has to admit to his baby sister who's attending a top-ten university on a partial scholarship, who talks Chaucer and Hesse, that he's never even known how to write a check? A man as proud as Jake? How do you expect him to do that?"

"But we could have helped!"

Finally Amanda went to her. "I know, honey," she soothed, enfolding the girl into her arms. "I know. He just couldn't bear to see you three lose faith in him."

"I humiliated him," she sobbed. "Oh, God, Amanda, I feel like I'm dying inside. He has to hurt so badly."

He does, Amanda thought, shutting her eyes against her own tears. You can't know, little girl, just how badly he feels. "We'll all get by this," she promised. "Maybe this is what he needed to get him started."

Lee lifted her head. "You knew," she breathed. "You figured it out. How? We've lived here all our lives and we didn't know."

Amanda's smile was sad. "Because Uncle Mick was illiterate. Nobody knows that but me, because I was the one who interceded with the world for him. Just like you guys did. *You* read his mail for him before he hired Betty, didn't you?"

Lee nodded, surprised. "He just said he was so tired from riding. And that he couldn't write letters and stuff because his handwriting was so bad. I mean, we always laughed about it, because his signature was so awful.... Betty," she said. "Wouldn't she know? Would she really know and not help him?"

Amanda could only offer a shrug. "Maybe she suspects. Maybe she thinks she's helping him by keeping his secret."

Still Lee shook her head, trying to comprehend the years of painful deception. "But, Amanda, there were so many things. How could he get by? How could we not know?"

"Lee, there are a truckload of tricks you can use to get by. And if you set yourself up as a man who does things just a certain way—"

Lee's abrupt laughter was bitter and lost. "Jake's way," she protested feebly. "We all say it about him. Oh, God, Amanda. What are we going to do?"

"We'll wait here for him, so we can talk before anybody else on the ranch shows up in the morning. Now, why don't you go on in and wash your face? He's probably down in the barn. Let's give him a little time alone, and then we can go talk to him."

"What do I say to him, Amanda? How do I face him again?"

Amanda took a big breath and fought the terrible frustration of impatience, of fear, of hurt. "Tell him you love him.

Tell him thank-you for getting you to that fancy school of yours. Whatever you do, don't tell him you're sorry."

Amanda thought maybe she should do the dishes, but her hands were shaking and her mind was down at that barn. She could build a new fire in the fireplace. If she hadn't left her dulcimer at the cabin, she could have attacked that for a while. Jake needed his room, and Amanda was going to give it to him if it killed her. Then she heard the rumble of a truck engine turning over.

"Where's he going now?" Amanda demanded, more to herself as she peeked out the front window to see the truck back away from its slot.

"The cabin," Lee said, walking back out of the bathroom. "Whenever he's really upset about something he heads right up there. I hope he's taking Buck. Buck doesn't mind him in bad moods."

"He's not taking a horse," Amanda said, turning back. "He's taking the truck."

"The truck?" Lee demanded, coming to a stop. "He can't take the truck."

"Why?"

"The bridge is out over Parson's Creek. Snow melt and the storm, I guess. The creek's a mess. That's why I came back, because I couldn't get by. There's a—" suddenly the color melted from Lee's face "—a sign." She breathed in horror. "My God, Amanda, he won't be able to read it."

"Yes, he will," Amanda reassured her. "He's learned to recognize road signs. The color and shape will alert him."

"No," Lee protested, as she headed for the door. "That's just it. There is no road sign yet. Just some hand-painted thing on cardboard at the side of the road. Amanda, he won't realize it in time. That creek bed's twenty feet down!"

They reached the lawn to see the taillights to the truck disappear around a bend.

"I'll get my car," Amanda decided, turning for the door and her keys.

Lee followed right on her heels. "No! You won't reach him in time. You know how that road is, Amanda. It's twisty and narrow, and the rain's made it too slick." Just inside the door, she grabbed Amanda's arm. "Grayboy," she said. "He can get me across that meadow faster than Jake can take the turns. I'll head Jake off."

"Lee, it's a mess up there. You can't really outrun a truck."

"It's not even a fourth of the distance," Lee protested. "And Grayboy's still the fastest thing on four legs. Please, Amanda."

Amanda spent precious seconds vacillating. Finally she nodded. "Come on," she commanded, shoving her out the door. "I'll follow Jake in my Jeep. And be careful!" she yelled to the girl's fleeing back. "It's getting dark!"

As she turned out into the drive, Amanda saw Lee swing onto Grayboy's bare back and spur the horse into a full gallop up the meadow. The sun teetered along the edges of the mountain, throwing the valley into shadow. Water glistened on the grass, and the last of the storm clouds blotted out the other half of the sky. A dazzling sunset, like all sunsets in Wyoming. Amanda never noticed.

The rain had left the road slick and dangerous. Jake fishtailed the truck a couple of times turning onto the mountain road that led up to the cabin. He didn't see the deer skitter back into the woods to his left, or the hawk make its last turns for the evening high over his head. He didn't see the sun strike sparks off the gleaming white snow on the mountains or the gem-blue sky west of the last clouds. All he saw was the look in Lee's eyes.

The horror. The betrayal. The confusion.

He'd done that to her. He'd done it year after year, lying to her, breaking her fragile trust as surely as if he'd stolen something away. The fact that it hadn't been his choice didn't matter.

He couldn't face her again. He couldn't face Amanda, knowing that he'd left her to clean up his mess. She'd probably held Lee in her arms while she'd told her about her brother's little problem. She'd soothed and instructed, as compassionate and pragmatic as always. Taking over the job that had always been Jake's. Assuming the privilege he'd always cherished more than any other. Because he hadn't been there. Because he'd been the problem.

Jake rubbed at his face, at his eyes that burned unbearably. He slammed through the gears and skidded along sharp curves, the truck protesting like a freighter in a storm. It didn't matter. None of it mattered. He just had to get away. He had to get up to that meadow where no one else walked, where the old dreams still lived. He should have gone up on Buck, but Clovis would have been in the stables with all his questions and assumptions. Buck had stayed in his stall and Jake had taken the truck.

It would be dark by the time he got up to the cabin. Too dark to go in where Amanda's aroma, her books and her dulcimer would keep him company. He'd be fingering his memories in there, remembering what that comforter had felt like against his back when he'd had her in his arms.

He couldn't bear that he'd lost the peace of that cabin by finding happiness there. Even so, it was the only place he knew to go. The only isolation that would suffice. So today he would settle for the meadow.

Almost too late, he slammed on his brakes rounding a corner. There was a slow-moving pickup ahead of him. The truck whined in protest as Jake geared down, riding his gas and brake pedal unmercifully, edging too close to the slower truck in front. He was usually a careful driver. He saw no sense in risking his neck or anybody else's on a road, when the feeling of speed was much more satisfying on a horse.

Tonight was different. Tonight, he wasn't in the mood to share the road. He wasn't in the mood for tact or understanding or common sense. Which was why he needed to be alone.

Which was why he'd needed to run.

An addiction. Amanda had been right. Hiding his disability was an addiction, consuming more and more of his life until there just wasn't anything else left. It ate away freedom and made a joke of choice. Every day the lies that surrounded his deception got a little bigger, that supported it got a little stronger, until they were prison walls no man could scale, and Jake was left with nothing but the taste of futility in his mouth.

And once in, there was no way out. He'd met the face of humiliation once; he didn't have the courage to do it again.

And so he ran. And he'd keep on running the rest of his life, from Amanda and Lee and Zeke and Gen, until he'd end up alone and frightened and frozen on that ranch with no way out.

He noticed the car behind him just as he finally lost patience and pulled out to pass the truck. The car was coming on even faster than he was. Jake's smile was grim. Maybe somebody else had worse news than his. Well, they wouldn't catch up. By the time they wanted to pass him, he'd be on the service road that led to the cabin. Another two turns and he'd arrive at the bridge over Parson's Creek.

He already had his blinker on when he saw the sign. A crude cardboard square hung to a light post with big scrawled letters. Probably somebody with a lost cat. Behind him the approaching car was flashing its brights. Jake figured the driver had just come up to that other truck back there. He took half a second to notice and wonder what kind of luck he'd have getting around where the only shoulder was a steep grade straight down the hill. When he turned back, it was too late.

"No!" he screamed, jamming on the brakes. The truck spun into an arc on the blacktop, skidding over toward the steep drop to the right. He jerked the wheel hard, trying to miss her, trying to send the truck right over the side if he could just miss her.

He missed her. It didn't matter. Somehow Lee had appeared in the middle of the road seated atop Grayboy. Waving frantically at him. Yelling. The sudden appearance of the truck around the bend spooked the horse. The screech of tires sent him straight up into the air.

Jake battled the truck to a stop inches from the horse. He pulled the door open even before he'd stopped, trying to get to Lee. Trying to stop it from happening.

"Lee!"

She scrabbled to stay upright. Grayboy's shoes slid across the slick road. His forelegs flailed in the air. His whinny was shrill and terrified. Lee fought him, trying to regain balance. Jake ran for them both.

"Jake!" was all she was able to scream before the two of them toppled backward into the yawning hole in the road.

* * *

The hospital was too bright, too noisy and impersonal. Amanda hated it. She hated the brisk nurses and the stern doctors and the machinery that kept her from Lee. She hated most of all the lights that betrayed just what kind of toll this was taking on Jake.

He sat for a few minutes and then he paced. Then he sat again, rubbing at his face as if he wanted to abrade something away. Drinking cup after cup of coffee and then crushing the plastic cups in his hands. Blaming himself, torturing himself for what had happened.

And Amanda had no choice but to sit alongside and watch.

She couldn't even see the night outside. Couldn't tell what time it was except by the institutional clock on the wall. They'd been at the hospital for three hours. It had taken an hour and a half to get Lee there. During that time, Jake had been like iron. He was the one who'd battled the swollen water to drag her out of the riverbed. He'd held her in his arms all the way back to the ranch and then kept her warm until the rescue unit had arrived. He'd ridden all the way to the hospital with her, refusing to be parted from her or treated for the cuts and bruises he'd sustained getting to her.

He'd only begun to fall apart when they'd arrived and Lee had disappeared into that sterile, alien place. He curled tighter and tighter into himself, refusing to speak, refusing to listen, until Amanda was terrified that it would be Jake they would lose tonight instead of Lee.

"Excuse me, Mr. Kendall."

Both of them looked up to see a nurse in scrubs standing in the door to the waiting room. Beyond stretched the intensive care units—doors beyond which one had to be invited. Amanda and Jake had not been yet.

"Can I see her?" he demanded, already on his feet. "Is she awake?"

His voice was raw and bleak. He still carried his hat in his hands, and Amanda could see that they shook. She climbed to her feet and stood beside him.

The nurse held a clipboard in her hands. She looked anxious. "I'm afraid not, Mr. Kendall. There's a problem. We had to call the trauma surgeon back in."

Jake froze. "Her head?" he asked. "Is it her head?"

The nurse shook her head. "No," she said. "The scan didn't show anything acute there. Like I said before, we're just going to have to wait to know about that. It's her belly. She's bleeding. The tests we've done indicate that it's her spleen and liver. Dr. Goldman wants to take her down to surgery."

"She's been here three hours," Jake protested. "Why didn't you know this before?"

"She was stable until now," the nurse said. "It happens this way sometimes."

"What do you need me to do?"

She handed over the clipboard. "If you could read this surgery permit. I'd be happy to answer any questions for you. Since she can't sign permission herself, we need you to do it as her next of kin."

Jake just stared at the clipboard, his face like stone, his eyes empty and lost.

"Mr. Kendall?" the nurse prodded.

"My...uh, sister," he stammered with a little shake of his head. "She's a doctor. She should be here in a couple of hours. She'd know about this stuff. I just..."

But the nurse was shaking her head. "I'm sorry. We really can't wait. The surgery has to be done immediately, or we might lose her."

Amanda took a step forward and held out her hand for the clipboard. "If you'd just give us a minute," she asked quietly, trying her best to smile.

The nurse looked at her, looked at Jake. Finally she answered Amanda's tentative smile and handed over the clipboard. "Surgery's preparing right now," she cautioned. "Everything is ready."

Amanda scanned the form. It was standard, requesting permission for any eventuality, warning that any of the procedures may still result in death.

Amanda faced the nurse again. "We'll be right out with it."

That was all the nurse needed.

Amanda waited until she'd closed the door behind her and faced Jake. "We don't have a choice, Jake. They have to do the surgery."

He motioned to the paper, his eyes so bleak that it was all Amanda could do to meet them. "What does it say?"

That was when her heart finally broke for him. She wanted to go to him. She wanted to run. She wanted to weep. Instead, she faced Jake with calm consideration and then bent to the task of reading the form aloud as he stood before her, his hat clenched in his hands, his pain a living thing.

He signed it, just like he signed everything at the ranch, with a big K and a scrawl. And then after the nurse had returned for the paperwork and disappeared back into the intensive care units with it, Jake sat down on a hard plastic chair and sobbed.

Zeke and Gen showed up almost at the same time, one trailing Clovis, and the other, Ed Deever. It was now closer to dawn, and Amanda held Jake's hand, as she had all along.

"What's happening?" Gen demanded without preamble. She was livelier than she appeared in her photos, with that same saucy cant to her mouth that Lee had. Now, though, that mouth was set in a grim line. Her eyes melted like chocolate when she saw what kind of condition her brother was in.

"Jake," she soothed, her arms automatically around him. "Honey, it's gonna be all right. The experts are in the field now. We'll keep an eye on her."

Jake couldn't even answer. He just closed his eyes and dropped his head onto to his little sister's shoulder.

"You must be Amanda," Zeke greeted her, hand out. Another handsome Kendall, with Gen's dark features and Jake's rock-solid jawline. Tall and slim and windblown.

Amanda pulled out a smile for him as she shook hands. "Then that makes you Zeke."

"I heard you got Jake to wear the sweater. We consider that a minor miracle in this household."

"Any small help I can be," she answered, knowing that even now she was being judged for her worthiness for the Kendall big brother. If she hadn't been so thoroughly drained, so taut and miserable, she might have found the situation amusing.

"Gen," Jake was saying, and only Amanda could still hear the tears he'd spent in that lonely, cold room. "This is Amanda Marlow."

Amanda turned toward yet another appraising eye. She just smiled. "Thanksgiving would have been better," she allowed.

Gen's answering smile was genuine. "Lee's talked about you once or twice," she answered. "What's the latest word on her?"

"She's in surgery," Jake said, his voice cracking, his eyes lifting to battle the moisture that glittered in them.

Gen immediately shot to attention. "Surgery? They weren't talking about it when I left to get here. What happened?"

But Jake was reduced to shaking his head again.

Back at the door Clovis and Ed stood in mute tandem, hats in hands.

"The nurse said possibly her spleen and liver," Amanda offered quietly, so tired of waiting, of worrying, of being the only shoulder to carry this weight. "Said that sometimes they look stable at first, but later something happens?"

Right before her eyes, Gen metamorphosed from little sister into medical resident. Gathering a kind of cool authority about her, the young woman bobbed her head and turned to her older brother.

"Yeah, well, we'll just see about that. You guys sit tight for a minute. I'm going in to talk to that ICU crowd."

"The door says authorized personnel only," Zeke offered laconically.

Gen's smile was piratical. "I just aced my finals in medical arrogance. Watch this."

"Boss," Clovis offered diffidently from his position as Gen swung through the doors no one else thought to breach. "I brought you and Amanda some dry clothes. You wanna change?"

Jake didn't even seem to hear him. Amanda saw that Zeke wasn't nearly as nonchalant as he appeared. She knew that he saw exactly what toll this was taking on Jake. The only comment he made was a worried lift of the eyebrow in Amanda's direction.

"Why don't you leave the clothes, Clovis?" Amanda asked. "Maybe when the word comes down on Lee . . ."

His nod was abrupt and uncertain. "She's a tough little filly, boss. She'll be just fine."

"I know," Jake answered, not bothering to turn his attention from where Gen had disappeared.

Amanda surreptitiously took his hand back in hers and exerted the gentlest of pressure. "Time doesn't pass any faster standing up," she offered gently.

His lip curled a little. "That another one of those quaint little sayings you two collect?" he demanded.

Amanda actually chuckled. "No," she admitted. "That's an original. Now, sit down."

Amazingly enough, he did.

"What happened?" Zeke asked, getting himself some coffee. "All I got was that it was an accident."

"It was an accident," was all Amanda would say.

"Jake," Ed spoke up, brushing his magnificent handlebar with nervous fingers. "Anything else I can do?"

It caught Jake's attention. He looked up at the store owner who had driven to Jackson Hole airport for Gen in the dead of night, and his expression lightened. "You've been a real friend, Ed. Thanks. I don't—"

He couldn't finish. Embarrassed, Ed ducked his head. "You just let me know. And let us all know how little Lee's doing, hear?"

Jake nodded. Amanda was going to have to tell Jake how his neighbors and friends reacted. There were four more of them out at that ranch who had organized the transportation in for Gen and Zeke, and another half dozen had offered everything from food to horse care during the crisis. The nurses had told Amanda that the entire town of Lost Ridge had been on the phone at least once asking after Lee, and asking to pass along the word that all Jake had to do was ask. More would have been there except that the hospital was so distant.

"Clovis," Jake said. "You might go with Ed. It'll be time to feed the horses soon."

Clovis jumped to attention, glad for the order. "You bet, boss. You want me to cover Target Watch with Grayboy like we'd planned today?"

Amanda's heart froze. Her hand closed more tightly around Jake's. But it was Jake who answered.

"Grayboy's dead."

Amanda heard Clovis gasp. She knew that Ed and Zeke went very still. No one knew yet. They'd brought Lee back to the ranch in the back of the truck, so the paramedics could be called. No one except Jake and Amanda knew that Grayboy's body still lay down in that ravine where he'd broken his neck.

"Boss!" Clovis pleaded, his face screwing up in distress. "What're you talkin' about?"

"Lee was riding Grayboy last night," Jake said. "They fell."

"But it was dark!" the little man protested. "What was that girl doin' ridin' a valuable animal like that in the dark?"

"Clovis!" It was a roar, and it shook the room to silence. Amanda felt the shudders race through Jake. She saw the threadbare control fray even further.

"I'll explain tomorrow," she said, trying her best to convince the foreman to go with only the message in her eyes.

He understood. With only one more jerky nod, he resat his weatherbeaten old Stetson and turned for the door. "I'll take care of things till you get back," was all he said in farewell.

Left behind, Amanda and Zeke watched Jake from either side. The clock ticked inexorably, and the truth remained caught between Jake and Amanda. Zeke's jaw was working. Even so, the young man kept his silence. He stretched, got to his feet and poured another round of coffee.

The three of them spun the minute the door opened.

It was Gen. Still in her professional persona, still grim-faced. Striding across the floor instead of strolling.

"What?" Jake demanded, already on his feet.

Gen waved aside the question. "Nothing new, I'm afraid. I was just catching up. She was awfully lucky that she didn't have a neck injury the way you guys played cowboy and dragged her back in a truck, for God's sake."

"Gen," Zeke admonished.

Gen waved him off, too. "Force of habit. I'm sorry. The sum total is, a broken forearm, a dandy of a laceration on her head—by the way, Jake, I like the model that you're sporting. We should get that treated while we're here—"

"Drop it, Gen."

She just nodded. "Yeah, right. Who am I to talk medicine to you? Anyway, she doesn't have any bleeding in her head, just some swelling, which we'll know if it's going to get better in a few hours. As to the belly, it was definitely spleen and liver. So far, she's a lucky little girl."

"So far?" Jake demanded.

Gen did her best to flash him her most unconcerned smile. It didn't quite work. "They know what the problem is. They're still trying to fix it. They're also giving her quite a bit of nice, new blood."

"Which means what?"

"We wait. You read the op permit. They have a lot of stuff to do, and all of it's tricky."

Jake grew, if possible, more rigid, until Amanda was sure he'd just snap in two. She couldn't believe he was still standing up. She couldn't believe he was conscious. Even so, when Zeke shoved a cup of coffee into his hand, he could hardly raise it to his lips to drink.

"You really should get some sleep, baby," Gen coaxed him, her eyes as eloquent as her sister's. "You'll scare the hell out of her if she sees you this way."

Jake just shook his head.

"Do you want to tell us now?" Zeke asked.

Gen looked over at him. Amanda didn't.

"What?" Gen asked.

Zeke turned to his sister, and then his brother. "Exactly how Lee fell in the dark and killed Grayboy and landed herself in surgery."

"Grayboy?" Gen demanded, whirling on Jake. "Grayboy's dead? My God, Jake, what happened?"

Amanda couldn't draw breath. She couldn't move or think. Jake hummed next to her like a tuning fork. She couldn't bear anymore. She simply couldn't. If this had to go on again and again, she couldn't do it.

"It was a freak accident," she said, anyway, instinctively fulfilling the function she'd had all those years ago.

But before she could finish constructing her lie, Jake turned on her. "No," he disagreed, determination flickering amidst the wasteland of his grief and guilt. "It wasn't a freak accident."

"Jake," Amanda protested instinctively, knowing what he was going to do, what it would cost. Knowing how little he could afford it right now.

"What was it?" Gen asked.

Jake wrapped his fingers around Amanda's and turned back to his family. And Amanda, sudden tears blinding her, held her breath.

Chapter 16

Amanda was all that held Jake together. Amanda's fingers twined through his, the only thing he felt; her support the only thing he recognized. She'd stood by him all night, when he was silent and when he was raging like a frightened child and when he was running again. She hadn't betrayed pity or disappointment or disdain. All Jake had seen in her eyes had been love and pain and support.

She was still willing to let him lie, to stand by his deception until he was ready to admit the truth. She was willing to take the weight from his shoulders until he was ready to bear it himself.

Well, he couldn't run anymore. He couldn't stand the thought of hiding behind her deception. Of having to think of her feeling she had to perpetuate something that had gone on far too long.

Far, far too long.

"Lee was trying to head me off," Jake said simply. "She knew the Parson's Creek bridge was out. And she knew I wouldn't realize it until it was too late. She cut across the meadow on Grayboy."

"You're kidding," Zeke protested. "Wasn't there even a sign up there warning people? No wonder—"

"There was a sign," Jake told his brother. "I couldn't read it."

Amanda held on tighter. Zeke and Gen turned to their brother, not understanding.

"I can't read anything," Jake told him. "I never have. I'm illiterate."

There was a dreadful silence. Jake held on to Amanda, knowing nothing else would help. Knowing it was the only way to face the stunned disbelief in Gen and Zeke's eyes.

"What?" Zeke demanded.

"I can't read," Jake repeated calmly, his insides twisting in dreadful anticipation.

"That's ridiculous," Gen objected instinctively.

Amanda held on tighter. Jake could feel it. He drew on her strength when he had none left, and knew that no matter what else happened he could never let her get on that plane back to Boston. No matter what he had to do or give up or learn, he had to make sure she stayed where she belonged. On the Diamond K with him.

If she'd have him.

"No, it's not, Gen," Jake admitted, too tired to cover the weary resignation in his voice. "I never learned to read. I've been too ashamed to let anybody know all these years. Amanda realized it. She's been trying to talk me into doing something about it."

He saw both Gen and Zeke swing stunned looks at Amanda and then back at him. He saw their identical denial, their wavering balance, just as he'd seen in Lee's eyes, and knew now that it couldn't hurt any worse than it had. After what had happened to Lee, it just didn't matter so much anymore.

"It was my fault Lee was hurt," he admitted.

"Jake Kendall—" Amanda immediately protested, a fist headed for her hip.

He turned the best smile he could on her, even knowing that it probably looked grim. "Stop sticking up for me, Amanda. It's the truth. I couldn't face it when Lee found out. I ran. And I ran so fast I didn't think. You two were trying to keep me from breaking my fool neck down that ravine."

Her answering smile was delivered through tear-swollen eyes. "Okay," she agreed. "I'll accept that. You do have a fool neck."

"But I don't understand," Zeke protested. "You were always reading to us. Homework and books and stories and the paper."

Jake smiled at his little brother. "You were reading to me," he corrected him. "Or to each other. Think hard, Zeke. It'll come to you."

The two of them—hotshot professionals, top of their classes, out to set the world on its ear—looked like ten-year-olds standing there trying to understand. Jake didn't blame them.

"You always had us reading, Jake," Gen protested. "Everything we could get our hands on. You rode us harder than the teachers did when we didn't get assignments in on time."

Jake shrugged. "I didn't want it to happen again. Dad couldn't read, either."

It wasn't the place he'd ever intended to reveal that. He'd never intended to reveal it at all. He'd seen what illiteracy had done to a man, reducing him to quiet isolation, scratching out a living on a farm, sentencing his son to the same. He wasn't going to do it to his brother and sisters. It was a vow he'd made a long time ago, and one he'd never regretted keeping.

Gen sank straight into her chair. "I didn't know."

Jake reached out a hand and tousled her hair. "You weren't supposed to. Mom always covered for him. She covered for me, too, while she could."

When Gen lifted her face to him, there were tears in her eyes. "Oh, Jake." She sighed, reaching up for his other hand. "I always wondered if you weren't pushing us out because you really didn't want us there."

Jake hadn't thought he'd survive this. He did. He sat down, settling Amanda next to him, and faced his family with the first real truth he'd ever shared with them.

"I wanted you free of the cycle," he said, taking his little sister by the hands. "You deserved choices, all of you. I wouldn't trade a minute of it, knowing that you're doing what you want."

"But what about you?" Gen demanded. "You're not doing what you want."

Jake could actually offer her a smile. "I'm doing exactly what I want," he told her. "Even if I were Einstein I wouldn't want to live anywhere else than right where I am. I wouldn't do anything but raise and break horses."

"But you'd read," Zeke prodded.

Jake took a second to restore himself with the sight of Amanda sitting next to him. Even exhausted and disheveled, even caught beneath the glaring hospital fluorescents that sapped skin color, she looked more alive than anyone Jake had ever known. More beautiful. The classiest woman he'd ever known, and it wasn't until she was in ripped jeans and a T-shirt that he'd really understood it.

"Yes," he finally admitted to Zeke, thinking how he wanted to go visit those isolated sites where Zeke dug out pottery shards and arrowheads. "I'd read. But that seems to be the next major project to be undertaken at the Diamond K." He felt the tension seep out of Amanda at his words and took his turn holding her hand.

"I'm sorry, Amanda," he apologized. "I haven't been fair to you, either."

"We can make amends later," she assured him.

He met her gaze then, excluding everyone, everything else. Bathing in that green, offering his own strength where he'd thought he'd had none, his promises when he'd thought she wouldn't want them. Far away from his ranch, from the peace and majesty of his mountains and the chatter of his stream, Jake Kendall rediscovered its worth in the eyes of a woman.

"I don't know, Zeke," Gen quipped dryly. "Next we'll be hearing that this here writer woman has him going to the theater or something."

"Museum of Modern Art," Jake offered, never taking his gaze from Amanda's now amused one. "New York."

She nodded. "I know a great little restaurant nearby. . . ."

His brother and sister made rude noises, and that made Jake smile even more.

Nurses came and went. The doctor stopped in, as bedraggled and sweat-soaked as one of Jake's old hats, to say that Lee

had made it through surgery. He still wouldn't promise anything, but he did offer to let them see her when she woke up
enough to appreciate their presence. Jake stood silently,
Amanda's arm holding him up as the doctor and Gen dueled
with medical terminology.

Somewhere beyond the windowless walls of the waiting room
the night struggled to morning, and the day shift filtered in.
And still, they waited.

By the time the nurse came back, Jake had to wake Amanda
from where she'd fallen asleep with her head in his lap. He fingered her hair where it lay tangled across his leg and bent down
to her ear.

"Hello, Amanda."

Her smile was quick and telling even before she opened her
eyes. "Hello, Jake."

"We can go in and see Lee. Wanna come?"

She bolted up so fast he almost lost a couple of teeth.

"What do they say?" she demanded, pushing her hair back
out of her eyes with trembling hands.

Gen was already on the nurse's heels, with Zeke quickly following.

"They say, come on in and see your sister before we throw
you out. Now, come on."

Jake still held on to her hand. He did it selfishly, knowing
that he wasn't prepared for seeing Lee like this. Knowing that
he was still depending on this small, slim woman next to him for
his strength, that somehow he always would. Even so, he
walked in feeling better than he had in years. Curiously at peace
for what he'd gone through in the last twenty-four hours.

There was equipment everywhere, all of it beeping and
blinking and threatening. There were monitors and IV bags and
pumps, and a nurse checking everything. And in the middle,
nestled in a stark white bed and swathed in bandages, Lee almost disappeared into the white sheets. Jake's heart lurched
when he saw how pale she was, how small and young and suddenly fragile. He held on to Amanda, and made it on in.

"You don't have to go to all this trouble just to get us home,"
Zeke assured the girl. "A phone call would have done."

Gen was too busy checking settings and harassing the nurse for a proper greeting just yet.

Still groggy, Lee took a minute to focus on everybody in the room. Finally she found Jake, and his heart dropped. Her face automatically folded into distress.

"Grayboy?" she asked, her voice not much more than a rasp. "Jake, is he all right?"

"You're all right," he retorted, bending past his other sister and all the machinery to deposit a kiss on the girl's forehead. "I think that's plenty for one night."

"Oh, he's dead, isn't he?" she asked, tearing up. "Jake, I'm sorry—"

Jake battled the harsh ache in his chest as he finally let go of Amanda to take his sister's hand in both of his. "Grayboy is a horse, honey. As much as I like horses, I happen to like my baby sister a hell of a lot more. I'd say I still made out great on the deal. Although we do need to talk about the fact that you were much too close to the edge of that ravine—"

"Jake—" his siblings and Amanda admonished together.

He nodded. "Good point. I'll have plenty of chances to chew you out while you're home getting better." He lifted a hand to her cheek, to that face he'd thought he'd have to close into a casket and almost choked. "Thanks, squirt. You pretty much saved my worthless hide."

She still didn't look relieved. "I shouldn't have gotten that close," she whispered. "But there wasn't room around that curve. And I'd just gotten there—"

"Will you knock it off?" Gen demanded, finally pausing long enough to see her sister in all the machinery. "He just told you he owes you his life. If I were you, I'd be thinking of something astronomical for paybacks. This is the only time you're gonna get it."

"Oh, Gen, I—"

Jake couldn't leave her that way. "All right," he offered. "How 'bout this? How 'bout I give you what you've always dreamed of?"

Gen smiled like a pirate. "Oh, this could be very good."

"I changed my mind," Lee whispered to Jake, "about what I always dreamed of."

Jake arched an eyebrow at her. "You don't want your very own sister-in-law?"

"What?" she demanded.

"What?" Gen echoed, almost bumping her head on the monitor as she came upright.

"What?" Amanda squeaked from behind him.

"Of course I want that," Lee insisted, affording Amanda a heartfelt glance. "I just . . . want more."

"You want me to be able to read your congratulatory telegram," Jake said.

Lee's eyes widened. She looked over at her brother and sister and saw the truth in their eyes. She turned back to Jake, and he let her know in silence what he should have let her know last night. That everything was all right. That it would be better.

Finally her expression eased. "Heck, no," she retorted with some of her old sauce. "The message I scrawl on your back window in soap."

Jake turned to Amanda. "I've raised a terrorist," he complained. "How encouraging."

"Is it a deal?" Lee demanded.

Jake pretended to think about it. "I guess I wouldn't mind finding out if that Amanda Marlow character's the writer she's cracked up to be."

As much as she could, Lee beamed. "Can I be maid of honor?"

"Depends on if I can hold out that long," Jake said.

"Depends on if I say yes," Amanda amended.

They all turned on her.

"What would work better?" Zeke asked. "Threats or bribery?"

"If you don't marry him," Gen echoed, "who will?"

Jake stiffened in outrage. "I beg your pardon. I'm quite a catch."

"You're a ten-dollar Stetson on a five-cent head," Lee informed him archly.

Jake turned that outrage on her. "Oh, God. You are feeling better."

Lee grinned at him. "I got plenty more where that came from."

Amanda actually giggled. "Yeah. Right here."

Jake turned to her, took her two hands in his, met her amused gaze with his suddenly intense one. "Will you?" he asked.

"Will you?" the other three echoed even more intensely.

"Hey," he protested, not bothering to turn from where Amanda was answering him even without words. "I do my own proposing."

Gen turned to her sister. "This from a man who wouldn't even accept a date to Sadie Hawkins Day."

Jake didn't even hear the teasing. He didn't see the ten-dollar bills being pulled from pockets behind him. He just saw Amanda, just suddenly saw walls tumble and the fresh spring sunlight pour in, and he trembled with the heady rush of freedom.

"I'm sorry," he said to her. "I've been bullheaded and afraid and confused. I promise not to be anymore if you marry me."

Amanda grinned. "Don't make promises you can't keep. All I want is the important one."

"To love, honor and all that?"

She nodded. "That's the one. And to keep a heater up in that cabin all winter in case I need to get away to write."

Jake didn't exactly answer her. He pulled her into his arms and reminded them both of what lay in store for them. He heard the crinkle of money behind him, but he decided to ignore it. He knew exactly who ended up with it all, anyway.

"I told you guys she'd be the one," Lee crowed.

Epilogue

" "My mama was a pow-wow woman. Why, she could say the words to stop bleeding or conjure the fire right outta burns. She were a right holy woman, citin' scripture for the power to heal. And when she conjured, she'd say, three times, 'cause three times is important—*Out fire, in frost, in the name of the Father, the Son and the Holy Ghost.*' "

"Who was that again?" Mick asked.

Jake looked up from the book he was reading aloud and considered the question for his son. "Let's see," he mused, counting generations on fingers. "Your great-great-great grandmother."

"And you put her in your book, Mom?"

Amanda looked up from where she was researching Scottish folklore and smiled for her precocious seven-year-old, but it was Jake who answered.

"Mom put all of them in the book," Jake assured the towhead who looked just like the pictures of his grandfather on the piano. Some day Amanda would tell Mick about him. He already knew about his namesake, and now he was learning about his genealogy. "Bart and Hattie and all the first generation of Kendalls in Wyoming," Jake continued. "Along with Willy's ancestors from up near the Wind River Reservation."

Mick nodded solemnly. "That's cool, Dad. Maybe some day she'll write a book about us."

"Maybe she will," Amanda agreed.

Sooner than Mick thought. She'd already been throwing ideas off Jake about writing a modern story about a proud man with a silent handicap, of the impact it had on him and the people he loved. Jake had been all in favor of it.

It had been such hard work. There had been more strain in the first year of her marriage than in the years after she'd been orphaned. Jake was, after all, a proud man, and it tore at him to have to struggle through a children's primer. Even with the help of computer programs, he'd fought and fumed and spent a lot of time on horseback up in the high meadow.

But Jake Kendall was not a quitter. In anything. And the first time Amanda had been able to share New York with him, had seen him order from a menu and read street signs he'd only heard of his whole life, she'd truly understood what the two of them had accomplished together. They had laughed through the whole trip, and had celebrated by testing comforters in some of the best hotels in town.

Amanda heard the back door slam and knew it could only be one of two people. Lee was currently visiting the cabin, and Clovis was due back from town.

"Boss?"

"In here, Clovis."

"No, Daddy," three-year-old Melissa objected from his other side. "My turn."

"Hang in there, pard," Jake suggested, tousling her thick, dark hair.

Amanda grinned again. Who could have pictured this that first afternoon she'd met Jake? Comfortably ensconced on the couch with his two children, his reading glasses sliding down his nose, for a moment forgetting the ranch. He'd never quite made it to sweaters and corduroy slacks, but that wasn't something Amanda missed. Especially when jeans still looked so very good on him.

"You want to come on down for Sidewinder and Gray-lady?" Clovis asked, hat in hand. At the last moment, he turned a sheepish smile on Amanda. "Afternoon, Amanda."

"Clovis," she greeted him. She didn't have to say anything. Clovis understood ritual, and he'd just interrupted one of the most sacred Kendall rites. It was just a matter of whether Jake would be able to withstand the lure of seeing his best cutting stallion cover his award-winning Grayboy get.

Amanda shook her head. Sidewinder. Of all the surprises. Seven inches away from being gelded, bought from Bill Nelson as incorrigible, the horse had finally let Jake channel all that energy and rage into cattle. It had proved a more impressive find than Grayghost with Jake Kendall himself rewriting cutting horse history on the big palomino. He'd been waiting a long time to start this new dynasty.

"Clovis," he objected, an eye to his wife, "this is reading time. You know that."

"But, boss, I sure think she's ready."

"Well, Sidewinder's a pretty attractive devil," Jake countered. "I'll bet she'll still be interested in another twenty minutes."

Clovis dipped his head in acceptance. Amanda knew Jake thought Clovis was disappointed. Only Amanda saw those sly smiles he gave her. A smoothly run ranch had become a real sparkler in the last few years.

"Daddy," Melissa persisted, pulling on Jake's shirt. "Now."

"Don't you want to hear more about the Kendalls?"

She shoved a brightly illustrated, oversized book straight at his stomach. "No. Binkleys."

Jake huffed. "Aren't you tired of reading about monsters yet?"

Melissa's smile was angelic, coy, and purely calculated. Amanda fought the laughter that bubbled up in her chest. She'd thought they'd have trouble with Lee. Melissa was going to be pure hell. That is, if Jake ever let her out of the house.

"Oh, okay, baby. Monsters it is."

"Then can we go riding?" Mick demanded.

"Yes, Daddy, please!"

Jake's smile broadened noticeably as he shot his wife a triumphant smile. "They're my kids all right."

"We're going to have to change the name of the ranch," Amanda quipped. "To the Three *R*s. Reading, Riding and Roping."

Jake slanted her a look of pure deviltry. "What about writing?"

She arched him a scowl. "That's a *W* word, Jake."

"I knew that. I just wanted to see if you did."

"If you do," she challenged, meeting that suddenly warm blue gaze with her own, "then you might want to use that *W* word on your brother. He's a little upset that he hasn't heard from you."

"My handwriting's still a mess," Jake protested.

"Daddy!" Melissa objected, tugging again and giving him another nudge with the book.

Amanda knew he wasn't paying attention anymore. "You're still using that as an excuse," she accused, struggling against the smile that his challenge was provoking. A smile of combat, of imminent skirmish. Although, Amanda knew all too well by now, the contest wouldn't be verbal. And, with two children sitting on the couch, it wouldn't be immediate. They'd tease each other with it for now, meeting in odd places to cast barbs, to join in a few steps to heighten the tension until they could be alone. Until they could spark the embers that always throbbed between them.

Never taking his gaze from her, Jake disentangled himself from the kids. "Excuse me a minute," he apologized absently. "I have to go have a few words with your mother about a man's prerogatives."

"Prerogatives?" Amanda countered, eyebrow arched. "Getting pretty snooty on me, Mr. Kendall."

"Daddy!" Melissa protested in a rather disgusted voice. "Mommy!"

"They're fighting again," Mick informed her.

"Yes, they are," Jake and Amanda answered at once. And smiled.

Amanda didn't move from where she sat on the easy chair, her feet curled up beneath her, the books piled around her. She shot an expression of amused anticipation at her husband.

"Aunt Lee says they fight just so they can make up," the little boy informed his sister.

"We have to stop letting her baby-sit," Jake told Amanda.

Amanda chuckled as his hands rested on the arms of the chair alongside her. "She's *your* sister. Besides, who else is going to watch the kids while we're gone?"

He leaned closer, his eyes darkening, softening. His scent seeping into her senses. "Clovis. He loves kids."

Amanda ran her tongue over her lips, loving the reaction it set up in her husband. "Only if they whinny."

"Aunt Lee says they have a bet," Mick offered. "That you'll find a new baby in Scotland, just like you found me in New York and Melissa in Venice. What was I doing in New York, Mom? Are we going to have a new baby?"

Amanda felt Jake's proximity right down to her toes. Her heart skittered in welcome. Her chest tightened. Her hands ached for the taste of his taut belly beneath them.

"What do you think?" he asked. "Is it a good bet?"

Amanda offered him a smile that held everything he was to her in it. "I already put ten dollars down with Lee. Is that okay with you?"

His smile softened. He lifted a hand to her cheek that cupped her in strong, callused warmth. "I already put down fifty," he said. "I guess it's finally time to stop bucking the odds."

"I think you've done your share already," she agreed, lifting a finger to play with a button, holding his gaze with hers.

Her husband. Her charming, challenging, infuriating husband who could hold his own at a literary party just as easily as he could in a corral. Her husband who had taught her all over again what it meant to discover the world around her, and then return to cherish her home. Amanda awoke every morning amazed and fell asleep every night grateful. And still it kept getting better.

"So, we do it my way, huh?" she asked.

Jake lifted an eyebrow, the game as old as their relationship. "Your way?"

"Yeah," she countered, feeding on that bright, sharp blue, fortifying herself with that strength and fire and beauty. "Amanda's way. One step at a time."

Jake bent down and kissed her, a slow exploration that promised more. "It's worked so far," he admitted.

"You're right," she said. "It has."

And Amanda Marlow Kendall, award-winning author and screenwriter, quoted in textbooks and newsprint, relished with her husband a silence that carried everything they had shared between them, the passion and dedication, the struggles and successes, the dreams and mistakes. And most of all, the love. Because what Amanda felt for Jake could never be captured any other way. It went beyond description, beyond reason or intelligence. It was a sharp, scintillating, secret devotion that was returned tenfold. A rare life that showed itself in such a way, that when the townsfolk of Lost Ridge saw them together, they would just smile fondly and say, "It's their way."

Amanda couldn't have put it any better if she'd tried. Because some things simply went beyond words.

* * * * *

NORA ROBERTS

Love has a language all its own, and for centuries, flowers have symbolized love's finest expression. Discover the language of flowers—and love—in this romantic collection of 48 favorite books by bestselling author Nora Roberts.

Starting in February 1992, two titles will be available each month at your favorite retail outlet.

In February, look for:

Irish Thoroughbred, Volume #1
The Law Is A Lady, Volume #2

Collect all 48 titles and become fluent in the Language of Love.

LOL192

THE LANGUAGE of LOVE

YOU'VE ASKED FOR IT,
YOU'VE GOT IT! MAN OF
THE MONTH: 1992

You just couldn't get enough of them, those sexy men from Silhouette Desire—twelve sinfully sexy, delightfully devilish heroes. Some will make you sweat, some will make you sigh . . . but every long, lean one of them will have you swooning. So here they are, men we couldn't resist bringing to you for one more year. . . .

A KNIGHT IN TARNISHED ARMOR
by Ann Major in January

THE BLACK SHEEP
by Laura Leone in February

THE CASE OF THE MESMERIZING BOSS
by Diana Palmer in March

DREAM MENDER
by Sheryl Woods in April

WHERE THERE IS LOVE
by Annette Broadrick in May

BEST MAN FOR THE JOB
by Dixie Browning in June

Don't let these men get away! *Man of the Month*, only in Silhouette Desire.

is pleased to present

A GOOD MAN WALKS IN
by Ginna Gray

The story of one strong woman's comeback
and the man who was there for her, Travis McCall,
the renegade cousin to those Blaine siblings,
from Ginna Gray's bestselling trio

FOOLS RUSH IN (#416)
WHERE ANGELS FEAR (#468)
ONCE IN A LIFETIME (#661)

Rebecca Quinn sought shelter at the hideaway on Rincon
Island. Finding Travis McCall—the object of all her childhood
crushes—holed up in the same house threatened to ruin the
respite she so desperately needed. Until their first kiss . . .
Then Travis set out to prove to his lovely Rebecca that man
can be good and love, sublime.

You'll want to be there when Rebecca's disillusionment turns
to joy.

A GOOD MAN WALKS IN #722

Available at your favorite retail outlet this February.

SEGG

DONAVAN
Diana Palmer

Diana Palmer's bestselling LONG, TALL TEXANS series continues with DONAVAN....

From the moment elegant Fay York walked into the bar on the wrong side of town, rugged Texan Donavan Langley knew she was trouble. But the lovely young innocent awoke a tenderness in him that he'd never known...and a desire to make her a proposal she couldn't refuse....

Don't miss DONAVAN by Diana Palmer, the ninth book in her LONG, TALL TEXANS series. Coming in January...only from Silhouette Romance.

LTT192

Take 4 bestselling love stories FREE

Plus get a FREE surprise gift!

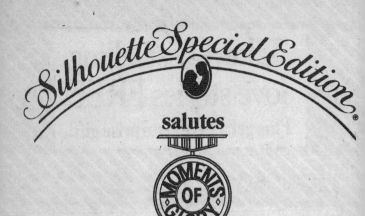

Silhouette Special Edition

salutes

MOMENTS OF GLORY

from Lindsay McKenna

In a country torn with conflict, in a time of bitter passions, these brave men and women wage a war against all odds... and a timeless battle for honor, for fleeting moments of glory, for the promise of enduring love.

February: RIDE THE TIGER (#721) Survivor Dany Villard is wise to the love-'em-and-leave-'em ways of war, but wounded hero Gib Ramsey swears she's captured his heart... forever.

March: ONE MAN'S WAR (#727) The war raging inside brash and bold Captain Pete Mallory threatens to destroy him, until Tess Ramsey's tender love guides him toward peace.

April: OFF LIMITS (#733) Soft-spoken Marine Jim McKenzie saved Alexandra Vance's life in Vietnam; now he needs her love to save his honor....

SEMG-1